me

"Welcome to the Future Widows' Club."

Sophia stood and made her way to the front of the room. "Now, before we begin tonight's meeting, I'd like to take a moment to introduce a new member." The older woman's gaze swung to Jolie. "This is Jolie Marshall. For those of you unaware of her story, it's a sad but familiar one. She married the wrong man. He's a thief, a liar, a cheater—" her voice hardened "—and, as you can see by the bruise on her cheek, a bully as well." She lifted her shoulder in a negligent shrug. "Basically, he's a bastard."

The women all nodded knowingly, sending Jolie encouraging smiles and woebegone glances.

"And, as such, she needs our help," Sophia continued. "We've all lived with one—and some of us still are—and we know what it's like. Our men were horrible. Looking forward to their deaths is what made our lives bearable. Doing the things in your handbook—fellowshipping with other widow-wannabes—it's how we cope, how we survive. So let's get this party started." She sent a meaningful look around the room. *"Our un-dearly departed—"*

"May he never rest in peace," the rest of the women finished.

Dear Reader,

The editors at Harlequin and Silhouette are thrilled to be able to bring you a brand-new featured author program beginning in 2005! Signature Select aims to single out outstanding stories, contemporary themes and oft-requested classics by some of your favorite series authors and present them to you in a variety of formats bound by truly striking covers.

We plan to provide several different types of reading experiences in the new Signature Select program. The Spotlight books will offer a single "big read" by a talented series author, the Collections will present three novellas on a selected theme in one volume, the Sagas will contain sprawling, sometimes multi-generational family tales (often related to a favorite family first introduced in series) and the Miniseries will feature requested, previously published books, with two or, occasionally, three complete stories in one volume. The Signature Select program will offer one book in each of these categories per month, and fans of limited continuity series will also find these continuing stories under the Signature Select umbrella.

In addition, these volumes will bring you bonus features...different in every single book! You may learn more about the author in an extended interview, more about the setting or inspiration for the book, more about subjects related to the theme and, often, a bonus short read will be included.

Watch for new stories from Vicki Lewis Thompson, Lori Foster, Donna Kauffman, Marie Ferrarella, Merline Lovelace, Roberta Gellis, Suzanne Forster, Stephanie Bond and scores more of the brightest talents in romance fiction!

We have an exciting year ahead!

Warm wishes for happy reading,

Marsha Zinberg

Marsha Zinberg
Executive Editor
The Signature Select Program

SPOTLIGHT

RHONDA
NELSON

the

Future
Widows'
Club

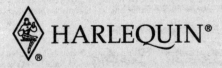

HARLEQUIN®

TORONTO • NEW YORK • LONDON
AMSTERDAM • PARIS • SYDNEY • HAMBURG
STOCKHOLM • ATHENS • TOKYO • MILAN • MADRID
PRAGUE • WARSAW • BUDAPEST • AUCKLAND

ISBN 0-373-83646-5

THE FUTURE WIDOWS' CLUB

Copyright © 2005 by Rhonda Nelson.

This edition published by arrangement with Harlequin Books S.A.

® and TM are trademarks of the publisher. Trademarks indicated with
® are registered in the United States Patent and Trademark Office, the
Canadian Trade Marks Office and in other countries.

www.eHarlequin.com

Printed in U.S.A.

Dear Reader,

The Future Widows' Club is my very first single-title release. I was thrilled with the wider scope and depth of the story, and the end result. And that isn't always the case. Writers constantly second-guess themselves, and when a project comes together the way you've envisioned it—when you get to the end and you're actually *happy* with what you've written—there's a rare level of satisfaction that makes the book extra special. For me, this has been one of those books.

Jolie Marshall made a mistake that many women make—she married the wrong man. She was swept off her feet by a man after her mother's money and the only way she can retrieve it is to stay married to the thief until she can manage to steal it back. When other members of her small hometown recognize the hell she's going through, they decide to help her and invite her into a secret society of women—The Future Widows' Club—who have been treated like trash by their horrible husbands, and prefer waiting for widowhood over divorce. But things turn sticky when Chris does end up dead and Jolie's alibi for the time of the murder is an FWC meeting. Then things get even more complicated when her old flame Jake Malone is named lead detective on the case.

I hope you enjoy Jake and Jolie's story, and would love to hear from my readers. Be sure and drop by my Web site—www.booksbyRhondaNelson.com—and sign my guestbook.

Happy reading!

Rhonda Nelson

PROLOGUE

"IF EVER a woman needed to be a widow, it's that one," Sophia Morgan said from the side of her mouth with a significant look across the crowded dining room.

Bitsy Highfield and Meredith Ingram leaned slightly back in their chairs and followed her line of vision. Looking sleek and polished as always, her short dark hair coifed in a flattering bob, Meredith instantly recognized the woman in question and her mouth curved knowingly. She shot Sophia a shrewd look.

Bitsy, as usual, wore her typical vacantly bewildered expression. "What woman?" Her penciled eyebrows formed a wrinkled line above her purple cat-eye glasses. "I don't see a woman."

"Jolie Marshall," Meredith hissed. "There." She gestured with a willowy bracelet-clad arm. "See her?"

Bitsy adjusted her bifocals, peered across the room. "Ah, yes. I see her. But if you ask me, her husband looks near enough to death as it is." Her wrinkled brow folded into an exaggerated frown. "Rather pasty-looking fellow, isn't he?"

Sophia swallowed a long-suffering sigh. "Not her, you idiot. *Her.* The young woman with the long auburn hair, wearing the cream suit. And that guy's not pasty looking, for heaven's sake," she snapped. "That's a statue of Poseidon."

And a poor one at that, but it was in keeping with the owner's taste. George Brown fancied himself an expert on all things Greek. His restaurant, *Zeus'*, was crammed with Greek statuaries and pictures of mythological gods, murals of Prometheus, Athena, Persephone and Zeus.

Which might have been appropriate were it not a steak house.

Sophia sighed, resisted the urge to roll her eyes. But it was the best Moon Valley, Mississippi, had to offer, so she ignored the tacky décor and carved off another bite of her filet.

Meredith snickered as Bitsy's blank look turned to one of dawning comprehension.

"Oh," she murmured. Then, "*Oh*. Why she's just a child!"

"Not a child, but a young woman," Sophia clarified. She harrumphed under her breath. "Too young to be shackled to that bastard of a husband of hers, that's for sure."

Meredith quirked a regal brow. "That's Fran Caplan's girl, right?"

"Oh, I've heard that story," Bitsy piped in, her voice dripping with gossipy innuendo. She was notoriously scatterbrained and clumsy, was blind as a bat—but her memory and hearing were sharp, both of which made her a valuable asset to the Club. "I heard Sadie talking about it a couple of weeks ago down at The Spa while I was getting my hair set."

That was hardly surprising, Sophia thought with a droll smile. Sadie Webster owned The Spa and the trendy hair and nails boutique, like most small towns, was the main hub of Moon Valley's gossip wheel. In order to satisfy her addiction to gossip and aerosol fumes, Bitsy kept a standing appointment. Much to the shampoo girl's chagrin, no doubt, Sophia thought with a wry smile. Bitsy was notoriously cheap, so tight that she tipped in coupons instead of cash. She and Meredith had tried to break her of the tacky habit, but alas to no avail.

"She and that Jolie are friends," Bitsy continued with a not-so-covert look at the woman in question. "I only caught part of the conversation, mind you—I was under the dryer—but apparently, from what I was able to piece together, she met that rounder on a vacation, she fell hard for him and he convinced her that he could take the proceeds her mother had gotten from her Daddy's life insurance policy and triple it."

Bejeweled fingers sparkling against the candlelight, Meredith calmly sipped her sherry. "I take it he didn't."

"No," Bitsy said. "That's what makes it so interesting. From what I gathered, he *has*—they own that new software company down on the square, something to do with business systems, the Internet and all that," she said absently. "He just refuses to give the money back. Somehow, despite the fact that they're partners, he's stashed it in one of those off-shore accounts."

"Still," Meredith hedged, the perpetual voice of reason, "I don't understand. If she's a partner, then why doesn't she do something about it?" She shrugged a slim shoulder. "If the company is so successful, why doesn't she just hire a good divorce attorney and take half?"

"What good would that do if he's hid the money from her?" Sophia pointed out. "If he can show that the company doesn't have it?"

Bitsy inclined her head. "I know that she's talked to Judge Turner about it. There's also a shady pre-nup, though I don't know the particulars."

"So what's she doing?" Meredith asked.

Bitsy smiled and a determined glint flashed in her pale blue eyes. She leaned forward, as though sharing a juicy secret. "Now that's the real mystery. If the rumors about her temper are true, then she definitely wouldn't sit idly by, but no one seems to know what she's doing about it. All anyone knows is that she is doing *something*. She's got a degree in accounting, she's on the board and has signature authority. My bet is that she's working that angle."

Sophia shifted in her seat, vainly wishing that she hadn't eaten that last bite of her steak. She firmly believed the *last bite* of every meal was what had made her pack on twenty pounds over the past two years. "Meanwhile," Sophia sighed, "he's making her miserable. He's a cheat and a liar. He's not the least bit discreet about his affairs and seems to delight in embarrassing her." She lifted her shoulder in a negligent shrug. "He's a bastard," she said glibly. Her gaze drifted significantly between the two of them. "And we all know what it's like to live with one of those."

Bitsy and Meredith both frowned, evidence of the truth of that statement.

Meredith gave Sophia another probing look. "So she's the reason we're here?"

Sophia nodded. "Her mother talked to me about it, asked us to intervene. I think she's a good candidate and I want to issue The Invitation." As founding members of the Club, they all had to agree. "Do either of you oppose?"

Bitsy snorted indelicately, her spiky gray curls bobbing. "I certainly don't. She's young. She could use some widow training, and from the sounds of it, the poor girl is going to need all the help she can get."

Never one to make snap decisions, Meredith's gaze slid to where Jolie Marshall sat across the room, seemed to take her measure. After a prolonged moment, she nodded. "I agree."

Sophia let go a breath, pleased. She lifted her glass, waited for the other two to do the same before readying their standard toast. The three shared a conspiratorial look, a secret smile. "To The Future Widows' Club."

CHAPTER ONE

"WOULD YOU LIKE to go ahead and order, Mrs. Marshall?"

Jolie forced a smile at the waiter and shook her head. "No, thank you, Charlie. I'll give Chris a few more minutes."

Charlie nodded, gave her an uncomfortable look, then swiftly moved away. A sigh stuttered out of her mouth as she lifted her water glass, the glass she'd like nothing better than to hurl across the room. But being as she'd like to aim it at her husband's head—and he wasn't here—she resisted the urge.

Chris, damn him, should have been here twenty minutes ago. The fact that he was late was no surprise—he enjoyed making her wait, another power play that she'd grown accustomed to over the past two years.

Two years—to the date—of sheer hell.

Though she was tempted to scream, then dive into a pool of self-recriminations, Jolie checked the impulse. Making a scene, calling herself every kind of idiot, wondering why she'd made the disastrous decisions she'd made, pondering the if-only's wouldn't change anything. It wouldn't make her feel any better and, more importantly, it wouldn't get her mother's money back, or the money of any of the other investors for that matter.

Every ounce of her energy, every thought, had to be directed to that end, and having a therapeutic temper fit, then mulling over the wreck her life had become wouldn't get her any closer to that goal. So no pity-party, dammit. She'd simply have to cope. She smiled at passersby, blew out a small breath to release some of her current pressure, and imagined blithely signing her divorce papers.

It was nobody's fault but her own that she'd royally screwed up and now she was left with the unhappy, nerve-wrecking, miserable task of fixing it.

Which, thankfully, was going better than she'd initially anticipated. So long as she stepped carefully— translate: didn't rock the boat with her son-of-a-bitch husband—she could recoup the rest of her mom's investment within the next three months, as well as that of the other investors. Then she'd swiftly, gleefully file for a divorce. She chuckled darkly. He'd live to regret that token appointment to the board, she thought with no small amount of satisfaction.

Her cell chirped, snagging her attention. It wouldn't be Chris, she knew. Though he was late, he'd never give her the courtesy of a phone call to let her know why. Things like courtesy, respect, fidelity and friendship had fallen instantly by the wayside the moment he'd realized that she knew he was a thief. She'd learned other things as well. She hadn't known him at all, she'd found out too late. Since then, he'd been a condescending, sarcastic control-freak who delighted in seeing how angry, how wretched, he could make her feel. Given present circumstances and her admittedly short fuse, she made it entirely too easy for him, a fact that she was desperately trying to rectify.

She'd started carrying a worry stone in her pocket, and though she'd been tempted to hurl it at him many times—not to mention the fact that she'd rubbed a blister on her thumb—she couldn't deny that she found it soothing.

She finally fished her cell out of her purse, then flipped it open. Her lips quirked. *Sadie.* "Hey," she answered.

"Don't bother ordering," Sadie told her by way of greeting. Her usually chipper voice throbbed with outraged anger.

Jolie rubbed an imaginary line from between her eyebrows, cast a subtle look around the restaurant, then let go of a sigh. "Do I want to know why?"

"No, but I'm going to show you. Take a look at this."

A picture of Chris's red BMW appeared on her cell screen. His vanity plate—*U WISH*—glowed in the dark, proof that it was definitely his car.

But it was what was hanging *out* of the car window that drew her attention—a pair of legs.

Feminine legs that definitely didn't belong to her husband. A dark shadow hovered just out of view—her husband heaving atop the woman who owned the legs, she imagined.

Jolie smirked, not the least bit surprised. Well, it *was* their anniversary. She should have known that he wouldn't miss an opportunity like this. It didn't hurt because she didn't care—she *hated* him. But she loathed being humiliated and he purposely chose whom he screwed around with to coincide with her maximum mortification.

"Jolie? Are you there?"

"Yeah, I'm here," she sighed. "Give me a minute. I want to send that to my e-mail account. It can go into The File."

Though Chris didn't know it, Jolie had amassed quite a bit of damning evidence for his take-down and her subsequent divorce. She'd need everything in order to invalidate the pre-nup she'd foolishly signed, the one he'd said was for *her* benefit. Another lie.

While Chris considered himself too smart to be double-crossed, his arrogance was actually working to her advantage. She'd been steadily documenting his shady business dealings as well as the infidelity, the worsening drug habit, and the mental abuse. She fully intended to ruin him, to make him pay for the way he'd treated her and her family. He'd picked the wrong pigeon this time and if it was the last thing she did, she'd make him live to regret it.

"That bastard," Sadie hissed angrily. "I swear, I don't think I've ever hated a man more than that son-of-a-bitch. Please tell me you're close to finishing up," she pleaded. "Please tell me that you can leave that bottom-feeder soon. Before I do something stupid, like kill him," she growled in frustration.

Jolie chuckled lightly, heartened by Sadie's outrage on her behalf. A vision of her friend's short brown curls bobbing with indignation flashed through her mind. Shirley Temple meets Katie Kaboom, she thought fondly. "I will," she promised. "Another three months, tops."

Thank God. She didn't think her nerves could stand anything else beyond that. She wanted her life back, wanted to be able to look at her mother without feeling the knee-buckling weight of shame hanging around her neck. In the meantime, she was avoiding her. Cowardly, she knew, but... The fact that her marriage wasn't a happy one was common knowledge in Moon Valley, so she didn't hold any illusions that her mother had no idea what was going on, but confirming the rumors then having to expand upon them was out of the realm of her ability at the moment.

Sadie grunted. "Another three seconds is too long. Honestly, I don't see how you stand it."

Jolie found her stone, absently rubbed it and smiled. "That's because you married the right man, and I married the wrong one."

Sadie had married her high school sweetheart, Rob Webster. They had two kids, a mortgage and a minivan, and were the picture of marital bliss. Did they have the occasional problem? Of course. Marriage, under the best circumstances, was still work. But they loved each other and they were both committed to the relationship, to their family.

Sadie sighed. "So what are you going to do?"

"Eat dinner," she said, forcing a lighter note into her voice, hoping her faux enthusiasm would prevent her friend from worrying. "I'm hungry."

Naturally, Sadie saw through the ploy. Hell, they'd been friends forever—since Kindergarten. Aside from one other person, Sadie probably knew her better than anyone else.

"Do you want me to come over?" she asked softly. "Because I can. I can order a pizza for Rob and the kids and I can be there in—"

"No," she Jolie interjected. "But thanks for offering. I appreciate it." And she really did.

"This sucks, Jolie," Sadie said heatedly, her ire renewed. *"This sucks."*

It certainly did, she thought as she palmed her worry stone, but she'd endured two years of it and was too close to being able to return the investor's money, most importantly her mother's. She could endure another three months. Then she'd turn her evidence in to the rest of the board, return the investors' money and she'd leave him. He should have paid more attention to the morality clause, Jolie thought with a small smile.

But she couldn't wait to leave him. Imagining that scenario was the only thing that made things bearable right now. She clung to it like a life line, dreamed about it, prayed for it.

"I, uh… I know it sucks, but I can't leave yet. You know the score," she said, unwilling to talk about it over her cell. The laundering technique she'd successfully implemented—her way of insuring that everyone got their money back—wasn't a topic of conversation one discussed over the airwaves.

Technically, it was embezzlement.

But Chris had started it first, and the difference between her and Chris was that she didn't plan to keep more than what she'd originally put in. She was giving the money back to its rightful owners, while Chris on the other hand was simply keeping it for himself. "I'm almost there, Sadie. I just need a little more time."

"I know." Sadie exhaled a resigned breath. "Call me if you need anything, would you?"

"You got it." Jolie disconnected, then snagged Charlie's attention once more. She ordered a house salad, the filet, and a bottle of expensive wine all without the slightest hesitation—she'd charge it to the company. The idea drew a half-hearted smile.

"I'll get that order in for you right away, Mrs. Marshall."

Charlie turned and walked away, and a woefully familiar profile, one that made her belly clench, loomed instantly into view. The brave smile she wore faded, and though the knowledge that her husband was currently boinking some whore on their anniversary didn't make her so much as flinch, seeing Jake Malone with another woman made her belly tip in a nauseated roll. Jolie's mouth went dry and her eyes stung. Her hands trembled and she had difficulty swallowing past the inexplicable lump that had formed in her dusty throat.

Oh, God. Not this. Anything but this.

Jake and Nicolette stood at the entrance to the dining room, presumably to wait for a table. Though she knew it was impossible, she thought she caught a whiff of fresh hay, the scent she'd forever associate with him. He loved horses, had an almost supernatural gift with them, one that had always fascinated her.

Rather than his usual T-shirt, jeans and boots, he wore a pair of khaki slacks and a white oxford cloth shirt open at the throat, cuffed at the wrists. Jolie imagined he'd ditched the tie as soon as his shift at the Sheriff's Department had ended. He'd worked his way up through the ranks, had finally earned his detective's badge, a feat she was certain he was proud of.

She couldn't know for sure, of course, because he

wasn't speaking to her—he hadn't since she'd thumbed her nose at his request for "more time" and married Chris—but she knew him well enough to know that he'd be thrilled with the promotion.

His dark brown locks were mussed, a shade too long by his usual standards, and those soft gray eyes were presently drifting over his date. Jolie knew that look—that sinfully carnal caress—knew what it promised and she envied Nicolette in that moment so much that it hurt—and hated Chris Marshall more than she ever had.

Of all the mistakes she'd made, setting Jake aside for the bastard she'd married was probably the hardest to bear. One way or another, she'd get her mother's money back—even when she'd realized how terribly wrong things had gone, Jolie had never doubted that—but Jake... Jake, she knew, was lost forever.

Still, though she'd been at fault, she couldn't accept all the blame. Wouldn't, dammit. Though Jake had been there for her practically her entire life—hell, they'd been grade-school sweethearts, been voted Best Couple, Prom King and Queen, had always been together—the one time she'd *truly, desperately* needed him—when her father had died—Jake had done the one thing she'd never, ever anticipated.

He'd let her down.

Instead of being her worry stone, her best friend, confidante and lover, he'd cooled things off between them and focused on his career. He'd been more interested in being a detective than being hers and had basically put their relationship on the back burner. He'd abandoned her at a time when she'd needed him most.

They'd ultimately fought about it, which was why she'd taken that ill-fated vacation alone…and the rest had been history. She'd been ready to start a family. Jake hadn't been. Then Chris had come along, showered her with attention, expressed the same interests as her, and in her emotionally overwrought state… Jolie sighed. A small town girl in the big bad world. In short, easy pickings. Furthermore, she'd never been able to do things half-way, had always been single-mindedly stubborn. And, for better or for worse, once she'd charted a course she never looked back, always saw it through. An admirable trait when she was right, but a bad one when she was wrong.

And choosing Chris had been wrong.

She'd later learned that he'd worked for the insurance company who'd insured her father. He'd apparently researched recent beneficiaries and decided to set his sights on her, and though she couldn't prove it yet, she firmly believed that he'd done this before to other unsuspecting women. Her lips twisted bitterly. He'd screwed her physically and financially and she'd made it easy for him.

Jolie would admit to many faults—she was impatient, hated to wait for anything and invariably squirmed through the three minutes she wasted at a traffic light. She had a horrible temper, one that had gotten her into trouble more times than she could conceivably count. But being *stupid* generally wasn't one of them, and it galled her to no end that she'd let that viper into their midst. That she'd brought him home into her insulated little world and created this mess.

The harried hostess finally arrived to show Jake and

Nicolette to their table and it was with sinking horror that Jolie realized they were headed in her direction. A quick glance confirmed that the table directly in front of her was vacant. She suppressed a whimper, resisted the urge to squirm.

Oh, shit. Shit, shit, shit.

Jolie looked from the table to Jake and she swallowed tightly as her gaze connected with his. A hum of static raced up her spine and a flock of swallows took flight in her belly. The urge to flee nearly made her bolt from her seat, but she forced herself to stay still and determinedly lifted her chin. Showing fear of any sort wasn't in her nature and she had too much pride to let him know how much he still affected her.

"Will this table be all right?" the hostess asked.

Jake's probing gaze held hers and for a nanosecond she thought she read something other than mockery and indifference. She'd seen a glimpse of anger, of pity. But it must have been her imagination, because in the next moment, a sardonic mask replaced the sentiment and he smiled a lazy sort of grin rife with something akin to triumph. "It's perfect," he drawled, his lips curled into a smirk. "Absolutely perfect."

His gaze slid away, purposely discarding her, and he focused his attention back on his date.

Oh, no, Jolie thought as she drew in a shuddering breath. She took a much-needed sip of water. This was not going to work. There was no way in hell she would be able to sit here and enjoy her meal with Jake crooning to Nicolette at the next table. Purposely crooning, too. He planned to torture her. Not that she could blame him, really. Like any thwarted female, when she'd first come home with Chris, she'd enjoyed the fact that Jake had been sorry, that he'd realized he'd made a mistake and she'd stupidly flaunted her new relationship. Were the circumstances reversed, she knew she'd undoubtedly want to inflict a little revenge as well.

But she just wasn't up to it tonight. Wouldn't ever be up to it, not where he was concerned. It was just too damned hard.

Aiming for covert, but probably looking frantic, she snagged Charlie's attention as he walked by. Lowered her voice to a near whisper. "I've changed my mind. I'm, uh, not hungry after all." The truth, as she'd just lost her appetite.

Charlie frowned. "You want me to cancel your order?"

Jolie inwardly winced. Was it just her or was he speaking especially loud? "Not the whole order," she muttered quietly. "I still want the wine." In fact, now more than ever. Getting drunk sounded particularly appealing at the moment.

"The whole bottle?"

She nodded. "Yes, please. Now," she added meaningfully. She withdrew her credit card from her wallet and handed it to him.

Looking completely bewildered, Charlie vanished once more. Thankfully, he made the return trip in record time. She added a generous tip and then signed for the bottle, anxious to get the hell out of there. Though she didn't remember Nicolette having an exaggerated sense of humor in high school, Jake was laughing silkily at every word she uttered. Jolie refused to look at them— at him, specifically. She was used to being manipulated—she'd been married to a master for the past two years—and she wasn't about to let Jake do it as well.

She gathered her purse and the bottle and was just about to stand when a trio of older ladies stopped by her table. She recognized only one of them, Sophia Morgan. She was a rather petite lady, a little round, with pale blond hair cut in a trendy layered style and kind green eyes. She and her mother were friends and, like most women in Moon Valley, both belonged to the Garden Club.

Jolie caught a whiff of lilies and steak sauce as Sophia bent low and smiled down at her. "I'm going to give you a card," she murmured through a fixed grin. "And I want you to read it, then hand it back. Okay?"

Thoroughly bewildered, Jolie nodded. "Er…okay."

The other two women huddled closer—one tall and willowy wearing lots of high-end jewelry, the other short and plump with spiky gray curls—seemingly to block her from the view of other patrons. Sophia slid a small card across the table. Intrigued, Jolie shot her a curious look, then picked it up. The card was heavy stock, pale pink and embossed with formal silver lettering.

The Future Widows' Club…
where a woman
prepares for widowhood before her bastard dies.
You are cordially invited to join the FWC
to prepare
and fellowship with other widow-wannabes.

Jolie felt her eyes widen with shocked delight, a disbelieving laugh tickle the back of her throat and a smile slowly rolled around her lips. *The Future Widows' Club?* What on earth—

Before she could ponder it any further, Sophia deftly withdrew the card from her hand and replaced it with another. This one simply had an address, date and time. "Come join us, honey," Sophia told her. "Trust me," she said direly, her voice a lilting old south southern drawl. "You need our help."

Looking equally concerned, the other two women shot her commiserating glances. "You definitely do," the short one said.

And with those words ringing in Jolie's ears, the three shuffled off.

Though she hadn't meant to, her gaze once again found Jake's. He wore a curious expression, and those gunmetal gray eyes dropped to the card in her hand, then jumped back up and tangled with hers. He quirked a questioning brow.

Smiling, Jolie neatly pocketed it out sight. Let him wonder, she thought. Served him right for torturing her.

Though her stomach was still in knots, Jolie calmly stood, grabbed her bottle of wine and just as calmly made her way outside. She didn't spare Jake or Nicolette so much as the smallest glance. The impulse was there, of course—it always was when Jake was around—but thankfully pride prevailed.

Pride kept her head high and her back straight as she strolled to her car, and pride kept her from looking back to see if Jake had watched her leave. The moment she slid behind the wheel, though, pride abandoned her, and it was all Jolie could do not to cry. She wilted into the seat. Her belly quivered, her eyes stung, and she instinctively bit her bottom lip to prevent the sob that beckoned in the back of her tight throat. She gripped the steering wheel and lowered her head.

She would not cry, dammit.

If she could cry prettily, without anyone being the wiser, then yes, she might have given in to the impulse and sat in her car and squalled. It's what she wanted to do, what she needed to do. But unfortunately, she couldn't cry prettily. Her nose streamed, her mascara ran, ugly red blotches formed on her cheeks and beneath her eyes, and her upper lip swelled to twice its normal size. She invariably looked like she'd had some sort of allergic reaction, and Chris, she knew, would instantly recognize the implications and wrongfully assume that her tears had been for him.

Which would be intolerable.

She'd cried her last tear over Chris Marshall—over the mistakes she'd made—and she'd be damned before she'd give him any more satisfaction at her expense. The thought bolstered her resolve, then triggered another.

The card.

She pulled in a shaky breath, let it go, then pilfered through her purse until she found it. She reread the date—just the day after tomorrow, she discovered, oddly relieved—and the time and address. For reasons which escaped her, the innocuous little piece of paper felt like a life preserver, offered a ray of hope in her dim existence.

The Future Widows' Club, indeed, Jolie thought, with a soft chuckle. The idea was intriguing to say the least. She harrumphed. God knows she'd entertained the widow fantasy many times over the past two years. She'd never been much of joiner, tended to make few friends and keep her circle tight, but now this…

This sounded like the perfect club for her.

CHAPTER TWO

JAKE FELT every muscle go rigid with tension as Jolie grew nearer, then slowly leak out of him like air from a punctured tire as she walked past. He inwardly swore, resisting the urge to put his fist through the wall.

More than two years and it was always the same when he saw her.

Like a sucker punch to the gut immediately followed by the unhappy sensation of falling face-first off a cliff. Regret would ultimately follow, then before his heart could explode right out of his chest—or he could puke, a gallingly too-frequent occurrence after she and Marshall had first gotten together—good old righteous anger would bubble up from the almost-dry well of self-preservation, and he'd push his lips into a smirk and think about how he'd felt the day she'd married Marshall.

Eviscerated. Just two little words—*I do*—to someone else, and she'd gutted him.

He forced a thin smile at his date, pretended to peruse the menu. Rationally Jake knew that he couldn't place all the blame for their break-up at Jolie's feet. In fact, were he able to be completely honest with himself—and he couldn't yet because it still hurt too much—he couldn't place *any* of the blame with her.

She'd acted completely within character. He'd been the one who'd stepped out of it.

After her dad had died, Jolie had looked to him to make good on all the promises and plans they'd made—marriage and a family—and, though he'd never doubted that they'd marry, for reasons he'd never been able to understand, he'd hesitated. Why? Hell, who knew? Some ignorant bachelor throw-back mentality, he supposed.

He'd looked into those clear green eyes, seen his future—the one he'd always wanted with her looking back at him—and he'd unaccountably freaked. He'd thrown himself into making detective, told himself that he didn't want to commit himself any further to their relationship than what he already had. Not the real reason, of course, but in the end, though, when all was said and done, it hadn't mattered.

He'd hesitated—and in that one moment of groundless uncertainty, he'd lost her.

Initially the knowledge that her marriage wasn't a happy one had been a petty balm to his battered ego and even still, at times—like now—when he felt like the scab had been ripped off a wound that hadn't quite healed, he couldn't always rise above his wounded pride. If he was miserable, then it was only fitting that she be unhappy as well.

If she could have just waited, dammit. Given him just a little more time to get his head on straight.

Jake drew up short and inwardly swore. He'd traveled the road named Pointless many times—backtracking was futile. But as time wore on and the ache numbed, the idea of her being unhappy ate at him even more than the fact that she wasn't—could never be—his. His jaw hardened.

Because her husband was a bastard of the first order.

In the past couple of years Chris Marshall had been arrested for DUI, charged with possession—the usual stuff, marijuana, ecstasy—and had been the cause of more than one domestic disturbance in town. He didn't exercise the least bit of discretion when it came to dipping his wick. Married or unmarried, it was all the same to him.

He'd been jerked up a couple of times by angry husbands, but rather than having the good sense to be chastened, the bastard seemed to get off on the thrill of bagging another guy's wife, seemed to delight in provoking them. Jake grimaced. Hell, it was a miracle he hadn't ended up in the morgue sporting a toe tag to go with that trendy suit and pretty boy smirk he usually wore.

Furthermore, it was a miracle—not to mention a mystery—that Jolie hadn't left him yet. Jake had heard the rumors, of course. Despite the fact that Jake had cited his long-term friendship with Sadie's husband and the fact that he particularly liked the way she cut his hair—that he'd hate to have to find another stylist—Sadie nevertheless tended to let things *purposely* slip. Would she bring up Jolie to him? No. She knew better. But that didn't stop her from talking about Jolie to other people while she had him captive in the chair.

As a result, he had a vague understanding of the life-insurance money Marshall had conned out of her mother—scheming ass, Jake thought, disgusted—and an even vaguer understanding as to what Jolie was doing about it. The best he'd been able to discern, leaving Chris was a foregone conclusion, but apparently there was no way to recoup the investment in a divorce settlement, and getting the money back had to come first.

"I guess my sense of humor left when she walked out, didn't it?"

Jake blinked, and looked across the table. "I'm sorry?"

Nicolette sighed, pushing a hand through her short pale blond hair. "You were laughing at every word I said for the first five minutes we were here, which is flattering, by the way, considering that a sense of humor has never really been my strong suit." Her lips tilted into a knowing smile. "But the minute Jolie left, you zoned out on me and haven't so much as responded to anything I've said, much less laughed."

Jake passed a hand over his face to hide a wince. Shit. "Look, I—"

"Here's the thing," she said levelly as she bent to retrieve her purse. "I'm not interested in sex for the sake of sex, and I'm sure not interested in being a substitute."

"You're not a substitute," Jake told her, swallowing the futile bark of laughter that hit the back of this throat. Substitute? There was no substitute for Jolie. Hell, he'd looked, had tried to invest himself in other relationships. It hadn't worked. Instinctively he knew it would never work. There wasn't another soul on the planet who could make him forget to breathe simply by smiling, who could set his veins on fire with a mere touch of her hand. Jolie had been it…and he'd screwed up and let her go.

Nicolette paused and gave him a look that bordered closely enough on pity to make him want to howl. "You're still in love with her."

Jake summoned a laugh and shook his head, felt a sickening jolt of alarm hit his belly. "No, I'm not." He took a healthy pull on his beer. *Liar,* a little-heeded voice whispered.

Again, that sad provoking smile. "Fine," she said, clearly not believing him. "But whether you love her or not, there's still too much feeling there for my liking. Definitely too much for me to ante up more than what I already have." She stood. "Goodnight, Jake."

Jake smiled grimly as she walked away, trying to muster the irritation he knew he should feel, but in the end, he couldn't. Hell, she was right and he couldn't blame her. If she wanted anything more than a few hours of recreational sex, then she was barking up the wrong tree because he didn't have anything else to offer.

Just superficial feelings, superficial sex, superficial time.

The corner of his mouth hitched in another grim smile. It was all part and parcel of the new Jake, courtesy of his own stupidity.

JOLIE AWOKE from a sound sleep—one brought about by several glasses of wine and enough Krispy Kreme carbohydrates to drop an elephant—to the two words she hadn't been the least bit interested in hearing.

At least, not from Chris.

"Happy Anniversary, baby."

Despite the fact that she'd locked her door, Chris—

even drunk and obviously high—had managed to let himself into her room, and had turned on her bedside light. His face was slick with perspiration, his eyes bloodshot and glassy. His pants were partially zipped, his shirt unbuttoned, and the beginnings of one helluva hickey was forming on his neck. He brought the stale scent of sex with him, making nausea curdle in her belly. A quick look at the bedside clock told her it was just after three. She grunted with disgust, then rolled over and attempted to ignore him.

It didn't work.

She felt the mattress shift as he dropped unsteadily onto the side of the bed. Then the sickening feeling of his hand sliding up over her hip, causing her flesh to creep. Repulsed, she instinctively jerked away from him. Jolie didn't know what the hell he was doing. She'd stopped sleeping with him the minute she'd learned the truth, absolutely refused to share anything beyond the house with him and looked forward to ending that arrangement as soon as possible.

Besides, she'd never liked this house. Located in a newer subdivision just outside the city limits it was cold and sterile, with designer grass and no trees. She had her eye on a little French Colonial fixer-upper on Lelia Street just off the square, one that would accommodate a cat, she thought, still miserably missing the long-time pet she firmly believed Chris had *made* disappear. Heartless bastard. After the divorce, she planned to put her accounting degree to better use, to take back her maiden name and hang a little shingle on the outside of the house.

Though many strip malls and shopping centers had cropped up on the main highway on the edge of town, the old town square was still the heart of Moon Valley. Fancy pavilions dripping with lacy fretwork and stocked with picnic tables anchored each corner and a beautiful fountain stood in the middle, paying tribute to a statue of Jebediah Moon, the town's founding father.

Every parade, be it Christmas, Homecoming, or Fourth of July, ended there, and the spot hosted their Annual Moon-Pie Festival each year. Between the Garden Club—Moon Valley citizens prided themselves on their ability to make things bloom—and the Civic Club, the quaint square was always dressed in her Sunday best. It epitomized Moon Valley life…one that her husband would never fit into.

"Get out, Chris," she said tiredly.

He slipped a finger down her arm. "I thought you might be feeling romantic."

Jolie barely resisted the urge to grunt in disgust. This just showed how completely out of touch with reality he could be. They weren't lovers, weren't in love. And whatever small amount of misplaced affection she'd thought she'd felt for him had gone by the wayside as soon as she'd realized what a scum-sucking, bottom-feeding thief he was.

She absolutely hated him—loathed him—with every fiber of her being.

And yet he thought she might be feeling romantic? If she weren't pretending to be half asleep, undoubtedly her eyes would pop out of her head.

He leaned over her and she felt his reeking breath hit

her neck. She shrunk away from him. "Why don't we try and fix things, Jolie? They don't have to be this way."

Had he lost his mind? she wondered. In order to facilitate getting her mother's money back, Jolie had suggested to Chris that they keep up appearances for the business's sake. After all, she'd reasoned, Marshall, Inc. was still a relatively new business, one that despite his lack of character, his drug habit and his other vices, he'd managed to make flourish.

Unfortunately, word of his penchant for illegal substances and alcohol had begun to leak out and, though she'd managed to handle damage control, she grimly suspected that, despite their good-old-boy way of doing business, their local investors—the ones she'd unsuspectingly lured into Marshall, Inc.—were beginning to get a wee bit unsettled. Until she recouped all the money, that was a bad thing.

In one of his rare reasonable moments, Chris had agreed that keeping up the pretense of the happy couple was best. After all, anything that was better for his bottom line was better for him. Jolie had instructed him to seek his pleasure elsewhere—like he hadn't been doing that already, she thought with an inward snort—and had indicated that the marriage would continue in an in-name-only basis. So far he'd honored their system with irreverent, purposely cruel, efficiency.

She rolled over, putting as much distance between them as she could. "Yes, they do," she insisted through gritted teeth. *"Now get out."*

"No," he said, his voice belligerent yet eerily calm. He lurched clumsily to his feet, staggered, then started fumbling with his pants. "It's our anniversary, *darling,* and I'm going to do what every man does on his anniversary—I'm going to fuck my wife."

The first inkling of fear quickened her heartbeat, prodding her out of the bed. The fact that he could make her afraid in addition to all the other things he'd managed to do to her lit her temper like nothing else could.

Jolie crossed her arms over her chest and summoned a sardonic smile. She cocked her head. "That's funny," she said, "because I have it on good authority that you've already fucked somebody else's wife tonight."

Sadie, bless her heart, had pulled sleuth-duty until she'd determined whose legs were jutting out of Chris's car. And she'd documented the proof with her handy picture phone. Jolie's lips quirked. The whore in question was one Emily Dean—*Sheriff* Dean's wife. Getting bolder and stupider by the minute, her unfortunate husband, Jolie thought with a wry twist of her lips. She just prayed he kept it together long enough for her to get everybody's money back.

Chris's sweaty mouth formed a sneer. "Jealous, are you?" He alternately stalked and stumbled toward her. "Don't worry. There's enough of me to go around."

"Then go spread it somewhere else," she threw back.

Though it nearly killed her, Jolie stood her ground. There was something about him tonight—a recklessness she'd never seen before—that absolutely chilled her blood. But she knew from experience that Chris fed off her emotions. If she showed him even the slightest hint of the fear currently chugging through her veins, he'd press his advantage…and she wouldn't care for the outcome.

His eyes were every bit as hard as his voice. "Now why would I do that when I have a tasty little piece like you at my disposal?" He twined a lock of her hair around his finger. "I mean, you aren't the best I've ever had…but you'll do in a pinch."

"Well, you won't, and I've developed higher stand-ards." She jerked back, pulling her hair in the process and moved to go around him. He grabbed her by the upper arm, his fingers biting painfully into her flesh. She swallowed a gasp, fighting back fear.

"Just what the hell is that supposed to mean?" His red-rimmed eyes narrowed. "Have you been screwing around on me?" he demanded. He shifted his weight, seemingly having a hard time remaining upright. "Let-ting somebody else have what I'm not getting?"

Common sense told her taunting him in this state wasn't the brightest course of action, but the fury tight-ening every muscle of her body wasn't in the mood to entertain reasonable thoughts.

She blinked as though confused. "You're getting it," she said sweetly, "just not from me."

"Are you screwin' around on me?" he demanded, shaking her for emphasis.

Jolie snorted, rolling her eyes. "Now that's the pot calling the kettle black if I've ever heard it." She looked pointedly at his hand on her arm. "Let. Me. Go."

"When you've answered the question." His expres-sion turned thoughtful, then shrewdly calculating. "I know you're not getting it from your old boy Jake. From what I've heard he's chasing every kitty *but* yours." He licked his lips, smiled. "But he leaves a fair amount of leftovers for the rest of us."

Jolie felt her stomach lurch. She'd shared her relationship with Jake with Chris when they'd first met— not everything, of course—but he'd managed to put the rest together once he'd moved to Moon Valley. It hadn't been hard. In a place where secrets were few and gossip frequent, Jake and Jolie's relationship had been almost legendary, their names linked since grade school, an extension of the other documented in yearbooks and newspaper clippings.

Chris had a way of ferreting out a person's weakness, then capitalizing on it. When he was feeling particularly spiteful, he'd invariably wield Jake like a knife, cutting little gashes into her already broken heart, occasionally parrying hard enough to puncture.

Like now.

She knew Jake had taken lovers—she'd heard and would never have expected him to remain celibate—but knowing it didn't prevent her from feeling like a rug had been jerked from beneath her feet when she thought about it. The idea of him touching another woman, of those big warm hands, that supremely carnal mouth doing the things they'd learned together to another woman…

Jolie tried to jerk free again and Chris smiled knowingly. He swayed on his feet. "That's what I thought. You're still my ever-faithful wife."

"I'm not your ever-faithful anything." Taking advantage of the various drugs—Viagra and ecstasy, she imagined—and alcohol wreaking havoc with his equilibrium, Jolie gave him a quick shove and wrenched her arm free. Chris wobbled, then his eyes flashed, and he did something he'd never done before, but something she'd recently feared was just a matter of time.

He back-handed her.

Clumsily, but the slap split her lip, made her ears ring and caused white spots to dance before her eyes. She reeled from the blow and her cheek blazed from the impact.

Seemingly spent, Chris fell back onto the bed, laid there and laughed. "Stupid bitch," he muttered. "I'll…teach you. I'll show you…who's boss." He flung an arm over his forehead, then passed out.

Though shocked and astounded, Jolie's first inclination was to *hurt* him. She wanted to slap him, claw him, beat him, pounce on him like a cat and not stop until every bit of the anger and frustration he'd dealt her had been given back three-fold.

When unconscious, he wouldn't feel a thing, and when conscious, he could hurt her far worse, so giving in to the fury would ultimately be futile, she knew. But she couldn't let it go completely. Couldn't let the incident pass without some form of retribution.

She decided on the passive aggressive approach, one she'd used many times over the past couple of years to make her feel better. Still breathing heavily, she marched into the bathroom, grabbed his toothbrush from the holder and, smiling grimly, scrubbed it around the toilet bowl. Then she put it back where it belonged.

Afterward, she calmly retrieved her overnight bag—the one she kept packed and ready for nights similar to this—and left. As always, her first inclination was to go home—home being her mother's small cottage on the other side of town—but like always she ruled out the option. Her mother had enough to handle without adding this newest development into the mix. Luckily Sadie had an empty apartment over the shop that had served as a refuge of sorts in the past, and it would certainly work again.

For the umpteenth time since this nightmare began, she felt the urge, the almost palpable need, to run to Jake, to lose the brave little soldier face and find solace in the safe-harbor of his arms. The thought made a whimper bubble up her throat and tears burn the backs of her lids, the ache of loss wrenching her insides until she thought she'd come apart. Unfortunately, Jolie thought as she sucked in a shaky breath, that wasn't a viable option.

Jake's arms were already full.

CHAPTER THREE

"THOSE WILL DO better if you plant them in the morning sun."

Feeling her hackles rise, Sophia gritted her teeth, straightened from the flower bed she'd been working in and turned to glare from beneath her straw hat at the infuriating man who'd issued the advice. Looking decidedly cooler than she, Edward Jennings leaned against her picket fence and regarded her with amusement.

Sophia made a grand gesture of alternately looking at the seven a.m. sun, her bedding plants, then him. She cocked a brow, silently questioning the validity of his eyesight, then twisted her lips into a superior smile. "Thanks, Edward, but I think I've been planting pansies long enough to know where they best thrive."

Honestly, she thought, exasperated. Just because he'd snatched the Garden Club presidency from her—a position she'd coveted since she'd planted her first petunia, dammit—the man had become insufferable. One who lived two blocks over and who'd developed the annoying habit of strolling by her house.

Every morning.

Which was why she'd wrestled herself into a girdle

this morning to go outside and work in her garden. Sophia pursed her lips.

Clearly, she'd lost her mind.

Edward inclined his snowy head and a wide smile split his tanned face. "Ah, I see that now." His light blue eye twinkled. "Your rump was in the way before."

A rebellious spurt of pleasure bloomed inside her before she could squash it out. Damn the man. He shouldn't be *looking* at her rump, much less letting her *know* that he'd been looking at her rump.

Sophia dusted the dirt from her gloves and regarded him coolly, no small feat when she was quaking inside like a virgin on her wedding night. "Are you suggesting, Edward, that my ass is so wide it blocked out the morning sun?"

He dipped his head, chuckled, the sound at once pleasing and masculine. Almost intimate. "Absolutely not. I was merely making conversation."

Sophia sidled forward, tugged her gloves off one finger at a time. "A word of advice then, Edward, since you don't seem to mind doling it out. If you'd like to initiate a cordial conversation," she explained patiently, "then you'd be better served to begin with a simple, 'Good morning, Sophia.'" She smiled sweetly. "Not offer criticism. People might get the impression that you're an arrogant know-it-all with an exalted opinion of your own wit."

He looked out over her garden, stroked his chin. When his eyes found hers once more she detected lingering humor and something else…something she couldn't readily discern. Uncertainty, maybe? He let go a small sigh. "Well, that would be most unfortunate," he said softly. "Thanks for the advice. I'll be sure and keep it in mind." He inclined his head and, whistling tunelessly, strolled away, leaving her standing at the fence.

Sophia felt her smile fade as she watched him go, and something akin to disappointment welled in her rebellious breast.

It most certainly *was not* disappointment, she told herself. With slightly shaky hands, she crammed her fingers back into her gloves, stomped back to the flat of pansies she'd been planting before he'd interrupted her. Disappointment indicated that she cared what he thought—about her and her rump, drat him—and that was simply not acceptable.

She buried the spade in the ground, flipping dirt aside with a little more vigor than was necessary. She was sixty-two years old. Widowed, thank God, she added silently. Her children were grown and settled. She had four adorable grandchildren, a nice group of friends, and a multitude of enjoyable hobbies to fill her days. She sat back on her haunches, and glared down the street at his retreating figure.

The last thing she needed was some Paul Newman look-alike to take an interest in her ass, making her long for something futile and elusive…like passion and companionship. A golden romance to gild her later years.

Romance, Sophia thought, with a huff of disgust. Now there was a pipe dream. Or at least it had been for her. Memories unwound like a spool of thread through her mind and her gaze turned inward. She'd met and married Charles Morgan all within the space of a month.

She'd been seventeen, just old enough to let those rip-ening teenage hormones over-ride what she liked to think was a fairly sound intellect, and that lone decision had shaped the course of her life as no other could have ever done. She'd thought she'd married a kind man with a good work ethic and a fine sense of family.

She'd thought wrong.

What she'd wound up with was a meaner-than-hell, lazy bastard who wasn't remotely interested in her or their children. By the time she'd realized that she couldn't change him, that no amount of prayer on his behalf was going to make him the husband she longed to have—the father her children needed—he'd had two blocked arteries and she'd already invested too much of her life in him to let him ruin her with a divorce. Every-thing they had, *she'd* worked for, and she'd decided she'd be damned before she'd give him half.

At the time, two friends, Bitsy and Meredith, had found themselves in similar situations, both of them married to men who made them wretched, and one night after one too many hands of rummy and one too many Bloody Mary's, the idea of the Future Widows' Club had been born.

Ultimately, it had saved her. Saved all of them. And now it offered hope to a new group of women trapped in loveless, miserable marriages. Women who needed a little vengeful humor to help them cope. Women like Jolie Marshall, Sophia thought, hoping that she'd come and join them. Women who, like them, preferred wid-owhood to divorce.

And why not? Sophia thought, particularly proud of

her brain-child. Being widowed definitely had the advantage. Instead of half—half your friends and half your assets—a widow got to keep it all. People sympathized and brought food. Black was slimming. A widow was pitied, not scorned. She was deemed a survivor, not damaged goods. Then there was the life insurance, Sophia thought with a fond smile. She harrumphed. Charles had definitely been worth more to her dead than he ever had been alive. Aside from the birth of her children, planting that miserable SOB in Shady Memorial—in the hottest patch of earth she could find—had been the single-most bar-none *best* day of her life.

Which was what made the idea of entertaining any sort of feelings for Edward Jennings absolutely insane. It had taken her twenty-three years to get rid of the first man that had ever caught her fancy. What in God's name would possess her to want to try that again?

She knew why, though it nearly killed her to admit it—sex.

It used to be that practically no one her age was sexually active. Waning sex drives and impotency had all but obliterated sex from her social scene, but with the advent of enhancement drugs—Viagra, Cialis, Avlimil, etc.—sex had made a huge comeback with people her age. And with it, the needs she'd forgotten—or had deemed too trivial to waste her time on—had come raging back.

Her own sex drive had been below the radar, lying like a dormant volcano for years, but now— Sophia smothered a frustrated groan. Dirt flew as she attacked her planting with renewed vigor. Now, a couple of smiles from a blue-eyed gentleman and some raucous talk of multiple orgasms and erections at the bingo hall had left her so wretchedly horny that her yearly trip to the gynecologist was actually something she found herself looking forward to.

It was crazy. Insane. And yet she couldn't deny the ache in her breasts, the throb deep in her womb, the desire for a warm male body at her back.

Both Bitsy and Meredith had taken lovers over the years, but Sophia had always abstained. She'd deemed herself above such needs and had secretly pitied their continued dependence on men. After Charles, though many had tried, she hadn't been remotely interested in forming any sort of relationship with a man. One had been enough, thank you very much.

But something about Edward Jennings shook that stalwart reserve, made her watch those sexual enhancement commercials with the sort of puppy-dog longing that was downright pathetic, even made her yearn for something as simple as sharing coffee over the breakfast table.

Sophia fingered the delicate bloom of a purple pansy, then closed her eyes as she caught the faint tune of Edward's whistle. For the first time in her life, she was lonely.

CHAPTER FOUR

ACHING AND ANGRY for her friend, Sadie aimed her picture phone at the side of Jolie's bruised face and blinked back tears. Chris Marshall needed his ass kicked, she thought. Needed the absolute hell beat out of him for doing this to her. "Okay," Sadie said, releasing an unsteady breath. "I got that side. Now let me get a close-up of your lip."

Jolie nodded, tilted her mouth up, but didn't speak.

Sadie leaned in and took the shot, made sure that all the photos were good, then with a few keystrokes sent them to her e-mail account. She'd pull them up and print them so that Jolie could have them on hand when she went to the Sheriff's department to file the official complaint.

Seeing Jolie's car in the parking lot this morning when she'd arrived at The Spa hadn't come as a surprise. Her friend had used the apartment above her shop as a sanctuary many times over the past two years, but seemed to be doing so with more frequency over the past few months.

But seeing the dark bruise—the imprint of Chris's hand and knuckles—against the side of her face had come as a complete shock. Up until this point, Chris had never hit her, had preferred to inflict psychological—

emotional—wounds. The fact that things had escalated to this point convinced Sadie more than ever that Jolie needed to be content with the portion of money she'd managed to secure so far, give that to her mother, and bail.

She wouldn't, of course, Sadie knew, equally irritated and exasperated. She was too damned stubborn, too determined that every person who'd invested in Chris because of her home-town credibility got their money back. Noble? Yes. But not at this price. It was too much. Too high.

Sadie swallowed, looked out over the square and watched the early morning sun glint off the arching waters of the town fountain. A group of older men had already plopped down on one of the benches—the very ones some of her patrons referred to as the Limp Dick Benches, she thought with a small smile—and had pulled out their pocket knives and wood. They'd whittle for hours, spit tobacco, trade secrets and tell lies.

"Look, Jo," Sadie said softly, "I know you're tired of hearing me say this, but give your Mom what you've got, and let it go. *Leave.*" She gestured toward Jolie's battered face, her gaze softening. "This— This can only get worse. He was too drunk to do more this time, but what's to say that he won't be the next time? And there will be a next time," she told her. *"You know it."*

Jolie had moved to a mirror, was presently rummaging through her make-up bag, and refused to look up. Her long auburn hair with its distinctive natural flash of blond at the widow's peak was tucked behind her ears and her normally envious complexion was leached of color save the bruising on her cheek. Despite the fact that she was too curvy to be called thin, Jolie looked smaller, more fragile than Sadie had ever seen her, and there was a sadness that lurked in her pale green eyes that seemed to be slowly snuffing out her usual spark.

Once again the desire to hurt Chris Marshall surged through her, made her hands involuntarily curl into fists. Sadie could honestly say that the need to inflict pain upon another person had never been something she'd ever experienced, an idea she'd ever entertained. But were she a man, there was absolutely no question in her mind what she would do—she'd hurt him. And the scary part was she'd enjoy it.

Jolie winced as she carefully applied concealer to her cheek. "Filing the report will make him think twice before doing it again any time soon," she said, seemingly unconcerned. "And it'll buy me the time that I need."

"That's what you said about the possession charge," Sadie argued, trying the keep the impatience out of her voice. God, it was so frustrating. She felt so powerless, so helpless. Watching this man do this to her friend… It was tearing Sadie up inside. Needing to do something proactive, she moved to the computer, logged on, pulled up the pictures and sent them to the printer.

"And it worked," Jolie replied. She slid a powder pad over her cheek, grimaced. "At least for a while, anyway."

"That's right," Sadie persisted. She leaned forward in her chair. "But only for a while, and not as long as you'd hoped. The fact that he's let his penchant for partying blind him to the bottom line ought to tell you something. He doesn't care anymore." She shook her head, gestured wearily. "There's no bargaining power left, Jo. No leverage. For the love of God, just leave," she implored.

Jolie turned, leaning against the faux marble counter. She chewed the unbroken side of her lip and, to Sadie's surprise, her eyes misted. "Sadie, I know you mean well, and I know that you don't understand why I have to do this. I know you're frustrated with me—" She looked away, shrugging helplessly "—but I *have* to do this. *I have to.*" She took a bolstering breath, sliding a knuckle beneath her eye. "Dad coughed up the money for that life insurance policy for over thirty years. Thirty years," she repeated significantly, her voice cracking with pain and determination. "When times were hard, he'd let the phone bill slide, or there might not be any meat on the table, but that life insurance was *always* paid. It was his guarantee for us, but mostly for her. It's *my* fault that Mom believed in Chris. *My* fault that he's here, that this is happening." She dragged in a bolstering breath, blinked back her moment of weakness. "I—I have to fix it. It's that simple."

No, it was that complicated, Sadie thought. Her shoulders sagged. Like her own family, Jolie had grown up one rung just above poverty level. Moon Valley had one main industry—steel—and the majority of its residents depended on it for their incomes. It was hard, particularly dangerous work, and every man who clocked in at Valley Steel was aware of the risks. Employees knew to invest in good work boots and sufficient insurance.

Sadie's father had worked alongside Jolie's—they'd

been lifelong friends—and though, thankfully her dad had lived long enough to see retirement, sadly, in a cruel twist of fate, Jolie's father had suffered a massive heart attack just two weeks before he was supposed to punch out for the last time. Her family had been devastated. Jolie and her mom had always been close, had shared a special, frankly enviable, bond, but something about that tragedy had changed them.

Jolie had turned to Jake and, despite the fact that their relationship had been forged on the playground in the third grade—had been the stuff of fairytales, had never once wavered—for reasons Sadie never understood, Jake had side-stepped like a spooked horse. He regretted it now, of course. She knew it. Could tell by the hollow look in his eyes, the harder edge regret had lent to his voice. But by the time he'd realized he'd made a mistake, Jolie had returned from Savannah with Chris in tow. Sadie sighed. And the rest, as they say, was history.

She shot Jolie a hopeful look. "Want me to have Rob kick his ass?"

Jolie chuckled softly, seemingly relieved by the subject change. "Thanks, but no." She rolled her eyes. "As gratifying as that would be—and God would it ever be," she said meaningfully, "there's no point in Rob going to jail." She pushed off from the counter and started tossing her makeup back into her purse. "I'm gonna go down and file the report before I head to work and I'd like to beat Chris to the office this morning." Her lips quirked and a spark of droll humor lit her gaze, along with her usual determination. "Get a little *laundry* done before he comes in."

Sadie felt a grin tug at her lips. "Want me to signal you if he beats you there?" From her vantage point just across the square, Sadie could look out her storefront window and see if Chris was in the office. When Jolie and Chris had started the software company, he'd wanted one of the newer offices in a complex away from the square, but Jolie had insisted on being downtown. It had definitely ended up being for the best.

Jolie nodded. "Yeah, I'd appreciate it. I don't look for him to make it in before ten, but—" she pulled a shrug "—I could be wrong."

Sadie snagged the pictures from the printer tray, came around the desk and handed them to her. She felt a sad smile shape her mouth as she looked again at Jolie's bruised cheek, just visible beneath the makeup. Her heart ached. "Let me know if I can do anything."

"You do enough." Jolie smiled and jerked her head toward the ceiling. "Like letting me crash upstairs when I need to."

A thought struck, popping another bubble of dread. "How are you going to hide this from your mother?"

Jolie hesitated, backed toward the door and managed a grim laugh. "The good-old fashioned way—by avoiding her."

CHAPTER FIVE

JAKE SNAGGED yesterday's paperwork and his thermos from the cab of his truck, then made his way across the parking lot and into the Sheriff's Department. His second home, he thought with a half-hearted smile. The scent of bad coffee, stale body odor and antiseptic cleaner greeted him as he pushed his way through the scarred double doors. Housed in the newer part of the county courthouse, the Sheriff's department had been dressed in the cheapest possible government-issue décor. Metal desks, plastic chairs, beige walls, and serviceable tile. His lips quirked. Only the best for the good citizens of Moon Valley.

Looking as happy as a hooker on a front church pew, Faye Kellerton manned the dispatch desk with her typical unwavering surly expression. Be it Botox or simply a perpetual bad mood, Faye rarely smiled. In fact, Jake wasn't so sure you could even deem the slight incline of the corner of her mouth a true smile. It was more of a painful, gassy smirk.

He conjured a grin and gestured toward the discarded newspaper on her desk. "You finished with that, Faye?"

"Sure. Take it," she said, her voice a long-winded sigh that implied that he was wasting her time. "Aside from the classifieds, it's just bad news from cover to cover."

A regular little ray of sunshine, Jake thought as he absently scoured the headlines and headed toward his office. The mayor was still having trouble with skunks, he noted—apparently, several families of the stinky creatures had taken up residence under his house—and there was the controversy over who should pay for the renovation of the statue of Jebediah Moon. The Civic Club or the city? The Civic Club had donated the statue to the town, so the city argued that since the Civic Club had been the original purchasers, they should pick up the bill for restoration.

The Civic Club took offense and said that the statue had been a *gift,* and as such, they weren't responsible for the upkeep. In the words of one of their esteemed members, "I gave my mail carrier a set of socket wrenches for Christmas. Does that mean I'm supposed to repair them if they break?"

"Jake?"

Still smiling, Jake paused and looked up. Looking grave enough to raise concern, Mike Burke, a deputy and his long-time best friend, waved him over. "What's up?" Jake asked, every sense going on point.

Mike passed a hand over his face. "Look, I took a complaint early this morning and I, uh…" He grimaced. "I thought you'd want to know about it."

Jake nodded, somewhat surprised by Mike's awkward behavior. Hell, he hadn't seen him this jumpy since the night they'd "borrowed" the principal's car and parked it on the fifty yard line of the football field. "Okay," he said cautiously. "What was it?"

Mike shifted a few papers aside and tapped his finger on a stack of photographs. "This."

Jake frowned, then looked down at where Mike had indicated and felt his body go numb with angry shock. He picked up the stack, and though his guts were boiling with sickening fury, managed to flip through them with what he hoped passed for professional detachment.

The first was a head shot of Jolie, the side of her lush mouth split and an ugly bruise marring the right side of her face. His jaw tightened. It was quite evident that she'd been slapped.

Hard.

The second was a close-up of her battered cheek, a large bruise, punctuated by three smaller more distinct discolorations—the bastard's knuckles, Jake decided. God knows he'd worked enough domestic dispute cases to recognize the pattern. The final photo was another close-up, this one of her mouth, and for whatever reason, this one managed to anger him more than the others, forcing him to swallow a curse.

God, she'd always had the sweetest mouth, Jake thought, tracing the familiar lines with his gaze. Full bottom lip, lush and suckable, and a slightly thinner upper lip with a distinct bow in the middle. Be it brimstone or a prayer, a smile or a kiss, he'd always had a thing for her mouth.

And Chris Marshall had broken it.

"What happened?" Jake asked, his voice low and throbbing with irrepressible anger.

Mike let go a breath. "Marshall came home around three this morning and broke into her room. He—"

Jake's gaze sharpened. "*Her* room?"

"Yeah, I'd wondered about that, too," Mike said, leaning a hip against his desk. "When I asked her about it, she said that they no longer shared a bedroom, that she'd moved into the guest bedroom over a year and a half ago." He paused. "Anyway, according to her he was drunk and high, said some ugly things to her," Mike said, being purposely vague, undoubtedly to keep Jake from getting angrier. "Then, when he wouldn't get out of her room, she tried to leave and he grabbed her. She jerked free, then he back-handed her, fell down onto the bed and passed out. Hell of an anniversary present, eh?" Mike added with a humorless laugh. "Sadie's given her a key to that apartment above her shop. Jolie went over there, spent the night, and from the impression I got, this wasn't the first time."

No, Jake knew it wasn't. Before he'd made detective, he'd worked the night shift patrol, and there'd been several times over the past couple of years when he'd seen her car parked in front of The Spa, the lights on in the upstairs apartment. Had he hit her then? Jake wondered as his guts twisted with angry dread. Or had she fled for another reason?

Seemingly following his thoughts, Mike shifted. "She says this is the first time that he's ever laid a hand on her." His mouth hitched into a half-grin. "And we both know she's not the type to put up with it."

Jake barely suppressed a snort. "No," he said, rubbing the back of his neck, a small smile tugging at his lips. "She's not." In fact, Jolie had a short fuse and, once it was lit, an even longer temper, one of the absolute worst he'd ever seen.

Unlike most people with a short fuse, however, Jolie didn't get angry over little things. She had to be thoroughly provoked, and it usually ended up being for someone else's benefit. Scrappy Doo, Jake remembered fondly. That's what he'd called her in grade-school. She'd been the number one champion for the underdog, always taking up for those too scared or too timid to take up for themselves.

Like in fourth grade when she'd pummeled the crap out of a boy twice her size for calling Jeremy Pickens "white trash." Or the year she spent walking three blocks out of her way to personally escort Lanni Wallace—a very small girl who had the unfortunate habit of wetting herself when she was frightened—to and from school to keep kids from purposely trying to scare her. Jake smiled, remembering. She was always the first to offer help, always a friend to the friendless. She was one of a kind.

Jake's gaze drifted over her picture once more, to the damaged side of her sweetly curved cheek, her busted lip and anger boiled to the surface once more.

There was nothing for it, Jake thought as he let go a tight breath. He'd have to hurt him.

"Mind if I ride with you to pick him up?" God, he hoped he resisted arrest. Then he could *legally* beat the shit out of him.

Mike grimaced, hesitated. "That's the thing. She filed the report, but didn't want to press charges yet. Just asked for a copy of the report."

Jake swore hotly, feeling his blood-pressure rocket toward stroke level. Surely to God she wasn't going to be this stupid. She knew better, dammit. As many times as she'd heard him complain about domestic abuse cases—particularly those where a woman refused to have the abuser picked up…

He squeezed his eyes shut, summoning patience from a hidden source. "You encouraged her to press charges, right?"

Mike nodded. "Of course I did. But she wasn't interested. Said a copy of the report was all she needed to make him back off."

Jake swore. A copy of that report wouldn't be enough, he thought ominously, but Jake certainly knew how to persuade him.

Mike shifted uneasily. "I, uh… I realize that your first inclination would be to beat the hell out of him, Jake—I admit it was mine—but it would be a bad idea."

Didn't feel like a bad idea, Jake thought. Felt like a *fantastic* idea. The best he'd ever had. Nevertheless, he thought, with an inward sigh as reason prevailed, Mike was right. While he'd no doubt take great satisfaction in slapping the hell out of Chris Marshall—repeatedly—it was against the law. Good cops upheld the law, they didn't break it, and he'd be damned before he'd let a scumbag like Marshall provoke him into doing something he'd regret.

But that didn't mean that he wasn't going to do anything…it just meant he'd have to get creative.

He glanced at Mike. "Did you get the impression that she'd eventually press charges?" he asked, unable to believe that she wouldn't at some point in the foreseeable future do the right thing.

"Yeah, I did," he replied, his brow folded in thought. "But she's biding her time."

Then she had a plan, Jake thought, which was more in character. He handed the photos back to Mike and thanked him for letting him know. "There's a lot of water under the bridge there, but…" His throat tightened. "Anyway, I appreciate it," he finished awkwardly.

Mike shot him an uncomfortable look. "There's more."

More? Shit. "Okay," Jake replied, drawing the word out.

Mike shot a furtive look toward Sheriff Dean's office, then leaned in closer to him. "She showed me a couple of pictures that she didn't let me keep," he said. "They were of Marshall and—" He looked around again, lowering his voice "—Emily Dean."

Jake squinted, cocked his head. Surely to God he wasn't suggesting—

"Naked," Mike added significantly. "And otherwise engaged, if you get my drift."

Dumbfounded, Jake felt his eyes widen. "Are you saying that Marshall is fuc—"

"That's exactly what I'm saying," Mike interrupted with another furtive look toward Dean's office. "Got a brass set, doesn't he?"

Or a death wish, Jake thought, stunned. Dear God, if Dean ever found out, he'd kill him. He'd rip him limb from limb. Jake shook his head, attempting to absorb it. "Where'd she get the pictures?"

"She wouldn't say. But they were time-stamped from last night. Around eight," he added.

Around eight? But how was that— Jake frowned as

the pieces clicked into place. His dinner reservation had been at eight and she'd been there, at the restaurant. Waiting for Marshall while he'd been shagging the Sheriff's wife. God, what a bastard, he thought again. He told Mike about seeing her at Zeus'. "So you know what that means?"

Mike nodded, shooting him a shrewd look. "It means she didn't take those pictures."

"Right. She couldn't have."

Mike arched a brow. "You think she's hired a private investigator?"

Jake shrugged, unsure. "It's possible." But knowing Jolie, he doubted it. He didn't see her putting that much trust into someone she didn't know. If he had to hazard a guess, he'd say Sadie—or maybe even Rob—was helping her out.

Only one way to find out, Jake thought.

Mike regarded him with a shrewd smile. "Your hair looks like shit, Jake."

Jake grinned. "You think so."

"Definitely. You could use a trim."

He agreed, nodded absently, and turned to leave.

"Keep me posted," Mike called.

"You got it."

AN HOUR LATER Jake walked out of Sadie's salon with a neat cut and the information he'd been interested in. Even if Sadie wasn't Jolie's best friend, The Spa was the first place to go to get the low-down on what was happening around town. Information was disseminated from within those walls with a frightening efficiency that would no doubt rival some of the FBI's best channels. Odd that the only woman who was capable of keeping a secret owned the place, Jake thought with a wry smile. Thankfully, in this instance Sadie wasn't interested in keeping one from him. In fact, she'd been very eager to share.

Just as he'd suspected, Sadie had taken the pictures—the ones of Jolie and of Marshall. In addition, she'd confided that she'd taken many more, that Jolie was amassing quite a case for her divorce and her husband's subsequent take-down as a partner of Marshall Inc.

While she hadn't filled in every blank, she'd shared enough to let him know that things were considerably worse than what he'd ever suspected, and the genuine worry he'd heard in every word she'd uttered had compounded his own. The more he'd learned, the madder he'd become, and as such, he'd cruised around town until he'd managed to put Chris in his cross-hairs.

Chris hadn't been at home and, on a hunch, Jake had cruised by the Sheriff's house. Sure enough, Marshall had parked his flashy little-dick compensation three houses down.

Jake had waited for him to come out of the house, then fell in behind him. Marshall had stopped by the bank, by the post office, and had presently disappeared into a convenience store.

Jake parked in front of the door and smiled. He'd been waiting for just this sort of opportunity. He stayed in the truck until he saw Marshall move to the register, then calmly slid from behind the wheel. Just as Marshall reached for the door handle to leave, Jake pushed open the door—with a little more force than was technically needed—and it slammed into Marshall's face, knocking him backward off his feet. Blood spurted from his nose and the coffee he'd been carrying had landed on his chest, scalding him. He rolled around on the floor, flopping like a fish out of water, howling with pain.

The clerk behind the counter squealed in belated alarm, grabbed a stack of napkins and hurried toward him.

Grimly satisfied, Jake stood over him. "Sorry," he said unrepentantly, his voice hard and menacing. "You should be more careful, Marshall. Accidents aren't fun and you don't appear to have a high tolerance for pain."

"Are you threatening me?" he asked, his voice an outraged nasal-like wail.

Jake cocked his head. "Merely stating the obvious. That looks like it might be broken. You should probably have it checked out." He picked up a package of M&M's, slipped a buck to the clerk, then smiling, made his way back to his truck. Not as satisfying as breaking the bastard's nose with his fist, Jake conceded as he pulled out of the parking lot, emptying M&M's down his throat, but it'd do.

CHAPTER SIX

ARMED WITH a marinated vegetable salad in a pretty cut-glass bowl—a good southern girl didn't show up for a party, meeting or any gathering of females for that matter, without having the consideration to bring food— Jolie stood on the front porch and, insides quivering, waited for someone to answer the door. The multitude of cars in the drive, not to mention the excited chatter coming from inside, told her that she had the right address. She'd successfully found the secret meeting place of the Future Widows' Club.

And after Chris's performance last night, the idea of being a widow had begun to sparkle with the shiny sheen of a brand new toy.

Evidently too hung over to work, he'd never made it into the office the day before—which had been a good thing because she'd managed to shuffle some things around and had netted another five grand for her cause—but he'd mustered the energy to go somewhere and had stumbled home at the relatively early hour of ten o'clock. His nose was broken, his eyes black, which had complimented both his mood and his soul, if you asked her, and he'd been fully prepared to finish what he'd started the night before—until she'd dangled the complaint she'd filed at the Sheriff's department in front of him.

For the time being, his desire to stay out of jail seemed to be greater than his desire to hit her, but in all honestly—like Sadie had pointed out—she didn't know how much longer that would hold true. He was becoming increasingly reckless, beyond caring. He'd been a hateful ass, so rather than laying into him the way she'd wanted to, she'd excused herself to the bathroom and gleefully used his toothbrush as a toilet bowl cleaner again. Petty revenge, but she happened to enjoy it.

The door finally opened, revealing the taller woman Jolie remembered from the trio at the restaurant. She wore lots of high-end jewelry and a stylish black hat over her short dark bob, one that would have looked nice with a sleek black dress, but hardly matched the trendy pink sportswear ensemble she had on.

"Ah, you made it," she said with a warm smile. Her gaze dropped to the bowl and her dark brown eyes gleamed with approval. "And you brought food. Come on in, dear," she told her, waving her inside, "and we'll get you settled. I'm Meredith by the way. Meredith Ingram."

Somewhat bemused, Jolie managed a smile and followed her into the foyer, where the chatter she'd barely heard outside rose to a delighted buzz. Meredith had stopped and was currently pilfering through a box, one filled with an assortment of little black hats. She decided on one, then swung around and, to Jolie's surprise, settled it over her head. "Oh," Jolie said. "Er…thank you."

Meredith studied her critically, made a face and shook her head. "Too round," she said as she whisked it off. "As you'll hear in a few minutes, finding the right hat is one of the first tasks on your list to prepare for widowhood—" she rummaged some more, pulled out another one and plopped it on her head "—but it can be a real pain in the butt, I tell ya, to find the perfect one." She inspected this one with the same thorough regard, then smiled. "But this one works nicely. It's a little big, and certainly not just anyone could pull it off, but with your hair and coloring it's trés chic. Prim and Proper down on the square carries it and it's a steal at under forty dollars," she confided, as though sharing a trade secret. "Let's put your dish on the serving table and I'll start introducing you to everyone."

Petering on bewildered, Jolie trailed behind her deeper into the lovely antebellum house. To the left of the foyer was a long living room and, just beyond it, separated by French doors, was the dining room. A dozen or more women were in each room, all of them wearing casual clothes and black hats. They were huddled in circles, chatted and laughed amiably, and the sheer pleasure they garnered from each other's company pushed Jolie's lips up into a small smile.

"Here we go, dear," Meredith said as she moved a plate of canapés aside. "Just set your dish here and I'll get a spoon from the kitchen." She turned and was nearly knocked down by a small, plump woman racing by on a motorized scooter. The shorter woman from the restaurant, Jolie realized with a start.

Meredith staggered and put a hand against her heart. "Dammit, Bitsy, you nearly ran me over," she snapped. "Go park that thing before you kill somebody."

Bitsy eeked to a stop and, multiple chins quivering, beamed at her. "Sorry, Meri," she said with a chuckle. "I'm still trying to get the hang of it." Her eyes rounded with delight behind her small purple glasses as her gaze fell upon Jolie. "Oh, you came!" she cried happily. "I'm so glad." She leaned in and inspected Jolie's cheek, which still bore the bruise, and tsked softly under her breath. "Heard about that, the bastard. Well, not to worry," she said briskly. "You're in the right place now. We'll get you trained up good until you can put that rounder out on his thieving philandering hide, or until he kicks it," she added grimly. "Whichever comes first." She gestured toward the table. "Go ahead and fix a plate, then come sit down. We're about to start." She tooted the horn and her head jerked backward as she shot off.

Smiling fondly, Meredith let go an exasperated breath. "The great fraud," she confided. "She doesn't need that thing. She's as healthy as a horse. She's just pissed because her kids wouldn't let her have a Harley. Now she's threatening to buy one of those mini-motorcycles." Meredith rolled her eyes. "As if that would be any better. She's blind as a bat."

Jolie chuckled, watching as Bitsy nearly upended an occasional table.

"Go ahead and load your plate, hon," Meredith told her with a glance at the table. "And be sure and try the petite fours before Bitsy spots them—she has a tendency to hide the whole plate, then take them home after the meeting. Sophia makes them and they're *divine.*" Meredith hurried away, presumably to get a serving spoon for Jolie's salad.

Rather than risk insulting anyone, Jolie managed to put a small dab of each dish onto her plate, ladled up a glass of punch, then nervously made her way into the living room and found an empty chair against the wall. She'd just popped one of the petite fours Meredith had told her to try into her mouth when Sophia sat down beside her.

"I'm so glad to see that you've decided to join us," she said, her face wreathed in a welcoming smile. She pulled a small pale pink booklet with a black hat and gloves logo on the cover from a tote bag and handed it to her. "This is your handbook," Sophia said. "It has a to-do list for becoming a full-fledged member—things like getting your hat, your outfit, additional life insurance and whatnot—as well as our official rules and regulations. For obvious reasons, we're a secret society, but I know you're going to want to tell Sadie about us. Since she's capable of keeping a secret, that's fine, but it would be best if you didn't mention it to anyone else, okay?" With another warm, commiserating smile, Sophia laid a hand on her knee and gave her a pat. "Trust me, sweetie. Things are about to get better. We're here to help you."

For reasons which escaped her, in that instant the weight and toll of the past two years seemed to come crashing down on her—for the first time since this all began she let herself fully acknowledge how *terribly awful* things had been—and though she'd only met Sophia a handful of times, Jolie suddenly wanted to drop her head onto the woman's round shoulder and sob with relief.

Because she got it. She understood.

Not to belittle Sadie in any way—Jolie knew she genuinely worried about her—but there was simply no way she could understand how wretched Chris had made her feel. She couldn't because she had a husband who doted on her, who loved her fully, completely, and without the smallest bit of reservation.

Jolie bit her lip, blinked back tears and cast a glance around the room. But these woman…she had something in common with them, and she fully believed Sophia, believed that, with their help, things would get better.

Jolie swallowed. "Thank you," she said, her voice tight.

Sophia gave her knee a squeeze. "You're more than welcome." She smiled. "Now let's get this party started." Sophia stood and made her way to the front of the room.

"Good evening, ladies," she called above the still-chattering crowd. Smiling, she waited for them to completely quiet before continuing. "Welcome to another Future Widows' Club meeting. Before we begin Confessional, I'd like to take a moment to introduce a new member." Her gaze swung to Jolie. "This is Jolie Marshall. For those of you unaware of Jolie's story, it's a sad but familiar one." Her lips curled with droll humor. "She married the wrong man. He's a thief, a liar, a cheater—" Her voice hardened "—and, as you can see by the bruise on her cheek, a bully as well." She lifted her shoulder in a negligent shrug. "He's a bastard."

The women all smiled knowingly, sending her encouraging smiles and woebegone glances.

"And, as such, she needs our help. We've all lived

with one—and some of us still are—and we know what it's like. We know how to help her. Now let's take a moment to introduce ourselves, state our status, and offer condolences." She looked at the woman seated directly to her right. "Margaret, let's start with you and form a line."

To Jolie's continuing surprise, all the women stood up and began to form a line in front of her. The woman named Margaret smiled and offered her hand. "Margaret Bendall, Future, looking forward to your loss."

"Lynn Willis, Official, may the worms feast on his privates."

"Cherry Hawkins, Official, may the devil rot his evil soul."

"Gladys Kingsley, Future, may he burn in hell."

On and on it went. One after another the women moved through the line as though this were a true wake and she a true widow, sharing their own particular condolences for the premature death of her bastard husband. Jolie felt her smile growing wider as the line wrapped up, felt her heart growing lighter with each sincere shake of her hand. It was magnificent, wonderful, and more cathartic than she could have ever imagined.

"Of course, you know Meredith, Bitsy and I," Sophia said when they'd all taken their seats once more. "We're the founding members and have since planted our miserable husbands." She shot a look at Bitsy. "Or, in the case of Bitsy, had hers cremated."

Bitsy grinned. "Ashes to ashes," she said. Her twinkling gaze found Jolie's. "Made excellent cat litter."

A shocked chuckle bubbled up Jolie's throat.

"All of this is in the handbook, but we meet once a week, here at Meredith's house."

"The neighbors think we're playing bridge," Meredith interjected smoothly.

"Now, so you understand, our group doesn't in any way wish to offend poor widows who had good marriages and actually miss their husbands. But we're not like those women. Our men were—are—horrible. Looking forward to their deaths is what made—and makes—our lives bearable."

"Here, here," someone called.

"Doing the things in your handbook—fellowshipping with other widow-wannabe's—it's how we cope, how we survive. So like any proper funeral," Sophia continued, "we always bring a covered dish, we wear our hats—they're fetching morale boosters," she said with a fond pat of her own. "And the Future's always confess the progress they've made in bettering their future position as a widow. Be it finding the perfect pair of gloves to go with The Outfit, adding additional life insurance, updating a will, or investing in a pre-burial plan. Any proactive effort is recognized, so when you come back next week, we'll need a full report."

"Finding the outfit is a bitch," one of the ladies, Lynn, if memory served, piped up. A murmur of agreement moved through the room.

"And there's a list of insurance companies that'll offer the highest payout and insure without a physical in the back of your handbook," another added. "You'll still need a signature, of course, but that's easy enough to get with a little muscle relaxant added to his scotch." She inclined her head and lowered her voice. "See me when we're done, honey, and I'll hook you up."

"Do you have a will?" Bitsy asked.

"Er…yes," Jolie answered, trying to absorb it all. "We had to have them for the business."

"And you know where it's at?"

She did. It was in a safety deposit box in Moon Valley Savings and Loan. Jolie nodded.

Bitsy beamed at her. "Excellent."

"Okay, then," Sophia said briskly. "Let's begin Confessional. We'll start on this side." She gestured to her left.

Margaret sat back in her chair. "Well, as you all know, Ed's cholesterol is through the roof."

The woman next to her nodded sagely. "Nothing like a good massive heart attack to do the job."

Margaret's eyes danced with mischief. "Yeah, well. I've been dumping his egg substitute down the drain and adding a mixture of real eggs and whole milk to the carton."

A diabolical "oooh" of pleasure moved through the room.

"Very crafty, Margaret," Sophia told her. "Excellent. What about you, Gladys?"

Gladys cocked her head. "Oh, I haven't been able to do anything like that. Robert's healthy as a horse, meaner than hell." Her gaze turned a wee bit sly. "But I did finally talk him into buying a burial package. We've got an appointment next week to go down and pick out caskets, vaults, and plots."

Everybody in the room beamed at Gladys as though

this was an absolute coup. "Oh, wow," Meredith breathed happily. "Gladys, that's fantastic."

The woman seated next to her—Lois if Jolie remembered correctly—nudged her. "Those pre-burial plans are great," she confided. "Just think. You get to plan the funeral in advance, so that's just one less thing you have to do when he kicks it. Gets you one step closer to independence and it's a lot of fun," she added earnestly. She leaned in closer, smiled. "I've got Howard lined up. The minute he finally checks out, I'm ready, honey. I'm sitting on G, waitin' on O."

Jolie felt her eyes widen and another chuckle vibrate the back of her throat. She sat back and listened as the other club members matter-of-factly talked about the efforts they were making toward their widowhood, and was struck by the camaraderie among the group. There was a chemistry here, a bond that defied description, and though she'd only been a member for an hour, she already felt like she belonged. She couldn't wait to get home so that she could flip through her handbook and start doing some of the things the ladies had talked about. It was liberating, empowering, awesome even, this incredible sense of purpose she now felt.

Granted she might have to live with Chris for another three months, but rather than looking forward to a divorce as she'd been doing, something about looking forward to being a widow in the interim appealed to her even more. Did that mean she wished Chris would die? No, not really. At least not yet, at any rate. But she wouldn't mourn him if he did, that was for sure.

Sophia cleared her throat, garnering everyone's attention. "Okay, ladies. Time to call it a night. I'll see you all back here next week." She grinned, sent a meaningful look around the room, which everyone returned. "Until then... *Our un-dearly departed—*" she began.

"—*may he never rest in peace,*" they all finished in unison.

Jolie's smile widened and she quietly echoed the sentiment.

CHAPTER SEVEN

SOPHIA LET GO a sigh and sailed her hat across the room like a Frisbee, where it landed on the couch with a quiet thump. Per tradition after a meeting, she, Meredith and Bitsy had pulled chairs up around the serving table and were currently gorging on leftovers and homemade muscadine wine. She liked to dabble with various berries and had earned quite a reputation as an amateur wine-maker.

"Well?" Sophia said, plucking a pig-in-a-blanket from a nearby plate. "How do you think it went?"

The remaining petite fours in front of her, Bitsy licked a bit of fondant icing from her thumb and absently selected a second. "Like it always does—good."

"I think Jolie enjoyed herself," Meredith said. She dunked a wedge of honeydew melon into a tub of fruit-dip. "She really started to smile once we moved into Confessional, and I saw her flipping through her book several times."

Bitsy tilted her head thoughtfully. "I liked that hat she was wearing. Looked good on her, didn't it?"

Sophia nodded. "She's a very striking girl. Always has been with that bizarre flash of blond in her hair." She selected a brownie, vowing to walk an extra lap around the square for it as penance. "Her grandmother had it, too, you know."

"I noticed that again tonight," Meredith murmured thoughtfully. She adjusted another chair, leaned back and propped her feet up. "I've seen it with dark-haired people—usually men—but I've never seen it on a red-head."

"Where'd you get that hat, Meri?" Bitsy asked, still more interested in what was *covering* Jolie's hair.

Sophia and Meredith shared a smile. "Prim and Proper," they said together.

Having eaten the rest of her favorite treats, Bitsy popped a sausage ball into her mouth and chewed bemusedly.

Meredith glanced at Sophia. "Are you going to call Fran and let her know how it went?"

"The minute I get home," Sophia said, letting go a sigh. "This latest incident has really upset her." In fact, she didn't think she'd ever heard Fran so angry, hurt and frustrated.

Like most children, Jolie was laboring under the incorrect assumption that, just because *she* didn't tell her mother something, that meant her mother didn't know.

Not so.

Though Sophia didn't know where Fran was getting her information—though she had her suspicions—her old friend was perfectly aware of everything that was going on. That's why Fran had contacted Sophia about inviting Jolie into the Club.

In a noble attempt to help protect her mother, Jolie was preventing her mother from directly helping her. Fran had been forced to do some behind-the-scenes maneuvering. If it had been her child, Sophia knew she would have undoubtedly done the same thing.

"Well, that's certainly understandable," Bitsy said. "If one of my son-in-laws ever raised a hand to one of my daughters, there'd be hell to pay." She nibbled on a cucumber sandwich, glowered at a plate of cheese straws. "There is absolutely nothing more despicable than a bully. Any man who hits a woman isn't a man at all—he's a coward. If I was Fran, I think I'd try to find someone to give Chris Marshall a good old-fashioned ass-kickin'. Did you see Jolie's lip?" she asked, outraged. "Poor thing."

"She filed a report, right?" Meredith asked.

Sophia nodded. "Filed the report, but is waiting to press charges. On what, nobody knows."

Bitsy grunted. "If she's smart she'll make sure *his* getting arrested coincides with *her* filing for divorce and finishing up with those sneaky dealings she's been using to get her mother's money back." She nodded succinctly. "That's how I'd do it if I were her."

Meredith and Sophia both blinked, startled at this abrupt pronouncement, then looked at each other. A bemused smile played on Meredith's lips and Sophia felt a grin tug at her mouth. Bless her heart, though there were times Bitsy could be as dim as a burned out bulb, occasionally a flash of brilliance emerged.

Like now.

Impressed, Sophia cast a glance at her friend. "Bitsy, that was inspired. I'd be willing to bet that's exactly what she's doing."

Bitsy shrugged, oblivious to the praise. "Just makes sense." She looked up as though another thought had struck and smiled. "Did either of you happen to see the paper this morning?" she asked, eyes twinkling.

Meredith chuckled. "I did."

Sophia shook her head. She'd been too busy fixing her hair and her face so that she could go out in the yard and plant petunias around her mailbox and wait for a certain blue-eyed know-it-all who made her old heart flutter like a doe-eyed virgin's. "What did I miss?"

"Oh, just another article about Mayor Greene's continuing skunk problem," Meredith chuckled. She bit her lip. "Apparently he decided to install a *small electric fence* around the perimeter of his house to keep them away."

Sophia felt her eyes widen and Bitsy positively chortled with glee. "I heard 'em talking about it at The Spa," Bitsy said. "Ginny Martin does the mayor's cleanin' and she was in there giving an eye witness account. Said the little suckers were hitting that fence and spraying like crazy." Bitsy did a comical impression—*jolt, freeze, jolt, freeze*—then slapped her knee and laughed harder.

"Needless to say," Meredith continued, "his plan didn't work."

Sophia chuckled quietly. No, she supposed not. For reasons unknown to Mayor Greene, the host of many professional exterminators he'd called in, and the entire town—with the exception of the three of them—couldn't understand why the crawlspace beneath the mayor's house had become Skunk Central. The pesky animals were digging holes in his lawn, making dens and alternately spraying, fighting and fornicating underneath his home and, as anyone could imagine, the odor was becoming quite…distinct.

But nothing less than what the old fart deserved, Sophia thought with a sanctimonious little nod.

For the past three years a city council member had been awarded the coveted Beautification Award. Her lips thinned. It was an appalling abuse of power, the height of political hypocrisy, and had been the scathing topic of more than one Dear Editor letter featured in the *Moon Valley Times*. Greene doled out the award to those who curried favor, and the rest of the town—who vehemently competed for the nomination—was left completely out the loop, their seasons of hard work ignored.

In Moon Valley that Beautification Award was the equivalent of a Nobel Prize. Gardening wasn't just a hobby in their little town—it was an Olympic sport. People guarded their tips and secrets with the sort of reverent regard worthy of the Holy Grail and having it handed over to unworthy candidates was blasphemous.

In fact, it stunk, so it was only fitting that the mayor should as well.

Sophia looked at the other two and quirked a brow. "Who has duty next?"

Bitsy, who admittedly had the best garden of the bunch, smiled determinedly. "I do."

"Throw out a few extra handfuls for our stinky friends, why don't you?" Sophia suggested slyly. "We want to make sure there's plenty for all of them."

CHAPTER EIGHT

"HEADED HOME, Malone?" Mike called as Jake unlocked his truck.

Jake turned. "Yeah," he said, dragging the word out. "I've got to feed, and I've got a mare I need to keep an eye on. She's due to foal soon." In the next couple of weeks if his calculations were right, Jake thought. He opened the door and tossed his case into the front seat, making a mental note to clean out his truck as the scent of stale fries and old coffee smacked him in the face.

Mike nodded, sucked in a breath and scanned the parking lot. "At some point we need to get together and talk about that information we received last week," he said, a significant implication hanging in his voice.

Jake grimaced. He knew Mike was right, but nonetheless found himself reluctant to get involved, and a week's perception hadn't given him any more insight than what he'd had when Mike had first mentioned the affair that Marshall was having with the Sheriff's wife.

Jake had made it a point to watch Marshall the past few days—one, he wanted to make sure that he hadn't hurt Jolie again—which was best for his continued good health, he thought ominously—and two, he'd wanted to see if Marshall was continuing to see Emily.

A couple of day-time drive-by's had concluded that he was.

Given the fact that the Sheriff had flexible hours and could arrive home at any time unannounced, Jake thought it was incredibly stupid for the man to risk getting his knob polished in the Sheriff's bed, but undoubtedly the risk held considerable appeal for the sadistic bastard.

Mike sidled over. "Any thoughts?" he asked.

Jake passed a hand over his face. "Should we tell him? Yeah, I think so." He winced, pulled a shrug. "But without the proof to back it up? I dunno, Mike. I'm not looking forward to telling him *with* the evidence," he told him. "Much less without it."

"I've been watching him, Jake," Mike said gravely. "The guy's going to *Dean's house.* He's banging his wife in his own bed."

"I know. I've been watching, too."

"If it was me, I'd want to know, and I'd be supremely pissed if a couple of my people knew it and didn't tell me." A muscle worked in his jaw. "He's a good man and they're making a fool of him."

Right again, Jake knew, but that still didn't silence the little voice that suggested he leave it be, that insisted it wasn't his business, much less his place. Technically, dammit, it was Jolie's. After all, it was her husband who was involved, her husband who couldn't keep his dick in his pants. Jake smirked. Of course, with that kind of thinking, she'd save a considerable amount of time and energy—if not ink—by simply running an ad in the paper and listing all of the women he'd had affairs with.

"Why don't you talk to Jolie and see if you can get her to give you a copy of the pictures?" Jake suggested.

Mike shot him an inscrutable look, then chuckled grimly. "You've got a better chance of getting them from her than I do. Why don't you ask her?"

While a part of him longed to jump at the chance for any reason to talk to her—to see her—Jake instinctively resisted. Just seeing her around town was hard enough. Talking to her, he knew, was beyond the scope of his abilities.

He hesitated, then gave his head a small shake. "She showed them to you. You took the report." Reasonable arguments, if not the complete truth. "If she'll give them to anyone, then it's you."

Mike nodded reluctantly. "All right," he sighed, rubbing the back of his neck. "I'll, uh… I'll give it a shot."

Jake shoved his hands in his pockets, leaned against the side panel of his truck and racked his brain for any sort of solution, preferably one that would spare Dean's pride and would prevent the Sheriff from spending the rest of his life in jail for murder.

Unable to find one, he shrugged. "I don't think we need to say anything without the proof to back it up."

Mike snorted. "As careless as that sonofabitch is, it wouldn't be too damned hard to get it ourselves."

He'd thought of that as well. With Marshall's reputation, a couple of pictures of him going in and out of the house would most likely suffice. That, or the next time Marshall paid Emily a visit, one of them could simply *forcefully suggest* that Dean go home. Though Dean was older than him and Mike, they'd nevertheless developed a friendship of sorts over the years, not to mention that Jake had a tremendous amount of respect for him. Keeping quiet felt wrong, but telling him didn't feel right either. It was just a bad situation all the way around.

"Last time I saw Marshall, I noticed he looked like he'd ran into a wall," Mike said slyly. "You wouldn't know anything about that, would you?"

Jake chewed the inside of his cheek, trying to suppress a grin. "It wasn't a wall. It was a door."

Mike chuckled under his breath, shot him a shrewd smile. "And you would know this because?"

"Because I was on the other side of the door. Clumsy bastard," Jake said amiably, pushing away from the truck. "He should really watch where he's going."

"Yeah," Mike agreed. "He could get hurt."

"Which is precisely what I told him." And precisely what he'd meant. If Marshall laid another hand on her, Jake wasn't so sure that a strong respect for the law would be enough to prevent him from hurting the louse.

Still laughing, Mike turned and walked away. "I'll let you know what happens with those pictures."

Good, Jake thought. Until then, he'd try to put it out of his mind.

CHAPTER NINE

"CAN YOU TALK?"

Jolie shouldered the cordless phone, walked down the hall and shot a look toward the bathroom. "Yeah. He's in the shower. What's up?"

"I saw Mike Burke come out of your office today," Sadie said. "Anything in particular that he wanted?"

Jolie grinned. Sadie didn't miss much and even if she did, she'd hear about it at The Spa. "Yeah," she said. "He wanted a copy of those pictures you took of Chris and Emily Dean."

"Did you give them to him?"

"I did," Jolie replied hesitantly. She'd shown Mike the pictures, hoping that he would let Dean in on what was going on, but Mike hadn't wanted to do that without the proof to back it up. Jolie understood, couldn't blame him really, and, though it was completely self-serving, she'd originally intended to keep the pictures in her own possession until she filed for divorce, strictly because she didn't want Chris aware of the fact that she was secretly documenting his behavior.

The less he knew the better.

But it was hardly fair to Sheriff Dean to hide the proof of the affair, and in good conscience, she simply couldn't tell Mike no. She'd made the copies and had felt better after she'd handed them over.

"Well," Sadie said. "For what it's worth, I think you made the right call. Dean's an innocent bystander in all of this as well."

"I know," she said heavily. They all were, except for her. She considered herself at fault for the original mistake in judgment. Jolie swallowed. "He, uh… He also shared something with me." Something that had made her heart alternately jump and squeeze, that had forced her to blink back tears long after Mike had left.

"Oh? What?"

Jolie let go a shuddering breath. "He told me who broke Chris's nose." She'd been curious about it, of course, but had refrained from asking because she knew Chris was just vain enough to draw the incorrect assumption that she cared. She'd just figured another pissed off husband had planted him a facer.

Sadie's voice positively vibrated with glee. "Oh, do tell? To whom do I owe my thanks? My gratitude? My firstborn?"

A broken laugh erupted from her throat. "Jake." Just saying his name aloud made something twist deep down inside her. Love and loss, regret and longing. His image rose readily in her mind, the slant of his cheek, that slightly full mouth, the very shape of his hands and the way his calloused palms felt against her own.

"Oh, Jolie," Sadie said, her voice tight with emotion.

She forced another laugh. "Last person I expected," she said. "I honestly didn't think he cared enough anymore to go to the trouble."

"I've told you all along that he did. He came in here the same day that you'd filed the report. Mike must have told him," she said, reaching the same conclusion that Jolie had.

"I, uh... I guess so," she replied haltingly, still having a hard time absorbing it, though he'd certainly come to her defense many times over the years.

One incident in particular stood out. Senior year, homecoming. They'd won. She'd been standing outside the locker room, waiting for Jake to come out when a couple of guys from the opposing team had walked by. One of them had mouthed off about her hair—she'd gotten that a lot over the years, particularly as a child. He'd called her a freak, then a witch. Jake had caught the tail end of the taunts and...

Jolie could still remember the way he'd looked that night. Dark hair wet from the shower, his face flushed from the heat and excitement of the game. He'd been muscled but rangy, a good-looking boy hovering on the edge of manhood. He hadn't uttered a single word, just walked up cool as you please, and slammed his fist into the guy's jaw. Then he'd dragged him up, hauled him over and shook him until he'd apologized to her. After it was over, he'd wrapped his arms around her. "Stupid idiot," he'd said. "Everybody knows that's the mark of an angel's kiss." Then he'd kissed her there as well.

Jolie released an unsteady breath. She could still remember the absolute bliss of that moment. He'd been her rock, her champion.

And she'd been too impatient. She'd given him up for Chris...and, though Jake might care enough to throw a punch on her behalf, she knew it was nothing more than what he'd do for anybody else. He hated a bully. Reading anything beyond regular human decency into it was an invitation for more heartache and, while she couldn't deny that she'd brought it upon herself, she'd had all she could stand of that for the time being.

She glanced at the clock and started. "Oh, crap. I've got to go. My meeting starts in fifteen minutes."

"You'd better hurry up then," Sadie told her, a smile in her voice. "After all, you've got *a lot* to report this time."

Promising to call with a full report once the meeting was over, Jolie grabbed her purse and the spinach quiche she'd made, then headed for the door. She didn't bother telling Chris good-bye. He was still in the shower and, since courtesy wasn't something he valued, she'd just as soon not waste her time.

Jolie had shared her new status in the Future Widows' Club with Sadie the minute she'd left the meeting last week. She'd been too pumped, jazzed and excited to wait and had driven straight over to her house the minute she'd left Meredith's.

Predictably, Sadie had jumped on board with gleeful enthusiasm. They'd pored over the handbook together, laughing at the darkly humorous instructions laid out by the founding members.

Things like, *FINDING THE OUTFIT: The perfect ensemble for the funeral is simply a must. It puts you in the "widow" mind-set and gives you something to look forward to. The perfect veiled hat—to hide your tears of joy and small satisfied smirk—is particularly difficult to find. Start early!*

And *SHOW ME THE MONEY: Regardless of present insurance and assets, another half-mil is prudent. Contact your agent at once.*

X MARKS THE SPOT: Think of a treasure map, and the will as your treasure. In this case, you don't want it to be a buried treasure that requires a long and possibly fruitless search. Make sure you're properly provided for—being sole beneficiary is best—and that the document is signed and stowed in a safe place.

PREPAY IS THE BEST WAY: Planning a funeral nowadays before one kicks the bucket is completely acceptable, even deemed considerate, thoughtful, and prudent. Take advantage of this perk, ladies! Have fun with it! Pick a plot, pick a casket, pick a service. Graveside or chapel? Efficiency now will make your special day run more smoothly. Your un-dearly departed...may he never rest in peace.

Jolie shook her head and laughed, remembering. But Sadie had been right—she *did* have a lot to report. She'd embraced the idea of being a widow with the sort of single-minded tenacity of a person clinging for dear life to the side of a cliff. The group had given her a purpose beyond getting her mother's money back. Being able to secretly thwart Chris made her feel empowered and alive—proactive. Better than she had in months.

Now, when he trickled acidic sarcasm over her, she merely smiled and thought about the additional life insurance she'd just purchased on him. She hadn't been able to get as much as the handbook suggested—that would have required a physical—but she'd added another hundred grand to what they'd already had. Getting the signature was simple enough. She'd slipped it in with other business which had required his careless scrawl and he'd signed the form without looking at it.

In addition to the life insurance, she'd found The Outfit. A black, fitted dress with sharp lines that accentuated her waist. A pair of long, sleek gloves and a pair of killer stiletto heels. The hat that Meredith had told her about at Prim and Proper.

And she hadn't stopped there.

She'd also bought a black merry widow corset, with a blood red bud nestled between the cups, matching lacy undies, and a pair of micro-fishnet thigh-highs. The fact that she'd never actually wear it hadn't kept her from dropping a small fortune on the outfit, nor had it kept her from trying it on. She'd felt like a femme fatale Mob widow…and she'd looked damned good, too.

Once she'd gotten the outfit, it had only seemed fitting to swing by the funeral home and pick up some literature on burial plans, and she had to confess that leafing through the little brochure had engendered satisfying visions of herself standing on a windswept hillside in her sexy widow gear, a mound of freshly dug earth at her feet.

The whole process had been wickedly fun, and now instead of merely surviving her current hell, she could feel the cool breeze of freedom beginning to blow through her life. Even Chris had noted the difference.

"What the hell's wrong with you?" he'd sneered earlier this afternoon. "What are you smiling about?"

The comment had pointed out two things. One, she'd been stunned to realize that she *had* been smiling—for no apparent reason, it would seem. And two, the fact that she'd been so miserable for months that he'd noticed a smile meant that things were definitely taking a turn for the better.

Jolie slowed to a stop outside of Meredith's house and eagerly anticipated the time she'd spend with these women tonight. It was ridiculous she knew, but she'd found it intensely comforting that an invitation into the Club meant life-time membership regardless of a woman's marital status. She'd worried that when she finally kicked Chris's worthless ass to the curb that she'd have to give up her membership.

Meredith opened the door again and promptly handed over her hat. "Oh, good," she said darting a glance over Jolie's shoulder. "You beat Bitsy here— she's out test-driving one of those little mini-motorcycles I told you about last week. Anyway, she took a real shine to your hat last week—even went down to Prim and Proper Wednesday to buy one for herself, but *someone* had just bought the last one." Her eyes twinkled knowingly. "My sources say that you've been busy this past week."

Jolie grinned. Sources, eh? she thought. This was Moon Valley. Nobody needed a source—all you had to do was make an appointment at Sadie's, walk around the square, or make a trip to the local garden center. "I've gotten a pretty good bit done," she finally confessed.

Meredith smiled at her as though she were a failing student who'd just aced an exam. "Excellent," she said warmly. Her gaze dropped to the dish in Jolie's arms and she sniffed appreciatively. "That smells wonderful. You know the drill, hon. Put it on the table, fix your plate and find a seat. We'll get started soon."

Jolie found an empty spot for her quiche next to a plate of mini-muffins, chatted amiably with Gladys, the woman who'd talked her husband into investing in the pre-burial plan. "It went smashingly well," Gladys said, positively aquiver. "You'll hear all about it soon enough. What about you, dear? Make any progress?"

Jolie nodded. "Quite a bit."

Gladys poured them each a glass of lemonade. "That's wonderful. Good therapy, isn't it? I remember when Sophia, Meredith and Bitsy first approached me about joining." Her gaze focused inward, presumably on the memory, then she blinked and looked at Jolie. "It saved me," she said simply. "Gave me something to do besides being miserable. I look forward to these meetings all week, have made some great friends. It's good to be with people who understand." She smiled. "I suspect that's what you think, too, isn't it?"

Touched by the insight, Jolie nodded. "Yes, it is," she murmured softly. She followed Gladys into the parlor where more and more of the women were slowly beginning to congregate.

Bitsy and Meredith were bickering over the scooter again—from what Jolie could gather, Bitsy had nearly run Meredith down again. Jolie stifled a smile. Bitsy had tricked out her little ride with a sewing basket and a couple of racing flags. She'd just noticed that Sophia was absent when she heard the front door open. A cake plate full of petite fours, tote and purse in hand, Sophia, looking harried but elegant as always, quickly made her way into the dining room to deposit her dish. Bitsy fell immediately in behind her and quickly loaded her plate down with Sophia's little cakes.

With an exasperated look at Bitsy, Sophia breezed back into the room. "Good evening, ladies," she called gaily. She wore a red pantsuit and had donned her hat. "It's lovely to see all of you again. I hope you all had a good week and that you have a lot to report." Her gaze drifted significantly over Jolie and a touch of humor curled her lips. "Unless there's any new business, we can start." She waited a beat, and when no one spoke, she let go a little breath. "Okay, then. Gladys, how about it? How did your meeting at the funeral home go?"

Gladys set her plate aside and smiled at the room at large. "Fantastic!" she chortled. "We took care of everything and get this," she confided, leaning almost off the edge of her seat. "I'd planned on suggesting that we economize based on being practical—when you're dead what's the difference between a three-thousand-dollar casket and a five-thousand-dollar casket, right? Well, I didn't have to say a word. Robert took one look at the price tag on those suckers and insisted that he be buried in the next best thing to a pine box. So not only did I get to plan his funeral, I saved several thousand dollars by letting him go with me."

A chorus of nods and praise for this accomplishment echoed around the room. "Just more for you, eh, Gladys?" Bitsy said. "Bank it for that cruise you're planning on taking."

"On the pretense of needing to 'get away', of course," Meredith chimed in with a sly smile.

"I *will* need to get away," Gladys said with a disgusted harrumph. She snorted. "God knows the old tight-wad has never let me go anywhere. When he's gone, I'm going to travel the world," she sighed dreamily. "I'm gonna go everywhere. See it all."

"I'm so glad that your trip to the funeral home exceeded your expectations, Gladys," Sophia told her. "I know you're thrilled."

Gladys sighed, patted her permed hair, then reached down and snagged a strawberry from her plate.

Sophia's twinkling gaze found Jolie's. "What about you, Jolie? I understand you've been very busy this week."

Jolie grinned. "I have been," she confirmed. "I've added one-hundred-thousand dollars worth of life insurance, found my outfit, and picked up one of those pre-burial plan packets from the funeral home."

The women all beamed at her, and Bitsy, Meredith and Sophia shared a proud look. "Oh, wonderful!" Sophia cried happily. "Wonderful, wonderful!" She laughed. "You certainly didn't waste any time."

Jolie poked her tongue in her cheek. "Yeah, well, I've wasted enough up until this point, haven't I?" she admitted.

"But you're making up for it now," Meredith replied. "And that's what's important."

"What are your plans for after your husband is gone, dear?" Bitsy wanted to know. "Anything you can share?"

Somewhat surprised by the question, Jolie tucked her hair behind her ear. "Er…yeah." She glanced nervously around the room. "I'm, uh… I'm looking at a lit-

tle house on Lelia Street and I'd like to start my own accounting business." It's the first time she'd said it aloud;
she hadn't even shared her plan with Sadie yet. Like a
secret gift, she'd been keeping it to herself, but actually
lending voice to her agenda made it all the more real,
made something light and happy expand in her chest.

"Oh, are you talking about Maudy Hawkins's old
place?" Lois asked fondly. "White siding, green shutters, big weeping willow tree in the front yard?"

"That's the one," Jolie said.

Meredith's face blushed with pleasure. "Oh, that's a
lovely old home. I can see you being very happy there."

She could, too, Jolie thought with an inward sigh.
She could see herself happy anywhere away from Chris.

Sophia moved the meeting forward, asked several
other Futures what they'd been doing this week to further their widow cause. Margaret was still slipping real
eggs and milk into her husband's egg substitute and
Lois had reported picking up a prescription of Viagra
for her husband. Initially Jolie hadn't understood the importance of this move, but Gladys had quickly explained
that men with heart conditions were warned against taking the drug. Apparently, Lois's husband was just a few
slices of bacon away from a good coronary and therefore didn't have any business taking the sexual enhancement aid.

"Dr. Gibson generally gives out the prescription regardless," Gladys told her. "The last time he refused to
dole out a free sample, his tires were slashed."

Jolie felt her eyes widen and chuckled softly.

"Let me tell you, women around here take that stuff

seriously. My daughter's a pharmacist and boy, has she told me some stories," she shared with a grim laugh. "Most of those women anchoring the front pew down at the Baptist church have acted like regular heathens when she's run out."

"Has anyone not shared?" Sophia called above the lively din.

On the far side of the room a thin woman with eyes the color of coffee gone cold raised her hand and blinked back tears. "I haven't."

Sophia's smile softened. "Sorry, Cora," she said. "I didn't mean to overlook you."

Cora shook her head, fished a mangled napkin from her pocket and wiped her eyes. "It's all right, Sophia."

"Tell us what's wrong, dear," Meredith encouraged. The room had gone silent, their faces somber as they waited for Cora to share her story.

"Jed took the checkbook from me again," she said, her voice thick with unshed tears. "He goes with me everywhere now—to the market, the gas station. Doesn't let me have so much as a nickel of my own," she said bitterly. "Doles it out like I'm too incompetent to be trusted with his hard-earned money."

Sophia and Bitsy shared a look. "Cora, there's only one solution for this, one that we've told you before. You've got to get a job. Make your own money."

Cora's shoulders sagged. "What am I supposed to do, Sophia? I've got no skills. I've been a housewife for thirty years. Aside from cooking and cleaning, what am I qualified to do in today's society?"

"Well, I don't know, but there's got to be something,"

Bitsy pointed out. "You make the best cakes this side of the Mississippi. You've taken first place at the county fair for as long as I can remember. That's certainly a skill."

"That's right," another lady pointed out. "Your fondant icing brought tears to the judge's eyes last year. 'Seamless,' he called it. 'Absolutely perfect.'"

"Why not see if Dilly's Bakery needs some help?" Jolie suggested. "She was covered up the last time I was in there. I can't imagine that she wouldn't welcome an extra pair of hands, and she certainly does enough business to support another employee."

Cora frowned thoughtfully, seemingly mulling it over and when she looked up at Jolie there was a hint of hope in her melancholy eyes that hadn't been there before. A tentative smile shaped her thin mouth. "I do know how to bake," Cora confessed rather shyly.

"Well, of course, you do," Meredith told her. "If you think the fact that you're married to a tight-assed old bastard was the sole reason we invited you into the Club, then you'd better think again," she teased. "We wanted your baked goods."

Startled, Cora chuckled.

"You did bring a cake, didn't you, Cora?" Sophia asked, her keen gaze zeroing in on the dining room table.

"I did," Cora said with a wavery smile. "But it's all gone."

Sophia's shoulders fell and she let out a heavy, lamenting sigh. "Five minutes late and I missed it." She grinned warmly at Cora. "Now that's a marketable skill. Do as Jolie suggested and check with Mary Dilly." She nodded succinctly. "Dollars to donuts she puts you to work. Then you'll have your own money and you can tell that stingy husband of yours to shove it up his ass."

"Won't be easy, though," someone pointed out. "It's too damned tight."

The remark drew a hearty laugh from around the room and the pleasant sensation of being able to help another person settled warmly over Jolie's heart. Poor Cora. She couldn't imagine being that dependent on another person. Chris may have stolen money from her mother and their investors, but she still earned a salary at Marshall Inc. Still had her own money.

Sophia cleared her throat. "Well, ladies, we should probably wrap things up for tonight. We'll see you all again next week. Until then." Her lips twitched. *"Your un-dearly departed—"*

Jolie grinned. She was ready this time, lent her voice to the mantra.

"—may he never rest in peace."

CHAPTER TEN

SOPHIA WAITED until the last member walked out before turning to Meredith and Bitsy, and grinned. "She's coming along well, isn't she?"

Meredith nodded and her eyes twinkled with humor. "She certainly is. Jumped right in and started getting things done."

"Just showed how much she needed us," Bitsy said. She pulled a face. "I heard a little more about that husband of hers this week." They made their way into the dining room and took their seats around the table.

Arching a brow, Meredith dragged a cracker through a cheese ball. "Oh, really? Do tell."

Bitsy chewed the inside of her cheek, then shot them both a you're-not-going-to-believe-this look. "Suffice it to say that he's been seen coming in and out of the Sheriff's house."

Sophia and Meredith frowned.

"When the Sheriff's not at home," Bitsy said meaningfully, playing her trump card.

Sophia's mouth dropped open and Meredith gasped

sharply. "He's sleeping with Sheriff Dean's wife?" she asked incredulously.

Bitsy nodded, pursing her lips. She selected a tea cake. "That's what I've heard."

"He must enjoy pain," Sophia said, struggling to comprehend that sort of stupidity, a wedge of cantaloupe virtually forgotten in her hand. "If Dean finds out, he'll tear him apart."

"Yeah, and Chris has already gotten his nose broken this week," Bitsy said. She waggled her brows. "I overheard a little talk down at The Spa. Jake Malone accidentally-on-purpose opened a door into his face."

Sophia nodded and smiled. She'd heard about it from Fran, who'd been eternally grateful to Jolie's old boyfriend for quietly coming to her daughter's defense.

"Jake Malone?" Meredith asked, evidently baffled. "Who's he? Somebody else's husband?"

Sophia shook her head. "No, he's Jolie's old boyfriend. He's a detective with the Sheriff's department. They were together for years—since third grade according to Fran—but things went bad after her dad died. Her mother's not altogether sure why—Jolie's never really talked to her about it—but she's hoping that they'll eventually get back together."

"Well, they can't until that vermin she's married to is out of the picture," Meredith pointed out.

Bitsy popped a cherry tomato into her mouth. "Heard a little more about that, too. Three months."

Meredith's brow folded. "Three months until what?"

"Until she's got her mother's money back and files for divorce."

Impressed, Sophia cocked her head. "How *do* you find these things out?"

Bitsy just grinned. "I have my ways."

CHAPTER ELEVEN

WITH EVERY INCH that put her closer to home, Jolie felt the dread of her return sucking at her, dragging at her spirits and generally making her miserable but she'd put if off as long as she could. After leaving Meredith's, she'd gone to Sadie's. Rob had been pulling a double shift at the steel mill, so it had been just her friend and the girls at home. They'd had the television in the kitchen tuned into Emeril Lagasse, icing cupcakes and screaming "Bam!" at the top of their wee little lungs.

While other kids were interested in Cartoon Network, Nickelodeon and Disney, Sadie's girls—little curly-haired miniatures of their mother—were watching the Food Network, HGTV, and the Style Channel. Jolie felt a smile tug at her lips. They were undoubtedly going to be a force to be reckoned with when they grew up.

Jolie had hung around and pitched in, then helped clean up the kitchen, bathed the girls, and put them to bed. Tucking them in had been particularly bittersweet, their little round faces bathed in the glow from their angel night-lights. It had conjured back-burner dreams of having her own family, but she couldn't help but be eternally thankful that she hadn't brought a child into the mess she'd created with Chris. In addition to everything else, she didn't think that she could bear the guilt of making such a poor choice for her child.

After the girls had gone to bed, she and Sadie had talked about her meeting, her plans for after she left Chris—which had gotten Sadie's enthusiastic stamp of approval—and regular Moon Valley gossip.

Sadie had updated her on the continuing problem the mayor had been having with skunks. Reeking of skunk perfume and tomato juice, the mayor's wife had come into The Spa for her regular set and had bemoaned her lack of sleep due to the "screeching, howling and humping" going on beneath her house. Evidently the mayor had called in the County Agent, and after investigating, he couldn't find any particular reason why the odiferous animals had decided to burrow beneath the mayor's home, nor could he suggest any further technique of removing them that hadn't already been employed.

As for the continuing debate over the restoration of the statue in the town square, the city council and Civic Club were engaged in the proverbial Mexican standoff, with neither party inclined to acquiesce. In the mean time Jebediah's stately bronze body was slowly oxidizing, turning black a result of the process. Jolie figured the Civic Club would blink first. A feeble smile caught the corner of her mouth. They'd been too proud of him to let him stand there and ruin.

Jolie wheeled her car onto her street and winced when she saw Chris's BMW in the drive. "Damn," she muttered, supremely disappointed. She'd hoped that he wouldn't be home—he usually wasn't—but, alas, it wasn't meant to be. What the hell, she thought, unwilling to let him wreck what had been a nice evening. She'd just do what she usually did—burrow in her room, curl up with a good book, a block of chocolate and try to avoid him. If he annoyed her too much, she'd pack her bag and spend the night in Sadie's apartment.

She didn't remember locking the door when she'd left earlier this evening, so evidently he'd been out and come back, she decided as she let herself into the house. With luck, he'd be passed out, sleeping off whatever he'd managed to get into tonight. A quick look in the living room confirmed that he wasn't holding down the couch—his preferred pit-stop after a night of drinking and whoring, she thought with an uncharitable smirk—and her first thought was that he'd probably gone on to bed. But then a curious sound reached her ears. Jolie stilled.

The shower.

Again? Jolie thought, her brow folding into a puzzled frown. Granted Chris was rather meticulous when it came to his daily grooming habits, but three showers in one day was a little excessive, even for him. Jolie didn't know why, couldn't account for it, but the oddest sense of foreboding shivered down her spine. Her gut hollowed, then filled with a combination of fear and dread. Oh, God, she thought. What had he done this time? She carefully set her purse on the couch and slowly made her way toward the back of the house to the master suite.

The first thing she noticed were the clothes he'd carelessly discarded before she'd left. They were left in an untidy heap at the foot of the bed. His wallet, too, didn't appear to have been moved from the dresser. Strange, because if he'd gone out, his things shouldn't be in the same place.

In the nanosecond it took to make this observation, her gaze darted to the bathroom door, from which no steam billowed out, and she noticed something that *did* look different. The bathroom door—which had been slightly ajar—was wide open…and from her vantage point she clearly saw something that made her stomach lurch with alarm.

Chris's leg was stuck at an unnatural angle out the shower stall door and a puddle of pink water had pooled on the floor.

Unable to stop herself, she gravitated toward the bathroom, moved though she suddenly couldn't feel her feet, could barely remember to breathe…and the rest of the scene came into view. The shower beat down on Chris's prone body. His eyes were open, unblinking, and a small hole cut through his chest. A silent shriek formed in the back of her throat. Then her voice caught up with the horror and she screamed.

SINCE BEING PROMOTED to detective, Jake had handled exactly three homicides, two of which had been crimes of passion, the other a drunken family dinner in which Frank Bolen had shot and killed his older brother Amos over a tub of butter. Amos hadn't passed it quick enough to suit Frank, so rather than merely waiting, Frank had reached for the snub-nosed thirty-eight he kept handy in the back of his jeans. Frank had later claimed the shooting had been an accident, but according to other family members present, he'd calmly buttered his corn afterwards, then asked for the salt and pepper.

When tonight's call had come in, Jake had been finishing up in the barn, his preferred after-work hang out. He'd spent some time watching Marzipan, throwing a little extra feed into her bucket. This was her first foal and while Mother Nature usually didn't need any help, he'd still feel better if he could be there during the birth in the event there were any problems. She'd started bagging up, so foaling was imminent. It was merely a question of when. Less than a week, he felt confident.

Mike had taken the initial call, arrived on the scene, then per protocol, had contacted the detective on call— Jake. He'd been grim and direct. "Chris Marshall is dead. Poplar Street. You need to get over here."

Jake had walked past Jolie in the living room, her face a white mask of shock, and followed Mike back into the master bathroom. Various men's toiletries littered the counter and shower stall, and the metallic scent of blood hung in the air. Chris Marshall lay sprawled on the floor of the shower, his brown eyes open and blank, a single gun-shot wound to the chest, right through where his heart should have been if the bastard had had one. But that wasn't the most startling injury.

Jake blinked, certain his eyes had deceived him. "Where's his dick?"

Mike passed a hand over his face. "We, uh… We don't know. It's gone."

"Gone?" Jake repeated, unable to process the information. He looked at the neat cut where Marshall's penis used to be, then back at Mike for an explanation.

"This is how we found him," Mike said, equally baffled. He scratched his head. "All I did was turn off the water, call you and the coroner."

Okay, Jake thought, numbly shocked. So their killer had taken a trophy. And a sick one at that. "Have you had a chance to talk with Jolie yet?" he asked, unable to look away.

"Just briefly. She made the call. Said he'd been in the shower when she left. She came home and heard the water still running, then walked back here, found him, and called us."

"Any sign of forced entry?" Jake asked.

"Not that I noticed, but I haven't done a lot of poking around. Jolie said she hadn't locked the door when she left, but it was locked when she got back. She'd assumed that Marshall had been out."

Jake nodded, mentally running down everything that needed to be done. The Sheriff should be there any minute as well as the Evidence Tech, Nathan Todd. Jake imagined the only reason he'd beaten them there was because he'd all but flown to the scene.

Sporting pillow creases and mismatched socks, Leon Turner, the county coroner, shuffled into the crowded bathroom. "What have we got?" he croaked tiredly, evidently suffering from a head cold. "Tell me it's natural causes. I'm too sick to handle a homicide."

"Sorry, Leon," Jake said. "I hope you brought your vitamin C. We're in for a long night." In homicide cases, the coroner and law enforcement worked closely together as it facilitated preserving the evidence, which led to solving the crime. Of course, in this case, some vital evidence was missing.

"Shit." Leon passed a hand over his feverish cheeks. "Oh, well. I couldn't sleep anyway. Hard to sleep when you can't breathe. Gun-shot wound, eh?" He squatted down, inspected the body, then his ruddy face went slack. "What happened to his—"

"It's gone," Mike said again. "Gone when we got here."

Leon blinked, seemingly certain he'd misunderstood. "I… Hmmm." He frowned, looked closer at the body, at the hole in Marshall's chest, then gingerly tilted him to look underneath the body.

"Good one," Mike said amiably. "We didn't think to check up his ass."

Though he knew it was inappropriate—the man was dead, after all—Jake had to smother a laugh.

"I'm not looking— I—" Leon stammered, flustered. The top of his balding head turned pink. "I'm checking for lividity." He pointed to some purplish discoloration on Marshall's left butt cheek. "See this?" he said. "He's been dead for hours. Long enough for the blood to pool and mild *rigor mortis* to set in." His thick brows formed a line. "Seems like there'd be more blood loss," he remarked thoughtfully.

"The water was left on," Jake pointed out. "Most of it likely went down the drain. What's your best guess on time of death?"

Leon shrugged. "Leaving him in a cool shower's gonna throw his core body temperature off. Based on what I see here, four to six hours, but the M.E. will be able to tell you more." He grunted as he stood, arching a brow. "Who found him?"

"Jolie," Mike said. Jake listened to him repeat the story.

"Well, he was alive when she left and dead when she got home," Leon said. He glanced back at Marshall's prone form. "Based on my best guess, that's consistent with what I see here."

Jake and Mike shared a brief look. Leon's shrewd gaze bounced between them and then his watery bloodshot eyes widened. "You don't think she did it?" he accused, his voice suggesting the very idea was blasphemous.

Did he think she did it? Jake thought. No. He couldn't imagine her ever being angry enough to kill someone. Knew instinctively that it wasn't in her nature. Hell, he'd seen her step over ant trails, nurture baby birds. As a girl, she'd taken in every stray, every unwanted animal—be it the two-legged or four-legged variety—and though he didn't know if she still did it or not, she used to volunteer at the local animal shelter. She hadn't killed him—couldn't have. She had too much respect for life, even Chris Marshall's, though he certainly hadn't earned it.

Nevertheless a good detective had to ask the hard questions, examine the evidence. And in most cases when a spouse was murdered, it was the husband or wife—whoever stood to benefit the most—who was responsible. And unfortunately, everybody in town knew that Chris had given Jolie a number of reasons to want to see him dead. Jake grimaced. Then again, that could be said of many people aside from Jolie.

He and Mike shared another look, one that Jake knew suggested they'd each reached a simultaneous deduction—Sheriff Dean.

Christ.

"We can't rule out anyone just yet, Leon," Jake told him, rubbing a hand over the back of his neck. "Hell, you know that." He could already feel the tension creeping into his skull. This was going to get nasty.

Leon leveled a hard look at him and despite the fact that he bore an unfortunate resemblance to Boss Hogg, he looked quite impressive in that moment. "Just like you know she isn't capable of this."

"She said she'd been at a meeting," Mike interjected. "That sounds like an alibi."

He'd find out when he talked to her, which he wasn't going to be able to avoid much longer. The very idea made his stomach knot with anxiety. He hadn't actually spoken to her in almost two years, and these were… Hell, these were hardly ideal circumstances. *Your husband's dead and his dick's cut off—you wouldn't happen to know anything about that, would you, Jolie?* Jake swallowed a morbid laugh.

On the rare occasions he'd actually let himself imagine talking to her again, he'd never been quite sure what he'd say. But he knew the coming conversation wouldn't remotely resemble anything he could have envisioned.

Leon passed a hand over his face. "Keep me in the loop, okay?" he asked Jake. "Her father and I were friends."

Jake nodded. "I will. Why don't you see if you can round up some coffee? This is going to take a while."

"Wonder where Dean's at," Mike said bemusedly after Leon left.

Possibly destroying evidence, Jake thought, wincing as the unchecked notion popped into his head.

Mike hesitated. "You, uh… You don't think he might have… That he…" He couldn't bring himself to finish, but Jake didn't need to be clairvoyant to know what he was suggesting, and the thought had certainly crossed his mind as well.

"We hadn't told him yet," Jake said, shifting uncomfortably.

"But that doesn't mean he hadn't found out. The guy's dick's missing, Jake. That's pretty damned personal."

Yes, it was. And whether Dean knew it before or not, they were damned sure going to have to tell him now. Had planned on it anyway, but what they hadn't counted on was having to bring it up because of a murder investigation. One which, for the moment, their boss was considered a suspect.

"If you'll wait on Nathan, I'll go ahead and talk to Jolie."

Mike nodded. "Sure."

Jake felt every muscle in his body atrophy with stress, mentally braced himself for the coming conversation as he made his way back into the living room.

Jolie looked up and her pale green eyes tangled with his. That phantom sucker-punch hit him in the gut and for all intents and purposes the ground shifted beneath his feet. He cleared his throat and uttered the same words that had ended their relationship.

"We need to talk."

CHAPTER TWELVE

"I JUST HEARD on my scanner that Chris Marshall has been found dead," Meredith said, her usually cool modulated voice panicked.

The words had filtered through Sophia's sleep-muddled mind, and sat bolt upright in bed when their implication set in. "What?" she breathed into the phone.

"Shot," she said. "Leon estimated time of death four to six hours ago."

That ruled Jolie out, Sophia thought, because she'd been with them. Not that she'd truly suspected her, of course—if Jolie had wanted to kill her husband she could have done that a long time ago.

But she'd need an alibi, which was undoubtedly what had put Meredith into a tailspin.

"I haven't called Bitsy yet," Meredith said. "But I will."

"Yes, call her," Sophia agreed, climbing out of bed. "We'll need to get over there."

"Oh, Sophia, what are we going to do?" Meredith asked, her voice weak and wavery with worry. "I don't mind outing our Officials—they don't have anything to lose. But what about our Futures? It'll ruin them. Ruin the Club."

Sophia wedged the cordless phone between her shoulder and ear, then shimmied out of her gown and blindly groped in her closet for something to wear. "We'll stick to the same story we've told for years. We were playing bridge. They can't prove otherwise, can they?"

"No, no, you're right, of course," Meredith said. "Still, I just have a bad feeling about this, Sophia. A very bad feeling," she said ominously.

Be that as it may they couldn't afford to lose sight of the immediate problem, Sophia thought, and that problem was that Jolie didn't know what to say, which was why they needed to get over there ASAP before she inadvertently outed them to the entire community.

Meredith was right—it could be disastrous.

"Don't worry, Meri," Sophia soothed. "Everything's gonna be fine. Call Bitsy, and then come pick me up. We'll hash it out on the way over."

She just hoped they made it before it was too late.

CHAPTER THIRTEEN

WE NEED TO TALK.

Jolie looked up, her gaze tangled with Jake's and for the first time since she'd walked into that nightmare in the bedroom, she felt the hot rush of tears hit the back of her eyes. If her legs would have supported her, she would have launched herself into his arms. Someone had walked into her house—the place where she normally slept—and killed Chris. She kept seeing his face, his eyes, in particular, and though she'd honestly hated him, she couldn't—would never—wish death upon anyone. Any life, even his misbegotten one, was too precious.

Jolie cleared her throat. "Okay," she said.

His expression somewhat dark, Jake came around the sofa and sat down in front of her. "I need to ask you a few questions, and later, if you're up to it, we need to go down to the Sheriff's department and do an official report."

She swallowed, then nodded.

Jake's gaze darted over her shoulder and she heard the scuff of footfalls hit the hardwood floor. She followed his gaze and discovered Sheriff Dean and another man, one she vaguely recognized but couldn't name, standing in the room. Looking solemn, the Sheriff nodded at her, but didn't speak.

"Excuse me just a minute," Jake told her, pushing up from his seat. He walked over to where they stood, briefing them, she supposed. She heard phrases like gun-shot wound, time-of-death and odd trophy, the last of which she didn't understand, but couldn't make her numb mind process anything beyond breathing at the moment.

After a moment he returned and took the seat in front of her once more. He braced his elbows on his knees and let his hands dangle in the deep vee between them. His bleak expression didn't match the kind, concerned and somewhat helpless look in those silvery gray eyes. "Can I get you anything?" he asked. "Maybe some coffee? Water? A soda?"

Jolie shook her head. Her mouth was dry as dust, but her stomach would undoubtedly protest so much as a grain of salt at this point. "No, thanks."

He nodded. "All right. Mike gave me the abbreviated facts, but I need you to start at the beginning and tell me everything, okay?"

Jolie chewed her bottom lip and with difficulty, found her voice. "He was home when I left, in the shower."

"What time did you leave?"

"Er…a little before six. I was running late."

"Did you notice anything odd when you left? An unfamiliar car? Anybody walking a dog, or hanging around?"

She thought back, trying to picture the scene when she'd walked to her car, then shook her head. "No, nothing, but I… I didn't really look. I was in a hurry."

Jake shifted. "Mike said you didn't think you'd locked the door."

That was the thing that really bugged her, Jolie thought. She was almost certain that she hadn't. In fact, she rarely locked the doors. There'd never been a need. Moon Valley had always been a safe place, one virtually untouched by the ugly violence of bigger cities. "I can't say beyond a shadow of a doubt that I didn't lock the door, but I'm 99.9% sure that I didn't. I'm not in the habit of it."

He arched a brow. "But it was locked when you got home?"

"Yeah." She moistened her dry lips. "I thought he'd been out."

"And what time did you get home?"

"A little after eleven. After my meeting, I called Sadie and dropped by her house to visit with her and the girls. Rob was pulling a double shift. She was lonely and…" Jolie hesitated, then she looked up, met his gaze and managed a ghost of a smile. "And I didn't want to come home," she admitted truthfully. "It's no secret that my marriage hasn't been a happy one."

Another flash of unreadable emotion lit his gaze, but he quickly blinked it away. "So you unlocked the door. Then what?"

Jolie thought back, replayed the memory, but had a hard time focusing on anything prior to finding Chris. That image—the absolute horror—was so stark it made everything else seem muted and unimportant in comparison. She closed her eyes tightly, hoping her lids would erase the vision.

Evidently sensing her train of thought, Jake cleared his throat. "You came in the living room," he coaxed softly. "Tell me what you saw, Jo. What you heard, what you noticed."

"I, uh…" Jolie scrubbed a hand over her face. "I noticed that Chris wasn't on the couch. He usually is, if he's home."

"Then what?"

"Then I heard the shower," she said woodenly, feeling the dread creep into her belly, infect her bones. "I thought it was odd because he'd been in the shower when I left. He showers in the morning as well, so I thought three showers? What's he gotten into this time? And I set my purse down and walked back to his bedroom."

"The master bedroom?"

"*His* bedroom," Jolie repeated. "We didn't share a room. Haven't since a few months into the marriage. Like I said," she repeated. "It's no secret we weren't happy."

Jake chewed the bottom corner of his lip and nodded, silently encouraging her to continue.

She cleared her throat, hugging her arms around her middle to stave off the chill residing there. She looked out the window, dimly noting the throng of cars parked in front of the house, hearing the ice-maker in the kitchen kick on, a wholly ordinary sound compared to the surreal, gruesome reality playing out around her. "The clothes he'd worn this afternoon were on the floor and his wallet was on the dresser. The bathroom door—" Jolie stopped short, resisting the image. She didn't want to see it again, *never* wanted to see it again.

"Was it open or closed?" Jake asked gently.

"Open."

"Had it been open?"

"No," she said, giving her head a small shake. "It had been partially closed. Just barely open. I'd glanced in there as I was leaving." She let go a shuddering breath. "There was no steam and… And it was cool." Nausea welled up the back of her aching throat. "Then I saw his leg. It was hanging out of the shower door and there was…there was b-bloody water on the floor."

Jake massaged the bridge of his nose. "Did you go into the bathroom, Jolie?"

She shook her head and forced herself to look at him, hoping that if she focused on his face she could push the other image away. She let go a stuttering breath. "Just to the door, close enough to realize that he was beyond help. Th-that he was dead. I saw the hole in his chest."

"What did you do next?"

She plowed a hand through her hair, tugging until it hurt to feel something besides the bizarre numbness that had invaded every nerve ending. "I got the cordless phone from the bedside table, then ran outside and called 911. I stayed on the porch until Mike got here. I didn't want— I couldn't be alone in here."

Jake nodded, seeming to mull over everything she'd said. He glanced up and caught her gaze. "You said you'd been to a meeting. What kind of meeting? Who were you with?"

Jolie let out a tired sigh. "I was at— I was with—" She blinked, stopped short and stared at him as a stark truth emerged through the fuzzy confines of her brain. She couldn't tell him where she'd been, she thought faintly. It was against the FWC rules.

Furthermore, even shell-shocked as she was, she had enough wits about her to realize that telling Jake she'd been to a *Future Widows' Club meeting,* of all places— when her husband lay dead in the next room—was going to sound…incriminating.

Her heart tripped and a new kind of fear, one borne of self-preservation, rocketed through her veins.

She'd undoubtedly be an initial suspect, Jolie thought weakly as more implications clawed their way through her foggy mind. She'd read enough suspense novels to know that, and had watched enough Law and Order to know how this would play out. She was closest to him, had the most to gain.

Oh, God. The life insurance. The outfit. The pre-burial plan.

She was going to puke. Or faint. Either way, she needed to be closer to the floor. She leaned forward.

Jake wore an odd frown and his gaze had sharpened. "Jolie, who were you with?"

"She was with us," Sophia said briskly as she hurried into the room. Looking harried and sympathetic, Meredith and Bitsy followed in her wake. "Jolie's part of our bridge club. We get together and play once a week."

Jolie wilted with relief. She'd never been more thankful in her life to see another person.

"We just heard, dear," Sophia said, coming around the sofa, shunting a startled Jake aside. She sat down next to her, draped an arm around her shoulder and squeezed. "We're so sorry," she soothed. "I hope you don't mind, but I called your mother. She should be here any minute."

Jolie nodded. The thought of her mom made the backs of her eyes burn. She'd missed her so much, but being around her after Chris had stolen her money had made Jolie feel so terrible, so unworthy, and so at fault she hadn't been able to stand the guilt. Until the debt was paid, it had been easier to avoid her. She knew her mom saw through the ploy, knew that she worried more about the money than her mom did, but that hadn't lessened the sizable weight of responsibility she'd felt.

"Is there anything we can do to help?" Bitsy asked. She tutted sympathetically. "Do you need a place to stay?"

"I hate to be rude," Jake interjected, "but you can help by leaving. You're not supposed to be here, ladies. This is a crime scene."

"But we just got here," Bitsy protested, shooting Jake a wide-eyed look.

"Nevertheless, I'm gonna have to ask you to leave."

Bitsy looked distinctly disgruntled, but Meredith merely nodded understandingly. "Of course. We just wanted to comfort Jolie."

Jolie thanked them, sending Sophia a significantly grateful look. "I'll go to Mom's," she told Bitsy. "But I appreciate the offer."

Smelling like cold cream and fabric softener, Sophia gave her another squeeze. "We'll be in touch tomorrow then, dear, okay? Don't worry. We'll help you get through this."

To the casual observer those words seemed innocuous, but Jolie knew they held a double meaning, one she desperately appreciated. She managed a grateful nod.

Sophia stood, and Bitsy and Meredith fell in next to

her. "Sorry to be in your way, detective," Sophia told Jake with a sweet smile. "We just wanted to be here for our friend." The three trooped out as coolly as they'd trooped in and even Jolie recognized that it looked odd.

Jake shot her an inscrutable look, one that led her to believe that he wasn't completely buying her story. "You play bridge?" he asked.

"I'm learning," she hedged, making a mental note to brush up on the particulars. She'd be in big trouble if he asked her any questions regarding the rules of play. She'd never been much of a card player, a fact he was perfectly aware of, she knew.

Jake continued to study her, then after a prolonged moment in which she'd suddenly developed a keen interest in the pattern on the sofa, he finally nodded. "You were learning to play bridge at—" He looked up, waiting for her to fill in the blank.

"Meredith Ingram's," Jolie said, quietly relieved that they were moving on.

"What time did you get there?"

"At six."

"And about what time did you leave?"

Jolie squinted, trying to remember. "Around eight, I think."

Jake chewed his bottom lip, giving another thoughtful nod. "Then you went to Sadie's, right?"

"That's right. I called her from my cell and she invited me over."

"What time did you leave her house?"

"Around ten-thirty. The news was going off."

"And you came straight home?"

She nodded, sliding her nerveless palms against her thighs in a vain attempt to warm them up. "I did."

Jake leaned back and passed a hand over his face. "Are you up to doing a formal statement tonight?"

Initially she'd planned on getting it over with, knowing the chances of her being able to sleep were slim to none. Every time she closed her eyes she saw Chris's lifeless body behind her lids. It was awful. But now that she'd begun to overcome the shock, she thought it would be best if she had a little time to think about things first. She needed a plan. Her involvement in and recent actions with the FWC were going to make things very…difficult. Now that was an understatement, Jolie thought, suppressing the hysterical urge to laugh.

She shook her head, struggling to pull it together. "If it's all right, I'd rather just go with Mom when she gets here. Could I come by in the morning?"

Jake inclined his head. "In the morning will be all right, but we really can't leave it any longer. We're gonna need to search the house and surrounding area."

"That's fine," she said, thankful that her Club handbook and the pre-burial plans were safely stowed in her purse.

Jolie stood and gestured tiredly toward her bedroom. "If we're done for now, I'll, uh… I'll go ahead and pack a bag."

"Make sure you get whatever you're going to need for the next couple of days," Jake told her. "You'll need to stay out of the house until we're finished up here, okay?"

That was fine with her. Other than a few personal mementos, she wasn't interested in taking anything out of this house. Wouldn't care if she never came back. It had never been a home—more like a prison.

Jolie nodded, then made her way down the hall to her bedroom. She packed enough clothes and toiletries to last for a couple of days as he'd suggested, then made the return trip to the living room.

Looking pale and worried, her mother stood talking with Jake when she walked in. Jolie's heart squeezed, and the tears she'd been holding back finally welled up. Everything she'd been holding back came to a head, and in that moment she might as well have been five again with a scraped knee. She didn't want to feel guilty or responsible, didn't want to be brave or in charge or anything else for that matter.

She just wanted her mother.

Fran Caplan's lined face folded into a sympathetic frown when she saw Jolie. She abandoned Jake, hurried forward and wrapped her in a tight hug. "Oh, honey," she said softly as Jolie quietly sobbed into her shoulder. "Don't worry. Everything's gonna be fine, okay? Let's get outta here," she murmured softly. "You don't need to be here, Jo. Let me take you home."

Home, Jolie thought, envisioning lavender gingham and a canopied bed, worn hardwood and high ceilings.

Finally.

CHAPTER FOURTEEN

FEELING EQUALLY USELESS and helpless, Jake watched Fran do the one thing he'd wanted to do since the moment he'd walked back into the living room and sat down with Jolie—comfort her.

Every broken cry, every slight shake of her slim shoulders chipped away at the professional demeanor he'd tried to keep in tact. He had to do things correctly here, had to make sure that every *I* was dotted, every *T* crossed.

With his and Jolie's past history he knew Dean would try to pull him off the case and appoint another detective, but Jake firmly intended to fight for it. One, he'd taken the call, so technically it was *his* case, and two—his gaze inexplicably slid to Jolie and he swallowed—she needed him.

Particularly since something was off with her alibi.

Jake didn't know exactly what yet, but knew she was hiding something. Hell, even the most unseasoned detective would have picked up on the way she'd mangled *that* particular question. Even if she hadn't cut her answer off mid-sentence, the frozen look of alarm that had captured her pale features had been enough to cause major concern.

Furthermore, he *knew* Jolie, was familiar with every nuance of her face—every expression—and the one he'd seen when he'd asked for her alibi was equivalent to "Oh, shit." Jake felt a smile catch the edge of his mouth. She'd worn the same look when she'd accidentally dropped his first badge off the side of the fire tower, one of their favorite old haunts. Or the time she'd backed his truck into the barn. She'd been "helping" him haul hay, had insisted that she could do it.

Fran caught his gaze as she absently patted Jolie's back and mouthed a thank you to him. For what, he didn't know. She gestured toward the door. "We're going to go now. You can get in touch with her at the house if you need to, Jake."

Jolie turned around. Her face was wet with tears and red with embarrassment. She hated to cry, always begrudging the presumed weakness. She used her sleeves to wipe away some of the damage, then pulled in a bolstering breath. "I'll, uh… If there's nothing else I should do tonight, then I'll see you in the morning."

Jake nodded. "We're good," he assured. "Go with your mom."

Fran took Jolie's bag and, murmuring soothing noises, ushered her outside. Jake watched her go, feeling the weight of impending disaster settle on his shoulders. At some point in the near future the other shoe was going to drop. He knew it. Could feel it.

"She's not doing the official tonight?" Mike asked.

After starting guiltily, Jake turned around. He hadn't heard him walk in. "Er…no. She wasn't in any shape," he said, releasing a pent-up breath. "She went with Fran tonight and will come down in the morning." He cocked his head toward the back of the house. "How's it going in there?"

"Todd's processing. Leon's getting worse. He needs to go home, but can't until the bathroom's done."

"What about Dean?"

Mike shot a quick glance over his shoulder, then looked back at Jake. "Oblivious," he said with a long whoosh of resigned air. "We've got to tell him."

A rectal exam would be more fun, Jake thought, grimacing, but Mike was right. It had to be done. "You've got the pictures?"

Mike nodded. "They're in my car, locked in the glove box."

"Get 'em," Jake told him. "Might as well get it over with."

Mike's mouth settled into a grim line as he strode past him and Jake silently echoed the sentiment. This sucked, but there was nothing for it. Dean had to be told, and the sooner the better given the current circumstances. If Marshall had been destined to have his dick cut off, it was probably better that it had happened postmortem. Had Dean found out about the affair before the bastard had gotten himself killed, Marshall wouldn't have been so lucky.

Manila envelope in hand, Mike walked back into the house. "Where do we want to do this?" he asked, glancing around the open living room. "He might not appreciate us whipping these out in front of Leon and Todd."

Jake considered the kitchen, but deemed it unsuitable for their purposes. He looked down the hall. "How about one of the other bedrooms? That'll give us a little privacy."

Mike bobbed his head in assent. "You wanna go get him, then?"

Want to? Hell no. But he would. "Yeah, I'll do it," he said resignedly.

Jake made his way back to the master suite. Dean and Leon—who did look worse, Jake noted—were standing outside the bathroom door, both of them watching Todd do his job.

"Twenty years on the job," Leon was saying, "and I've never come across anything like it. What sort of killer emasculates a man, Dean?"

The Sheriff merely shook his head. "A severely pissed off one, I'd say," he sighed.

Jake cleared his throat. "Sheriff, a word please."

Dean looked up, excused himself and followed Jake down the hall. "Mike and I need to talk to you."

"Yeah, I need to talk to you as well," Dean replied. "Look, Jake. You know I can't leave you on this case. You're too close. It's too personal."

Jake felt every muscle clamp with dread. He'd been expecting it, of course. Still, he'd hoped that Dean would let it be. "Er…that's one of the things I wanted to talk to you about." He continued through the living room down the hall that led to the other end of the house.

"Where's Mike?" Dean asked.

"Back here. We, uh…" He looked back over his shoulder. "We wanted a little privacy."

Dean nodded, seemingly baffled, but followed him all the same. They found Mike in one of the spare rooms, Jolie's, Jake knew instinctively. The faint scent of vanilla hung in the air and the room was littered with small reminders of her. A jewelry box—one he'd made for her in shop in their junior year, Jake noted, mildly surprised—and various perfumes, lotions and creams lined the dresser. A couple of books, a candy dish of Hershey's kisses, a tube of chapstick and a ponytail holder lay scattered on the bedside table.

A pair of black pumps had been kicked carelessly off next to the door and her bathrobe had been slung over the end of the four-poster bed. It was the only part of the house that remotely resembled *her,* that suggested that she lived here as well as Marshall. The rest of the house had a modern feel—sleek chrome and glass, lots of white, gray and black, trendy artwork—but not this room. It was warm, had heart. An old quilt covered the bed, mismatched plates had been grouped together on one wall and framed pictures of family and friends covered the top of the chest of drawers.

"What's this about?" Dean asked, settling his sizable hands at his waist.

Jake pulled his thoughts together, then glanced at Mike who wore a distinctly uncomfortable expression—one that plainly said, "You tell him."

Jake looked away, pulled in a deep breath to summon his nerve, then let it go and faced Dean. There was no easy way to say what had to be said. "Mike and I found out about something…and we thought you should know."

Dean nodded, acknowledging him.

Now or never Jake thought. "Emily's been seeing Marshall."

Dean's eyes narrowed. "What do you mean 'seeing him?'" he asked suspiciously.

Mike handed over the pictures. *"Seeing him,"* he repeated, evidently reluctant to elaborate.

Several emotions streaked across Dean's face as he flipped through the damning photos—shock, disbelief, outrage, then anger. His face reddened and he sucked in a harsh breath, then let it go. "Where did you get these?"

Jake stared at the jewelry box to avoid looking at Dean. It seemed disrespectful somehow to intrude on such a private sort of pain. "Jolie brought them in last week when she filed the assault report against Marshall."

His head jerked up. "Last week?"

"Yeah. She showed them to Mike."

A white line emerged around his thinned mouth. "If you've known about this for a week, then why the hell am I just hearing about it now?" Dean demanded. "For God's sake, Jake. Mike." He threw his hands up in futile frustration, swearing hotly.

Mike shifted guiltily. "She showed me the pictures last week—she was keeping them until she filed for divorce—but she didn't give them to me until a couple of days ago. We didn't want to tell you without the proof. It's…" Mike kicked awkwardly at a silver candy wrapper on the floor. "It's not the sort of thing you tell a man about his wife without proof, Sheriff."

Jake shoved a hand through his hair. "Look, Dean, I'm sorry. It's ugly business and I—" He shook his head. "I know we should have told you sooner, but given present circumstances—" Jake jerked his head meaningfully down the hall "—it's probably better that we didn't."

It took Dean less than three seconds to absorb that reality. Granted he'd just learned that his wife had been balling the deceased, but he was still a cop and they all knew that if he'd had prior knowledge of the affair, he'd have been a suspect. At least a temporary one. He swallowed. "Who else knows about this?"

"Besides us? Jolie, of course, and Sadie Webster—she's the one who took the pictures. But she's got a good head on her shoulders. She's discreet." Jake hesitated. "And whoever your wife or Marshall might have told," he reluctantly pointed out.

Dean nodded curtly, then indicated the photos still clutched in his hand. "When did Sadie take these?"

Jake told him and Dean seemed to be mulling it over. After a moment, Jake blew out a breath. "As far as this investigation's concerned, it never happened, Dean. It's dead and buried."

Dean shot him a considering look. He knew what Jake wanted in exchange and was obviously debating the merit of letting him have it. He finally sighed. "I appreciate it. It's your case," he said. "Keep me informed." He nodded at them, then, pictures still in hand, turned and strode out of the room. "Call me if anything comes up," he called without turning around. "I've got to go have a talk with my wife."

Mike glanced at him, released a deep pent-up breath and shook his head. "Cheatin' wives, missing dicks," he said tiredly. "This has been a busy night in Moon Valley."

Yep, Jake thought. And it was only getting started.

CHAPTER FIFTEEN

SOPHIA ADDED a shot of whiskey to her coffee and joined Meredith and Bitsy at her kitchen table. "Got there in the nick of time, didn't we?" she remarked, letting go a profoundly relieved sigh.

"I'll say," Bitsy confirmed with a significant eye roll.

"Don't kid yourselves," Meredith snorted. "If you think for one minute that he didn't notice that something was off, then you'd better think again." She dumped a teaspoon of sugar into her coffee. "I was watching him. He's smart."

Bitsy tsked, snagging a lemon cookie from the plate Sophia had automatically put on the table. "Oh, Meri, why do you have to be such a prophet of doom? What's he going to do?"

"Dig around," she direly predicted. "Mark my words. This isn't over. He knows her, knows her friends." A humorless laugh erupted from her throat. "Sadie, her very best friend in the whole world doesn't come to her rescue, but three old ladies who barely know her drag themselves out of bed and hurry to her side?" she asked skeptically.

"Sadie doesn't have a scanner," Bitsy argued, blithely unconcerned.

Nevertheless Sophia agreed with Meredith. This was

by no means over. Tonight they'd avoided immediate disaster, but steps were going to have to be taken in order to preserve the Club. So long as everyone kept their mouth shut—and she fully believed that Jolie was capable of that—then everything should be fine.

Despite the reassuring thought, she couldn't seem to shake the odd sensation that their world was about to suffer a significant shift. All of Moon Valley's for that matter. The last person to be murdered in their little town was Amos Bolen, but there hadn't been any mystery attached to his death. Sophia rolled her eyes. His ignorant, hot-headed brother had shot him over a tub of butter.

But this? This had all the makings of a real drama. Stolen money, adultery, a hated victim and the town darling. If word leaked out about the FWC they'd undoubtedly wind up in a made for TV movie, portrayed by fat, aging actresses with fake Southern accents, bouffant hair, mobile homes and muumuus. Sophia inwardly shuddered.

"So what now?" Meredith asked. "Should we call an emergency meeting? Maybe avoid having meetings until this is resolved?"

Seemingly horrorstruck, Bitsy appeared oblivious to the cookie crumbs tumbling out of her gaping mouth.

"No," Sophia said. "But we need to make sure everyone sticks to the story." She turned to Bitsy.

"I'll handle it," she said with a succinct nod. "As it happens, I *know* how to play bridge."

Staring unblinkingly into the distance, Meredith cocked her head. "I should probably pick up a few card tables."

"Good thinking," Sophia told her. "A few decks of cards would probably be good, too."

With everything seemingly settled—or as settled as it could be for the moment—Bitsy carelessly bit into another cookie, then slid them both a sly glance and asked the one question that they'd all been wondering. "So, who do you think did it?"

Sophia leaned back in her chair, grimacing. "I dunno. Jake's got his work cut out for him, that's for sure. The man had *a lot* of enemies. Any one of them could have done it."

Meredith arched a brow. "Sheriff Dean could have snapped."

Deciding that chewing would improve her ability to sleuth, Sophia gave into temptation and filched a cookie from the plate, then munched thoughtfully. Meredith definitely had a point. Marshall had been sleeping with Dean's wife. That would certainly incite some men to murder.

"Emily Dean's just who he's been seeing recently," Bitsy said. "We can't rule out a jilted lover. Or a jilted lover's husband."

"Then there's always the money trail," Meredith chimed in. "He's certainly screwed a lot of people over in that regard."

Bitsy grunted darkly. "If Jolie were my daughter, I'd want to see him dead, I know that. Especially after what happened last week."

Sophia felt her eyes widen. "Fran?" she gasped. She immediately shook her head, resisting the idea. "No, she wouldn't do that."

"I wouldn't be so sure, Sophia," Meredith remarked, surprisingly concurring with Bitsy. She lifted a brow. "Mother's aren't above killing to protect their young."

Sophia knew that. Still… If Fran had wanted Chris Marshall dead, the last thing she would have done was suggest that Jolie join the FWC. It would have been too risky. Her actions over the past week—the life insurance, the pre-burial pamphlets, the outfit—were going to be under intense scrutiny as it was without factoring in her secret membership in the FWC. Right now the only thing she had going for her was her "bridge" alibi and the fact that she truly was innocent. She related her thoughts to Bitsy and Meredith.

Bitsy who was able to be both fat and happy—unlike her, Sophia thought enviously—scarfed down another cookie. "I think you're worrying for nothing. She didn't do it. The truth will speak for itself."

"Ultimately, yes," Sophia admitted. "But in the mean time she'd better brace herself for sheer hell."

Meredith shrugged lightly. "She's been living in sheer hell for two years. She's trading one for another now, but without the primary source of her misery." She smiled shrewdly. "Which one do you think she's going to prefer?" She grunted as though it were a forgone conclusion. "I know which one I would."

And there was that, Sophia thought. She felt a smile flirt with her lips. "Spoken like a true Future Widows' Club member, Meredith."

"Don't forget that Jolie's one, too," Bitsy added knowingly. "Once *that* reality sets in, she'll be fine."

CHAPTER SIXTEEN

JOLIE'S HEAD JERKED UP as a knock rattled the glass. She leapt up from Chris's desk, moved to the window and peeked through the blinds onto the sidewalk. A sigh of relief leaked out of her mouth—*Sadie*. She hurried around to the front of the office and opened the door, quickly ushering her friend inside.

"You're here early," Sadie said, breezing into the room. She brought the faint scent of hairspray and strawberry jam with her. "You're not going to believe the crazy rumor I heard this morning. Bitsy Highfield called before I even left the house and said—" Her gaze caught Jolie's and stopped short. Her tentative smile fell. "Is it true?" she breathed disbelievingly. "My God, it's true, isn't it? He's dead."

"He is," Jolie told her.

Sadie's eyes widened. "Oh, my God," she said again.

"I, uh… I found him last night after I left your house." She shuddered, still feeling a chill land in her midsection every time she recalled seeing his face. "It was too late to call you and I didn't want to wake up the girls."

Sadie sagged against the reception desk, then shot her a shaky look. "What happened?"

"Other than the fact that someone walked into the house and shot him, I don't know."

Sadie sat there for a minute, seemingly absorbing the fact that they now inhabited a world where Chris Marshall no longer existed. She blew out a deep breath, then lifted her shoulders in a small unrepentant shrug. "Wish I could say I was sorry, but I'm not," she said bluntly. "I didn't like him when he was alive, and I'm not going to pretend to like him now just because he's dead." She scowled. "I hate it when people do that. He was a mean-spirited bastard who made you miserable. Dying doesn't make him a saint. Far as I'm concerned, it's the first act of kindness he's ever shown you."

Jolie knew that she should at least pretend to be outraged over her friend's hard-hearted reaction to Chris's death…but in all truth she couldn't because after the initial shock of last night, she'd begun to feel the same way. Sadie was right. Dying didn't make him a saint. She wasn't going to pretend to mourn him—she didn't own the necessary attachment, the emotion needed to pull it off. He'd made her wretched. She'd hated him. Those were the unhappy facts. Did that mean she was *glad* that he was dead? No…but it certainly made things easier.

Last night after she'd gone home with her mother, she'd had a good bone-wringing cry. She'd whimpered, wailed and sobbed, and not necessarily in that order. She'd cried for her mistakes, for the things she'd lost, the pointless time she'd spent away from her mother. She'd had years of despair built up and being able to simply let it go and finally be with her mom had been very…cathartic.

When the storm of emotion had passed—leaving behind a raging headache, a splotchy face and a mountain of soggy Kleenex—she'd felt unbelievably better, like she'd been baptized by her tears, cleansed of her guilt.

It had been the oddest thing. She'd been sitting there at the kitchen table—the Southern equivalent of a shrink's couch, Jolie thought wryly—watching her mom scoop coffee from a generic can into the pot. Her mother had never spared any expense when it came to buying good coffee. It had always been her little extravagance, the *one* thing she wouldn't compromise on. Jolie had inwardly winced, thinking that her mother wouldn't have to buy generic coffee once she got her money back.

The fleeting thought had triggered an epiphany and her brain, which had been numbed by the horror of finding Chris and by the lengthy crying jag, had suddenly been enervated with what needed—*had*—to be done.

Immediately.

She knew that Chris's assets would most likely be frozen—they usually were when a person was murdered—so she'd needed to act before that happened, which had only given her a narrow window of opportunity. She'd explained things as best she could to her mom, then left her standing in the doorway, wearing a frayed robe and worried frown. Armed with a sense of purpose and a thermos of generic coffee, she'd hurried down to the office.

She'd been here all night, going through files and folders, systematically scouring his office until she'd found the numbers and pass codes for the off-shore accounts—he'd cut a small hole in the leather beneath his executive chair and had tucked them there for safe keeping, where he could figuratively *sit* on the money—and she'd just accomplished the final wire transfer into her own account when she'd heard Sadie at the front door.

The minute Marge, their secretary, came in this morning, Jolie planned to instruct her to fill all open orders, issue checks to their creditors and pay their employees their last check along with a hefty severance bonus. She'd see to the investors, making sure that their original investment as well as their *correct* returns were given to them. Between what Chris had stashed in his private accounts and what she'd managed to slip aside, she'd have enough to do that as well as still have a nice little nest egg for herself.

It was finally over, Jolie thought, letting go a relieved sigh.

She relayed her plans to Sadie. "By five o'clock this afternoon, we'll close the doors and Marshall Inc. will be no more. I've got to go down to the Sheriff's office, file the official report, bury him, and that'll be it." Her shoulders sagged with relief and the first tentative bloom of hope blossomed in her chest.

Rather than looking impressed with her speedy efficiency, Sadie's brow folded into a small frown. "Jo, I hate to burst your bubble…but I don't think that's going to be *it*. He was murdered. There'll be an investigation."

Jolie nodded. "I know that. Jake's in charge. He, uh… He was there last night." And she'd never been more thankful to see another soul. He'd been amazingly kind, given the circumstances, and though she hadn't been completely herself, he'd seemed a little nervous talking to her. In retrospect, it was oddly endearing.

"That'll definitely work to your advantage, but you realize that you're going to be a suspect. At least, initially."

"I know," she said, undeterred. "But I didn't do it, so I'm not going to waste my time worrying about it." She let go a heavy but determined breath and crossed her arms over her chest. Not altogether true—she would worry to some extent—hell, she'd be a fool not to—but she fully intended to move on. "I've wasted all the time I intend to waste, Sadie. I'm washing my hands of it— all of it." She gestured around the office. "I'm moving out of that house and I'm putting in an offer on that little place over on Lelia Street I told you about. I want to move on. I *need* to. I want my life back." Not an unreasonable request given what she'd been through, Jolie thought.

A worried line wrinkled Sadie's brow and she weighed her words carefully. "Jo, nobody knows more than I do how difficult things have been for you, but…you might want to rethink this. Being hasty could give the wrong impression." She bit her bottom lip. "A *guilty* impression."

Jolie squashed a frustrated wail. She knew that, dammit, but frankly she didn't care. She was innocent. Being in an unhappy marriage didn't make her a murderer. More like a survivor. Chris Marshall had dictated practically every aspect of her life for the past two years and she'd be damned before she'd let him do it from the grave. His days of yanking her chain were over. She was taking her life back.

Effective immediately. And though she was vaguely concerned about being investigated for a crime she didn't commit, she didn't intend to lose one more moment of her life because of Chris Marshall.

"Jake knows I didn't do it," Jolie told her. "He's damn good at his job. He'll find out who did it and when he does I'll be exonerated."

"I'm sure that you will, but it would be better for you to make his job easier rather than more difficult. Dean will be looking over Jake's shoulder." She grunted. "Given the personal history between the two of you, Jake may not end up being the one in charge of the investigation. Dean may pull him and assign another detective."

Jolie paused as a note of alarm hit her belly. *That* scenario had never occurred to her. She completely trusted Jake to find the truth. Not only was he good at what he did, he *knew* her. Knew that she wasn't capable of doing what had been done to Chris. But another detective might not be so discerning and she'd definitely make a convenient suspect. Still, she hadn't murdered Chris and furthermore, she had an alibi.

She told Sadie as much. "I'm innocent. Regardless of whether I move out or close this company or anything else, nothing changes that fact." She shrugged, trying to cast off the weight of worry dragging at her determination. "They can investigate me until the cows come home for all I care. They're not going to find anything."

JAKE LEANED BACK in his uncomfortable desk chair, passed a weary hand over his face and futilely wished he hadn't taken this call. "Look, Andy, I wish I could help you, but I don't know when or even if you'll get the body. Once the autopsy is completed, Jolie will have to make those arrangements. I'm just the detective in charge. I'm not making the funeral arrangements."

"I realize that," Andy explained with exaggerated patience, "but after calling around all morning, you were the person I was directed to." He paused. "Has Randy already called you?" he asked with irritated suspicion. "Is that why I'm getting the run around?"

Dubbed "Double Death" by the citizens of Moon Valley, Andy and Randy Holbrook were identical twins who'd gone into the funeral profession. Together, to start with, but three years into a prosperous career, they'd had a falling out and had since started individual businesses.

Moon Valley could comfortably support one funeral home, but the population simply wasn't sufficient to support two, and as such, every time somebody died Andy and Randy fought over the body and the bereaved like a couple of mongrels over a soup bone. Dean had been called in to intervene countless times, and the issue had even been raised at several town hall meetings. People ought to be able to bury their loved ones in peace, they'd argued, not be harassed and hounded until they wished they were dead as well.

Jake swallowed a beleaguered groan. "No, I haven't heard from Randy," he told him, hoping to end the call.

"Good, because if he tells you that she's planning on using Eternal Rest as opposed to Heavenly Harvest then he's lying. She was in here just last week checking out pre-burial plans." He chuckled grimly. "Bet she wishes she'd gone ahead and purchased one then," Andy remarked somewhat gleefully. "Now it's *really* gonna cost her. Dying isn't cheap, Jake." He sighed sagely. "Not cheap at all."

Jake stilled as every sense went on point. "She was in there last week?"

"Yep, so this fish is dangling on *my* hook. Randy has no claim."

"Do you remember what day she came in, Andy?"

"I do. It was Thursday. I know because I always do a follow-up a week after initial contact. I tried to call her yesterday, but she wasn't available."

Less than a week before the murder, Jake thought with an increasing feeling of dread. That wasn't good.

"She took some pamphlets home, said she wanted to show them to her husband."

"These plans, were they for her and him?"

"Nope. Just him. But that's not really uncommon, I'm afraid. Lots of people have a hard time coming to terms with their mortality—to their detriment," he tutted woefully. "You should really think about having a little look-see yourself, Jake. It's never too early to make arrangements. Death is certain, you know."

"I'll think about it," Jake told him distractedly. He uttered an abrupt goodbye, then sat back in his chair and rubbed his gritty eyes with the palms of his hands. What the hell had she done? he wondered, absolutely flabbergasted. Why in the hell had she been scoping out a pre-burial plan for her husband less than a week before he was murdered? She hadn't killed him—he knew it.

Last night while Todd had worked his magic and

Leon had dozed on the couch, he and Mike had tossed some scenarios around and Mike had skeptically suggested that she might have hired someone to do it. That didn't fit either. Murder just wasn't in Jolie's character. Furthermore, a hired hit man wouldn't have cut off Marshall's dick. That was a personal attack, one that suggested the killer had some connection with the victim. If not an intimate connection, then at least one significant enough for the person to truly despise him.

And this case was going to be hard enough to crack without Jolie's bizarre behavior factored in. Leon had finally been able to take the body this morning around four. Last night, Jake and Mike had walked the perimeter of the house, looking for forced entry, discarded cigarette butts, footprints, anything that might indicate the presence of another person at the house.

They'd found nothing.

With the exception of the scene of the crime, their search inside had been equally futile. Jake had taken one end of the house, Mike the other. A glutton for punishment, he supposed, Jake had searched her room first. He'd found a box of sentimental mementoes stored deep in the back of her closet—a pressed posey necklace he'd made for her in grade-school, several cartoon Valentine cards signed in his untidy juvenile scrawl, pictures of them at various dances, an empty bottle of strawberry wine, the very one they'd shared the first time they'd made love. Jake swallowed. God, it had been so long ago, and yet the memory was still so vivid it could have been yesterday.

Graduation night. While other kids were hosting or

attending parties, most of them getting hammered, he and Jolie had strolled hand-in-hand off the football field and headed straight for his truck. They'd been waiting for years, planning this particular night for almost as long. He'd gotten an older cousin to buy the wine, had stopped at a gas station and fed the condom machine a handful of change until it had spit out ten of the damned things.

Jake grinned, remembering. What the hell, he thought, tapping a pen against his desk. He'd been optimistic.

Then they'd headed up to their secret spot at the lake. He'd built a fire, spread a blanket and they'd talked about the future for hours. They'd shared that bottle, laughed and cut up, had simply enjoyed the night…then on an old quilt under a blanket of bright stars and the promise of a bright future, they'd enjoyed each other.

To this day, nothing could compare to the absolute perfection of that time. He'd been head over heels in love, half drunk and nervous as hell, no longer a boy, but not quite a man. She'd been sweetly shy, but eager and trusting, and she'd made him feel like the most important guy in the world.

Jake released a slow breath. What he'd give to go back and have a talk with that boy, to tell him the things he knew now so that kid could avoid making the mistakes he'd made. But he couldn't, and no amount of wishing would make it so.

At any rate, aside from the bathroom, they hadn't found anything incriminating anywhere in the house. The best Jake could figure, the killer had walked through the front door, followed the sound of the shower to the bathroom, then shot Marshall at point blank range. The assailant had turned off the water—Todd had found smudges consistent with gloved hands—had cut off his dick, with what, no one knew yet. Nothing in the house, they were relatively sure. A hand towel was missing from the rack behind the commode. Todd figured—and he hoped Jolie could confirm—that one had definitely been there, that the killer had used it to transport their odd trophy. Afterward, the culprit had turned the water back on, presumably to alert Jolie when she came home.

Jake hadn't found any evidence to support it yet, but he firmly believed that whoever had killed Marshall had been waiting for Jolie to leave. Waiting *where* was anyone's guess. Probably the street. Not in the yard, he didn't think. He'd looked last night for clues, but planned on going back over this morning as soon as he finished taking Jolie's official report. He wanted to scour the house and surrounding area again today. Who knew? Maybe a few winks and the benefit of daylight would give him a fresh perspective.

Talking with Andy the funeral director this morning certainly had, Jake thought grimly. Those were not the sort of discoveries he was interested in, that was for damned sure.

Dean knocked a couple of times on the door frame, then walked into Jake's office. Lines of fatigue fanned out around his eyes and he had the pinched look that marked a night of too little or no sleep. "How's it coming?" he asked.

Jake relayed the pertinent facts, then told him about his conversation with Andy. He pulled a tired shrug. "My gut tells me it's a dead end, but it's still—"

"Odd," Dean finished. He arched a brow. "She's coming in this morning to file the official?"

Jake nodded.

"Are you keeping it under your hat, or are you going to ask her about it?"

"I'm gonna ask her about it," Jake told him. "I want to get a read on her." He rubbed his eyes. "Like I told you last night, she hated him—no question there—but Jolie's not a murderer. She's just not wired that way."

Dean hesitated. "You can't rule her out, Jake. You're gonna have to stick to her like glue. Given your history, can do you that? Better still, can you do it objectively?"

Jake nodded and felt his gut clench at the impending lie. Be objective where Jolie was concerned? Ha. "If I couldn't, I wouldn't have asked to stay on as lead."

"Keep me updated," he said. "And let me know when you find his dick," he added darkly. "I'd like to hold a separate sort of ceremony for it, if you get my drift."

Jake suddenly imagined Marshall's dick glued to the center of a bull's eye, a calmly furious Dean using it for target practice.

He cleared his throat. "Er…how did everything—"

"She's packing as we speak," Dean told him flatly. His lips twisted with bitter humor. "This wasn't the first time, Jake. It was just the last damned straw."

Surprised, Jake swallowed, then said the only thing he could think of. "Shit, Dean. I'm sorry."

"Ah, it's my own damned fault," he said wearily, leaning against the door frame. "I should have washed my hands of her the first time. She blamed the job, made me feel guilty. Said I wasn't paying enough attention to her." He pulled an offhand shrug. "I thought I owed it to the marriage to give it another go. So I did. At least this way I know I did everything I could to make it work." He shook his head. "Wasn't enough, but it wasn't my fault. She'll be the one to carry the weight of that mistake, and better her than me, eh?" He managed a half-hearted smile, then turned to go. "I'll expect daily reports and updates on all new developments."

Jake nodded. "You got it." He glanced at his watch, noting the time. He'd give Jolie another ten minutes and if she wasn't here, he'd run her to ground. If she'd checked into pre-burial plans, just what the hell else was she hiding? he wondered. What else had she checked into? Jake tensed as the obvious answer to that question dawned in his puzzled mind. He swore, pulled the phonebook from the desk drawer, flipped to the yellow pages—to the I section, specifically—until he found the listings he was interested in.

Insurance.

If she'd taken out any new policies on Marshall recently, things would take a nasty turn from bad to worse. Dread ballooned in his gut, anticipating what he feared he'd find.

Four calls later he found it. One-hundred-thousand. Added last Tuesday.

A stream of profanity spewed from his lips. He blew out a heavy breath, sagged back in his chair and felt the beginnings of one helluva headache claw through his skull. For someone he knew beyond a shadow of a doubt was innocent, she was certainly doing a damned bang-up job of looking guilty.

CHAPTER SEVENTEEN

SOPHIA POPPED a bite of maple link sausage into her mouth, shuffled over to her kitchen table and set the warmed blueberry syrup and stack of fresh, fluffy pancakes on the table. They joined a host of other breakfast favorites. Biscuits and gravy, grits, scrambled eggs, hot tea and orange juice. Stress tended to make her hungry and when that happened, she couldn't just settle for a mere muffin or a piece of toast—she had to eat buffet style.

This was particularly unfortunate as she was supposed to be dieting.

Sophia had battled her weight for years, diligently fighting every eager fat-storing cell in her body. The struggle would have been a whole lot easier if she didn't enjoy food—the sight, scent and taste of virtually any sweet, cake, pie, main dish or gooey casserole. Honestly, other than hominy—which she detested—she didn't cull much.

Furthermore, practically every occasion was celebrated with food. Holidays, birthdays, bad days and good days, deaths, etc.... Food played a prominent role in society and it was truly a pity—the height of injustice, dammit—that some metabolisms worked better than others.

Hers, for instance, seemed to be permanently stuck in neutral.

Sophia had always promised herself that when she turned fifty, she'd say to hell with it and eat whatever she wanted. She'd keep up her exercise—a good brisk walk was good for anybody—but once she hit the big five-oh, she'd trade her fat-free margarine for good old-fashioned butter, her low-fat frozen yogurt for rich, creamy pralines and cream ice cream. She'd take a sledge hammer to her scale, shatter it to bits before sweeping it into a dust-pan and gleefully throwing it away.

Two weeks beyond her fiftieth birthday however—a blissful two weeks in which she'd eaten everything that hadn't been nailed down and she'd gained seven pounds—she'd had a terrible nightmare. She'd dreamed that she'd had a heart attack and needed to go to the hospital, but she couldn't get out of the bed because she was too damned fat. The rescue squad had ended up taking a Sawzall to her bedroom wall and cutting a giant hole in the side of her house in order to accommodate her whopping girth. It had taken a wench and a back-hoe to get her out of the house, and they'd hauled her bloated, flabby hideous body away on a flat-bed truck, a melting king-sized candy bar clutched in her fist.

The next morning, Sophia had gloomily resumed her battle against the bulge.

She occasionally fell off the wagon—like now—but after last night, she felt like she deserved a little comfort food. She'd walk another lap around the block, two if need be.

Sophia started as a knock sounded at her back door.

She rarely had visitors this early, she thought, wincing as she walked away from her warm breakfast. She opened the door, then horrorstruck, barely resisted the urge to slam it shut in her unexpected visitor's face.

"Good morning, Sophia," Edward said dutifully.

Sophia patted her uncombed hair, painfully aware of her unmade face and tattered chenille robe. She felt her mouth work up and down, struggling to dredge a syllable up her tight, mortified throat. "Good m-morning, Edward. What can I do for you?"

"I just noticed that you weren't outside this morning. You're not feeling under the weather, I hope."

Sophia's first thought was to blast him with an icy remark about unexpected house calls, but the kind concern in those compelling blue eyes, plus the warm knowledge that he'd actually missed her, prevented the impulse.

She tightened her robe around her middle—the one not poured into a bulge-smoothing girdle—and resisted the urge to whimper. "No, I'm not, but thank you," she said, somewhat stiffly. After all, she wasn't accustomed to being nice to him. It had always been easier—safer—to be surly.

He sniffed appreciatively and his keen gaze darted over her shoulder to the spread on her kitchen table. A grin slid across his surprisingly attractive mouth. "That certainly smells good," he commented lightly. "Are those blueberry pancakes?"

Sophia felt a smile flirt with her lips. "They are," she conceded.

His eyes narrowed, seemingly zooming in on the syrup. "And is that your homemade syrup?"

This time it was her eyes that narrowed. How did he know that she made homemade syrups? "It is," she replied slowly.

"Oh," he sighed, rocking back on his heels. "That's some count there, Sophia," he said with just enough sincerity and awe to make her want to preen despite the fact she looked like a bag lady. "I bid on a bottle at the Civic Club's silent auction last fall and won. Best stuff I ever put in my mouth."

He was clearly angling for an invitation, and even more clearly hoping to garner one through flattery. One that, despite her unkempt hair and ratty robe, he was going to get. Still, she had her pride, so she pretended to look put-out. "As you can see I have plenty," she said grudgingly. "Would you like to join me?"

He grinned. "I was hoping you'd ask."

Betting on it, more like, she thought with a silent snort, but she wasn't going to quibble because a ridiculous thrill had whipped through her, momentarily gluing her tongue to the roof of her mouth. For the first time in fifteen years a man—one that captivated every sense and made her feel like her skin was stretched too tight over her old bones—was going to put his feet under her table.

It was a start, Sophia thought, her insides quivering with anticipation. A beginning, she cautiously hoped, to an ultimate end.

CHAPTER EIGHTEEN

JOLIE GLANCED at her watch and swore as she hurried down the hall toward Jake's office. She'd promised him that she'd be here first thing this morning, but she hadn't counted on having to awkwardly console a crying Marge when she'd learned of Chris's death. Chris had always treated Marge abominably, had criticized, shouted, and cursed her for the smallest of infractions, so she was the last person Jolie had expected to shed any tears over her late, unlamented husband. Jolie had heard herself muttering things like, "Oh, yes, it's terrible," and "Yes, it's such a loss," but the words felt weird and distasteful coming out of her mouth.

Probably because they were lies.

Playing the grieving widow was *not* a role that would come easily to her, which was just as well, because despite Sadie's dire warnings, she'd decided against it, and once she made up her mind, it was set. She'd been living a lie for two years. She was finished, a fact she planned to share with Jake this morning.

While she couldn't tell him about the FWC, she nevertheless intended to make her position perfectly clear. She hadn't killed Chris, but she wasn't exactly *sad* that he was dead. Relieved, quite honestly, was more accurate. He could deal with those facts however he chose and if he decided to judge her for them, then so be it.

She drew in a bolstering breath as she neared his office and felt her stomach do an odd little flutter, a physical reaction to the knowledge that she was about to see him. Under normal circumstances her reaction would undoubtedly be considered inappropriate—particularly since her husband's body was barely cold, Jolie thought with a wry smile—but these were hardly normal circumstances.

Jake had been the love of her life—the one she'd let pride keep her from reclaiming—and Chris had been the bane of her existence for the past twenty-four months.

There was no comparison.

Jake's door was open and, given the one-sided conversation she heard as she neared his office, she guessed that he was on the phone, a hunch that was confirmed when she peered into the room. He glanced up and motioned for her to come in and take the only other chair in the room.

His office was small with a functional metal desk, a single beat-up filing cabinet crammed in the corner and covered with magnets, business cards and the odd sticky note. A couple of photographs had been adhered to the wall behind his desk with thumbtacks. The sight drew a smile. True to form, framing them had been too much trouble.

One was a family Christmas photo, his Mom, Dad, brother and sister. The other was a candid of Jake that she'd taken during her photography phase and admittedly, *he'd* been her favorite subject.

This photo was one that she'd been particularly proud

of because it had captured him in such a true moment. He'd been standing close to Smoke, nuzzling the gray dappled horse's muzzle, and the respect and the love for the animal had been evident in every line of his face. The crinkles around those silvery eyes, the soft turn of his mouth. He'd been relaxed and unguarded…and sexy as hell.

Though genuine cowboys were scarce in Mississippi, Jake had always had that special spark, that easy grace and careless swagger brought about by hours spent in the saddle. While other men went to the gym or Roxy's Roadhouse after work, Jake had always spent his destressing time on the back of a horse, or at the very least, in the barn taking care of one. He had a keen understanding of the animals, a way with them that was frankly fascinating to watch.

His skills were somewhat legendary in their little part of the world and it hadn't been uncommon—even in his teenage years—for other owners to ask his opinion or seek his advice about a difficult animal.

Within months of her marriage to Chris, his grandfather had deeded twenty acres to him on the south end of the family property, a rolling landscape with hundred-year-old oaks dripping with Spanish moss, hearty maples and a clear swift-moving stream. In the spring hundreds of buttercups, wild poppies and Queen Anne's lace bloomed across the meadows, painting the hills and valleys with splashes of bright color.

He'd built the barn before the house, making sure that the animals would be taken care of first. Priorities, right? Jolie thought with a small grin. The house was a replica of his grandfather's old two-story farmhouse—the very one they'd always talked about having—but, according to Sadie and Rob who'd had the privilege of visiting, it had been updated with all the modern conveniences.

She'd occasionally torture herself by driving by, picturing him there before a crackling fire, book in hand. But as time had worn on, she'd stopped. Only a glutton for punishment would keep it up, and Chris had been punishment enough, thank you very much. Besides, it had just been too damned hard. It should have been her with him before that fire, her there sharing his bed. She'd never understand, never get over how terribly wrong things had gone.

Jolie took her seat, watched Jake scribble on a yellow legal pad, presumably taking notes.

"One-hundred-thousand, you say?" he said, shooting her a veiled look, one that had the dubious honor of simultaneously making her mouth dry and her stomach roll in a sickening pirouette.

Shit, she thought with ballooning dread. He knew already. Moon Valley was too small to accommodate discretion, so she hadn't harbored any illusions that Jake wouldn't find out about the life insurance and other things, but she damned sure hadn't counted on him ferreting out the truth so quickly.

"And she's the sole beneficiary, is that correct?" He hummed under his breath, tapped his pen against his notepad while she resisted the urge to squirm in her seat. "And this policy was taken out when?" Jake nodded, scribbled another note, then circled it. "All right, then. That's all I needed to know." He thanked whomever had been so bloody helpful then disconnected and shot her a considering look. "Have you slept?"

Code-speak for "You look like crap," Jolie thought, unreasonably perturbed. Evidently her concealer hadn't done the job.

"A little," she told him. "Have you?"

"I caught a cat nap this morning. I expected you earlier," he commented lightly. "Any particular reason why you're so late?"

"I ran by the office. I needed to let Marge know about Chris," she improvised, since it wasn't completely a lie. She could hardly tell him the truth. *I've been emptying Chris's accounts before you freeze them.*

He nodded, seemed to accept that excuse. After a moment, he blew out a prolonged breath, abruptly stood and shut the door. He leaned against it, crossed his arms over his chest and merely waited. For her to offer an excuse, she was sure, but she had no intention of obliging him. If he wanted answers, he'd have to ask the questions, otherwise he was outta luck. She certainly wasn't going to volunteer any more than she had to, at least not in the beginning. The more time she had to move the money, the better. With luck, she'd get everything done this afternoon. That was the plan, at any rate.

She felt the weight of that cool, calm regard for at least another sixty seconds before Jake finally muttered a hot oath and sat back down. He pulled a small black tape recorder from the desk drawer, spoke her name and date into the device, then turned it off and set it down between them.

He looked up and his gaze tangled with hers. "Before I turn this on, I need to ask you a question."

She knew he did—knew what he'd ask—and though a part of her resented it because he of all people should know better, undoubtedly the life insurance and her bizarre alibi had shaken his opinion. She couldn't blame him, but that didn't lessen the sting.

She returned that level stare, determinedly ignoring the flash of heat that hit her belly, and lifted her chin. "Sure. Go ahead."

"Did you have *anything* to do with this, Jo? Anything at all?" His voice was a mixture of exasperation and agony, indicating that he hated having to doubt her, which seemed only fitting because she hated it, too.

"No, Jake. I didn't. I hated Chris, which is common knowledge among my family and friends, but hating him and killing him are two completely different things. I could never have killed him."

A sigh of relief slipped past his lips. He sagged back into his seat, closed his eyes and rubbed the bridge of his nose. "Then please tell me why you were researching pre-burial plans last week?" he asked with weary irritation.

Jolie blinked. She'd been prepared to answer the insurance question, but she'd had no idea that he'd already heard about the pre-burial plan. How the hell—

"Andy called me this morning wanting to know when he could have the body," he explained, most likely as a result of her uncomfortable silence. His lips tilted. "He was afraid Randy would beat him to the punch and explained why he thought he had dibs. He mentioned the pre-burial plan—the one you investigated less than a week before your husband's murder," he added significantly. He leaned forward and shook his dark head. "I'm going to be honest, Jo. If it wasn't for your alibi— at least twenty of your bridge club members called this morning to verify your whereabouts last night, by the way—you'd be in deep shit. For someone who's innocent, you're doing a helluva job making yourself look guilty. Dammit, what gives? What have you been up to?"

Jolie cast around her semi-frozen brain and tried to think of any reason—aside from the truth, of course, which she couldn't share—why she'd been scoping out funeral arrangements last week for her perfectly healthy husband.

She forced an uncomfortable laugh. "There's nothing w-wrong with b-being prepared is there?" she asked, her voice a little too bright to be believable.

"Being prepared? No," he said. "It's the timing of your preparations that raises concern."

He did the waiting thing again, pinning her with that gray gaze until the silence practically screamed between them. Feeling like a kid who'd been called into the principal's office, Jolie barely resisted the urge to squirm, and to make matters worse, she could tell by the set of his jaw that Jake was disappointed that she wasn't going to confide in him. She hated that look, barely refrained from spilling her guts just to make it go away.

"Fine," he finally relented. "Don't tell me. I'm just trying to help you here." He blew out a breath. "What about the life insurance? Why did you add another hundred grand when you had enough to cover the business and your mortgage?"

"You can never have too much insurance," Jolie told him, quoting the agent who'd sold her the policy. "Furthermore, Chris owed debts that weren't on paper," she added darkly. Ones she firmly intended to take care of the minute she left here. Odd, though, she thought. When she'd been pouring through the accounts and tallying expenses early this morning, she hadn't factored in *any* of the life insurance. That would end up being a tidy little sum to add to her nest egg.

Jake quirked a dark brow. "By that are you referring to the life insurance money he swindled away from your mother?"

Surprised that he knew, Jolie glanced up. "Er…yeah, I am." She frowned uncertainly. "How did you—"

"Sadie," Jake interrupted, filling in the blank. "Don't be pissed. She only confirmed what I'd heard around town. After you came in and filed the report, I, uh… I went down and had a talk with her. She told me about the insurance money."

And everything else, most likely, Jolie thought, but curiously couldn't drum up any outrage that Sadie had confided in Jake, particularly after Chris had hit her. She'd never thanked him for that, Jolie thought suddenly. She bumbled her way through it. "I, uh— I appreciated what you did. With the door and all," she clarified.

A half-hearted smile caught the corner of his mouth and she felt that meager, woefully familiar grin in places that hadn't known a touch of emotion in years. "Wasn't as satisfying as using my fist," he said with a small lift of a muscled shoulder, "but I improvised." He paused, searching the side of her face for any lingering damage. "Bastard," he muttered.

"Yes, he was," she readily agreed. "Which is why I hope that you'll understand and not pass judgment when I move on. He made me miserable. Wretched. Am I sorry that someone murdered him? Yes. Am I sorry that he's out of my life? No. I know it seems harsh, but—" She drew up short, tried to find the words to frame the way she felt. She shrugged helplessly. "It's just the way it is."

Jake nodded. "Moving on is fine, Jolie. From what Sadie told me, you definitely need to." He hesitated. "That said, please keep in mind that everything you do, especially over the coming weeks, will be under intense scrutiny and—" he raised one eyebrow meaningfully "—it'll make my job a whole lot easier if you aren't doing things that make you look guilty."

"Like dancing on his grave?" she suggested innocently.

Surprise jimmied a chuckle loose in his throat and he shot her a startled look. "Yes. Dancing on his grave wouldn't be a good thing."

She made an exaggerated moue of disappointment. "There went that plan."

He passed a hand over his face, trying to wipe away his smile. "If there's anything you need to tell me, now would be a good time. I don't want anymore surprises."

Jolie felt a blanket of guilt settle over her shoulders as she shook her head. She hated lying to him, but she couldn't out the FWC. Too many members were still shackled to bastard husbands and the FWC was the only thing making their lives bearable. God knows the past two weeks she'd spent as a member had made her feel tremendously better. She couldn't tell him.

"Sadie seemed to think that Dean might pull you from this case," Jolie said, opting to change the subject. "Is that going to happen?"

To her vast relief, Jake shook his head. "No. He wanted to, but was, er, persuaded to let me remain as lead. I was given strict instructions to keep Dean up to date…and stick to you like glue," he added.

Jolie repressed a shudder as another inappropriate thought flitted through her head. Though she knew he'd meant to scare her—or warn her, most likely—her thoughts had instantly turned in another direction. She knew what it was like to have Jake stick to her like glue. In the past he'd been very adept at making her fall apart…then putting her back together. A bittersweet pang squeezed her chest. It was just one of the many things she missed about him.

She blinked, trying to pull her thoughts back together. When she looked up, Jake was watching her closely, an odd expression on his face. "Er…does Dean know about Emily?" Jolie asked, once again fishing for a subject change.

He leaned back once more. "He does. Mike and I told him last night."

"How did he take it?"

"She's moving out. They're finished."

Damn Chris's hide, Jolie thought, angry and disgusted. "I'm sorry," she said, wishing there was something she could do to make things right.

"For what?" Jake asked. "Wasn't your fault."

"Maybe not directly, but I'm the one who brought him here." She looked away, then picked at a loose thread. "You have no idea how much I regret it."

"It's still not your fault, Jolie," Jake insisted. "Emily's a big girl. She knew what she was doing and, according to Dean, this wasn't the first time. Don't beat yourself up about it."

"The sonofabitch never could keep it in his pants," she muttered, unable to let it go. Dean was a good man. He deserved better. And she didn't care what Jake said, while she might not be completely to blame, she was indirectly at fault. She'd brought him here and infected her town with his cancerous—

A bark of laughter erupted from Jake's throat. "And still can't. We still haven't found it."

Confused, Jolie glanced up. "Found what?"

Jake's eyes widened in belated regret, then he shifted and swore hotly. "Christ," he muttered. "I'm such an idiot."

"Found what?" she repeated. She had a sickening suspicion, but surely he didn't mean what she thought he meant.

"His penis," Jake finally told her. "His killer castrated him."

Jolie gaped, equally horrified and revolted.

"You, uh, must not have noticed."

She snorted. "No, I didn't. I lost interest in Chris's penis a long time ago. Other than documenting who he'd been sticking it to for my divorce file, that is." Jolie shook her head, unable to make it process and though she knew it was horrible, she had the almost overwhelming urge to laugh. There was something very satisfying about poetic justice.

"Do you have any idea who might have done this?" Jake asked her.

She snorted. "Anyone in particular? No. But I'll give you everything I've got in my file. I've been keeping up with everything—the shady business dealings and adultery—for the divorce. Dean's wife wasn't the only woman he was screwing around with. He wasn't particular, I can tell you that. Nor was he very smart." Jolie chewed the corner of her mouth and looked up. "I know he's your boss, but are you sure Dean didn't know about Emily before last night? I know Chris had been going to their house."

Jake shook his head. "He didn't. I'm sure of it."

Since it was that same assurance that told him she was innocent, Jolie didn't argue. Most likely Jake was right. Still, Chris's hijacked dick shed a whole new light on things. That was personal. Someone *really* hated him. Come to think of it, Jolie decided, lots of people really hated him and each one of them with good reason. Jake wouldn't find himself short on suspects, that was for sure. For her part, however, she just wanted it over with. And to that end, she needed to be able to bury him, her last official act as his wife.

"Er…any idea when I'll be able to arrange the funeral?" she asked him.

"The M.E. should be finished with the body in another day or so. Just get in touch with Andy and he'll handle that end of it."

Jolie nodded, relief melting her spine. A couple more

days, and then that would be it. Her life would be her own again. Or at least as much her own as she could make it while she was a murder suspect, at any rate.

"Did Chris have any family?" Jake asked curiously.

"No," she deadpanned. "He sprung fully grown from the loins of Satan."

Jake's lips twitched and he shot her a look. "That's cold, Jo."

She smiled, then let go a small sigh. "I honestly don't know. He told me a tragic story about his parents being in a car accident. At the time I bought it, but now…" She shook her head. "He told so many lies. If he's got any family, they've never contacted him or vice versa."

Jake seemed to be mulling that over. Finally, he gestured toward the tape recorder. "We should probably get started."

"Okay."

"Mind if I come by later and pick up that file you told me about?"

"Not at all," she replied. "It's in the apartment above Sadie's shop. Keeping it at the office or in the house was too risky."

"Makes sense. Had you contacted an attorney about the divorce?"

"I had. Lanny James."

Jake whistled low and his gaze seemed to sharpen. "Pulling out a big gun, eh?"

Jolie smiled, shrugged. "I was in for a fight. I knew Lanny had a better shot than most to handle him." Lanny had been looking forward to it, too, Jolie thought. He was an old dog who didn't bark, just bit, which made him one helluva divorce attorney. He'd given her invaluable advice; he was the one who'd encouraged her to start the file. He didn't go into a courtroom without the ammunition to annihilate an opponent. Chris's death had robbed her of that satisfaction, but at least this way she was spared the mess and expense.

"I'll have to talk to him," Jake said, shooting her a level look.

Her lips slid into an unconcerned smile. "Talk to whomever you have to, Jake. I'm innocent. Nothing you're gonna find will change that."

That silver gaze caught and held hers, momentarily sucking the air from her lungs. "Am I gonna find anything else that will *challenge* it?"

Depended on where he looked, Jolie thought, chewing the inside of her cheek. "Let's hope not," she replied, forcing a smile.

His gaze narrowed, instantly seeing through her flimsy, evasive answer and he muttered an exasperated curse. "Can't you see that I'm on your side? That I'm trying to help you? Why are you making this harder than it has to be?"

"You're the detective, Jake. Figure it out."

He managed a weak grin. "Very cute, Jo. I'm just not sure you understand the gravity of the situation. If any other guy had this case, alibi or no, you'd make a *very* convenient suspect."

She crossed her legs and leaned back in her seat, doing her best to ignore the frightened shiver that tripped down her spine. "I do understand that, but being a convenient suspect doesn't make me guilty. The truth will speak for itself." She had to believe that.

He lifted a sardonic brow. "And I'm sure all the innocent people on death row had the same opinion."

He was trying to scare her, and to her discomfort, it was working. Still, she couldn't tell him about the FWC. She couldn't betray her fellow Future Widows. Furthermore, telling him about them wasn't going to help him, because it wouldn't do one damn thing for his investigation. Jolie lifted her chin, but refused to respond.

Looking extremely put out, Jake heaved a long-suffering sigh. "Fine. We'll do it the hard way. What time do you want to meet me at the apartment?"

"When ever works best for you," she said sweetly, willing to be partly accommodating.

He grunted. "Six, then."

"I'll see you there."

Jake blew out another breath, rubbed his eyes, then to her vast relief finally flipped on the recorder. "Okay," he said. "Let's start at the beginning…"

CHAPTER NINETEEN

ARMS CROSSED over his chest, Jake stood in Sadie's shop and peered out her storefront window across the square, watching Jolie tape a sign to the inside window of Marshall Inc., presumably one announcing Marshall's death. She wore a pair of khaki slacks and a form-fitting ribbed shirt that hugged her curves, the very ones he's spent too much time thinking about this morning while she'd been in his office, Jake thought, doing his damnedest to ignore the commingled flash of heat and affection that warmed both his heart and his groin.

She'd pulled that thick, striking hair back into a sleek ponytail and secured it with a stylish patterned scarf. Gold hoops dangled in her ears and despite the fact that she'd had very little sleep, she looked curiously refreshed. Her lips were curled in the faintest hint of a smile and the tension she'd seemed to have carried around for the past couple of years had lessoned, making her, if possible, even more beautiful than she'd already been.

Last night when Mike had called him, Jake had realized then what he was in for. He'd known that he'd have to talk to Jolie, be around her, particularly if the investigation played out the way he'd assumed. And for the most part, it had. He'd been simultaneously filled with anticipation and dread, with longing and regret. He'd braced himself, had literally felt every muscle clench in preparation, for what simply being in her presence would do to him.

He couldn't be around her without going into sensory and emotional overload. Her smooth vanilla scent, that silky laugh, the sweet curve of her familiar face. Between those things and the ever-present hum of awareness—the sheer need to simply feel her body against his, the brush of her hair beneath his chin—he'd been in a state of weary but pleasant agony for the better part of twenty-four hours.

This morning when she'd walked into this office, every cell in his body had reacted to her presence. He'd felt her in his blood, in his very bones. At first he'd avoided looking at her because he'd known the instant his eyes met hers, he'd lose his breath. An odd, not altogether pleasant feeling, that was for damned sure, Jake thought with a silent chuckle. Even knowing about the life insurance and pre-burial plan, even knowing that she'd gotten herself into a helluva mess and that she planned to hold out on him, hadn't lessened the impact.

Nevertheless, focusing on the job ahead and keeping her delectable little ass out of jail had to take top priority.

He'd spent the majority of the day at the house, going over the scene once more. He'd combed the house from end to end and had spent a lot of time walking the yard, making sure that he hadn't missed anything the night before. He was convinced that whoever had entered the house had done so by way of the front door. It would have taken too much time to heave the garage doors up and out of the way to go in via the carport, and the back gate had been padlocked.

Which meant the killer had to have entered from the front and, given that, one could reasonably assume that *someone* had seen *something,* whether they knew it or not.

To that end, Jake had spent a couple of hours canvassing the neighborhood. Unfortunately, while none of Marshall's neighbors were particularly concerned that he was dead—and more than one had seemed almost ghoulishly delighted—not a single one of them had noticed anything out of the ordinary.

From her vantage point in the kitchen, Mrs. Dotson across the street had noticed Jolie leave, but had said that one of her children had decided to give their pet hamster swimming lessons in the commode and she'd been forced to abandon the dinner dishes. It was after dark when she'd returned to the sink and by then she said she'd been so tired that she wouldn't have noticed Freddy Krueger lurking in the bushes.

Whoever had waltzed into that house hadn't looked out of place, had looked as if they belonged there, or at the very least had a legitimate excuse for being there. Taking that into consideration had left him with the unhappy task of checking out Jolie's close friends and family, namely Sadie and Fran. Did he think either one of them did it? Gut instinct told him no. But the sooner he ruled them out, the sooner he could move on with the investigation. Jolie was the epicenter—he had to work the circle closest to her, then fan out.

He'd purposely arrived at The Spa a little early to get

a read on Sadie. Sadie loved Jolie, he knew. They'd been play-pen playmates—their parents had been friends—and had ended up having a sisterly bond as a result of that long-time acquaintance.

Sadie had been very emotional when she'd talked to him following the night Chris had hit her friend. She'd complained of Jolie's stubborn streak with exasperated affection—one he completely understood—and had called Chris a "mean-spirited snake." Jake had to agree with that assessment as well. It seemed wrong somehow to be questioning her for holding the same opinions he himself held, but her role as Jolie's most trusted friend entitled her to more knowledge of the situation than any other person, which gave her more of a motive to hate him than the rest of them.

Nose burning from the scent of hair color and perm solution, Jake waited for her last client to leave before posing the question he'd been waiting to ask. "What's she hiding, Sadie?"

Sadie, who'd been dropping coins into the cash register, stilled. "W-what do you mean?"

Pathetic stall tactic, but he'd caught her off guard and her reaction just confirmed what he knew—Jolie might not have killed Chris, but she'd definitely been doing something they didn't want him to find out about. Given the nature of his most recent discoveries, it was probably something incriminating.

He mentally swore.

"I know about the pre-burial plan and the life insurance she took out last week," Jake told her, a fact Jolie had probably already shared with her, but he felt com-

pelled to impart as well. "But there's more." He braced
a hand against the desk. "I know she's innocent, Sadie,
and I want to help her, but I don't want anything coming up and biting me on the ass on this. I need to know
everything."

She refused to look up. "I wish I could help you,
Jake, but I can't. You know she didn't do it. That's all
you need to know, right?"

Jake shook his head. "It doesn't work that way. I've
got Dean looking over my shoulder and the D.A. isn't
going to be too far behind. Come on, Sadie," he cajoled.
"I know she's your friend, but are you sure you're being
the best one you can be to her? I don't think she appre-
ciates the gravity of the situation."

Sadie shut the drawer and looked up. Worry lined
her forehead, but determination firmed her pert jaw.
"I kept her mom in the loop, Jake. That was a risk,
but I could justify it. I— I can't do anymore. I'm
sorry. As for the gravity of the situation—" she
shrugged helplessly "—you know how she is. Once
she makes her mind up, that's it. There's no changing it."

He'd gotten no more than he'd expected, he supposed. Still, it had been worth a shot. "So she came to
your house last night?"

"She did." Her brow folded into a thoughtful frown.
"She got there around eight—the girls and I were cooking—and left about ten."

"Were you home all night?"

Sadie's lips quirked with a hint of droll humor and
crossing her arms over her chest, she leaned a hip

against the desk. "I wondered how long it would take you to get around to it."

Jake shrugged, a sheepish grin tugging at his mouth. "I gotta ask, Sadie."

"I talked with Jolie last night right before she left to go to Meredith's—she mentioned that Chris was in the shower, by the way—then I left and went to Mom's for dinner. Rob was pulling a double, so the girls and I were on our own. We were there for about an hour…home by seven." She smiled and her eyes twinkled. "Does that cover everything? Does my alibi pass muster, Detective?"

"I'm sure it will once I've checked it out."

She shot him a look, then snorted indelicately. "You're barking up the wrong tree, Jake. I might have been tempted to cut his dick off, but I'd have never had the nerve to shoot him."

Jake winced. "She told you about that, eh?"

Sadie nodded. "She did. Only fitting, if you ask me. He'd never been anything but a dick, anyway."

Pretty much the consensus, Jake thought, unsurprised by the amusing observation. "What about you? Have you got any theories about who could have done it?"

Sadie paused to consider the question and her gaze turned speculative. "I don't know," she said thoughtfully. "He had a lot of enemies, but when you factor in the whole cutting-his-dick-off part, I'm thinking that you're most likely looking for a woman." She cocked her head and slid him a droll glance. "Can't see a man having the stomach for it no matter how much he might have hated him."

Jake had arrived at the same conclusion. Cutting off Marshall's dick had been the ultimate insult, the final salvo and the entire concept smacked of distinctly feminine revenge. He was most likely looking for a jilted lover, which meant that a trip to see Emily Dean would undoubtedly be on his agenda tomorrow. Now there was something to look forward to, Jake thought, as dread balled in his gut. If she was the one who'd murdered Marshall, she'd undoubtedly be entertaining similar thoughts about him and Mike for outing the affair which had ultimately ruined her marriage. A bulletproof vest and a cup probably wouldn't be out of order, he thought with a dark chuckle.

Sadie finished tidying up and slung her purse over her shoulder. "Jolie's on her way," she said. "Wanna follow me outside so I can lock up? Rob's got evening shift tonight and—" she glanced at her watch "—if I leave right now, we might actually have time to eat dinner together before he has to leave."

"Sure." Following her outside, he looked out across the square and tried to avoid staring at Jolie as she made her way closer to them…but it wasn't easy. With every step that put her nearer to him, he could feel her—feel his belly hollowing, then clenching, then hollowing again.

The faint scent of petunias, pine mulch and fresh-cut grass wafted toward him on the late afternoon breeze and the sun played hide and seek with low, smeared clouds. Despite the fact that he'd lost his pretty bronze sheen, Jebediah stood proudly on his little patch of marble, seemingly enjoying the soft gurgle of the nearby fountain. On the other side of the square an elderly couple held hands, strolled unhurriedly to some unknown destination.

Sadie jerked her thumb toward her car. "Hey, Jo, I'm heading out," she called out. "I want to catch dinner with Rob before he leaves for work."

Jolie waved her on. "Go on," she told her. "I'll call you later."

"You'll be at your mom's?"

"Yeah."

Sadie nodded, then slid into her car. She waggled her fingers at them as she drove away. Thirty seconds later, Jolie arrived in front of him. Several strands of dark red hair had pulled loose from her ponytail and whispered around her face. One in particular had swept across that lush mouth and clung distractingly. "You got here early," she remarked with a twinkling smile. "Checking out Sadie, were you?"

Jake's gaze slid away from her, and he felt a grin tease his mouth. She was too damned smart for her own good. God, how he'd missed that. "Just asking questions."

She headed toward the back of the building to the entrance to the apartment. "Well, Mom said whenever you get ready to *ask some questions* to be sure and call first. She'll put a blackberry cobbler in the oven."

A bark of laughter erupted from the back of Jake's throat as he followed her up the steep stairs. Blackberry cobbler was his absolute favorite dessert and Jolie's mother made the best he'd ever eaten. "What?" he joked. "You think you have my whole strategy figured out?"

She fished the key out of her purse, then threw him a look over her shoulder. "Not your whole strategy per se," she said drolly, "but we've read enough suspense novels to have a general idea of how things are going to go."

Jake felt a sigh slip through his smiling lips. "I'm just doing my job."

Jolie pushed open the door and made her way inside. Tall windows painted rectangular wedges of golden light on the worn hardwood floors. "I know. And if I haven't said it yet, I'm glad that it's you that's got this one."

Something warm moved into his chest. "Yeah, well, you might not be glad if I can't figure out who did this." He grimaced. "So far I've hit nothing but dead ends."

"But you're just getting started, right?"

Jake wandered into the living room part of the giant studio, noting the small touches which told him Jolie had definitely spent a lot of time here. A bottle of nail polish, a paperback book and a hair clip sat on an end table, and he could detect the faintest hint of vanilla in the somewhat musty air.

"I am," he told her. "Still, I'd like to have a little more evidence to work with. Other than a couple of smudges on the faucet, there's nothing." He shoved his hands in his pockets, shook his head. He told her about canvassing the yard, then speaking to the neighbors. "Naturally nobody saw anything."

"Chris hadn't exactly ingratiated himself with the neighbors." Jolie pulled a brown accordion file from one of the kitchen drawers, walked over and handed it to him. "But maybe this will help."

Jake accepted the folder, randomly flipped through it and felt his eyes widen. "The mayor's daughter?"

"Yep."

"Christ." What a friggin' nightmare. The sheriff's wife, the mayor's daughter. Was there any prominent citizen in Moon Valley that he hadn't screwed over?

"I'd like to get in the house tomorrow and get my things. Is that going to be all right?"

Still engrossed in the file, Jake nodded. "Yeah. We've gotten everything we're going to get out of there, I think, and everything else has been documented." He looked up. "You could actually move back in if you'd like."

She chewed the corner of her mouth and shook her head. "Nope. I just want to get what little is mine and move on, not move back," she added significantly.

"Technically it's all yours now."

"I don't want it. Everything that belonged to Chris can be sold with the house."

Jake nodded. Given what Marshall had put her through, he could easily see why she wouldn't want to live in the house anymore. Still, she should probably exercise a little discretion when it came to actually putting it on the market. He hesitated, then told her so. "I think that you should wait until this is resolved. Like I told you before, everything you do is going to be under intense scrutiny…and considering the fact that you took out an insurance policy last week and researched a pre-burial plan for him, you're being looked at pretty hard as it is."

"I'll think about it," she said evasively.

Jake felt his nostrils flare as he pulled in a slow breath. She obviously had absolutely no intention of following his advice. She had to be the most provokingly stubborn female he'd ever encountered in his life. "Think real hard, Jo."

"I will," she said, the tone of her voice adding a *not*. "Did you need anything else tonight?" she asked. She dropped a glance at her watch. "Because if not, Mom's cooking. You're, uh… You're welcome to join us if you'd like," she said, awkwardly issuing the invitation. There was something distinctly vulnerable about the tentative way she tendered it. "There'll be plenty."

Jake's first impulse was to accept, to latch on to any reason to be with her. And hell, as far as that went, he had a reason—Dean had told him to stick to her like glue. But somehow he didn't think enjoying dinner with her would qualify as true surveillance. After a moment, he shook his head. "Thanks, but I can't. I've got to feed the horses and, er… Marzipan is due to foal any day now."

Her expression brightened. "She is?"

Jake nodded. Marzipan had been "her" horse. She'd gone with him to the sale when he'd bought the sweet-tempered almond-colored mare. She'd even named her. After they'd broken up, Jake had been tempted to sell the horse, not wanting any unnecessary reminders of Jolie around, but he'd never been able to summon the nerve. It had just felt wrong somehow. "It's her first," he said, "so I want to be there."

And from the wistful expression on her face, she wanted to be there, too, Jake realized, feeling a tingly whoosh swoop through his midsection. The last damned thing he needed to do was even indirectly try to pick up where they left off, to spend more time with her than was absolutely necessary. Which made him the biggest fool in the world when he offered to call her when the foaling started. "If you'd like to be there, that is."

A big smile slowly dawned across her lips and she nodded. A bizarre charge passed between them, one that heralded if not a new beginning, then at the very least a truce. "I'd love to be there," she said, her voice somewhat strangled. "Thanks."

Jake nodded, unable to tear his gaze away from hers. Jesus, he'd missed her, still ached for her in places that he hadn't known could hurt. "Okay, then," he finally managed to say, and gestured toward the door. "We should probably get going."

Jolie nodded, seeming to come to her senses as well, and followed him downstairs. She locked up, then after a brief but awkward goodbye, Jake made his way back to his car. He slid behind the wheel and swore. Repeatedly. "Idiot," he muttered.

As if things weren't complicated enough.

Hell, her friggin' *husband* wasn't even in the ground yet and all he could think about was how much he wanted to feel the sweet curve of her cheek beneath his palm, the taste of her lush mouth against his lips. It was crazy, insane even. Jake pictured Dean's thunderous expression, could just hear him—*and you call this objective?*—and felt a burst of wry laughter well up in his throat.

He needed his head examined, Jake decided. He truly did. Just because Marshall was dead didn't mean they could just pick up where they'd left off. A lot of bitter water had flowed under the bridge—and he was responsible for most of it.

No matter how much he'd like to blame Jolie for jumping the gun with Marshall, for not giving him the time he'd asked for, he knew he'd been the one ultimately at fault. In the moment when she'd needed him most, he hadn't been there for her, had let her down. It had been his biggest fear and like a self-fulfilling prophecy, it had come true. Jake swallowed, still unable to account for the supreme ignorance of that hesitation. He lived with it, carried it around with him all the time. It was the height of idiocy to think that she'd ever truly forgive him for it, courting heartache to even hope that she might.

Furthermore—and he suspected he'd be reminding himself of this a lot over the next few weeks—he'd do better to spend his time thinking about how to clear her of possible murder charges. If he didn't, he could very well see himself trying to kiss her through a quarter-inch of Plexiglas.

CHAPTER TWENTY

"WELL?" MEREDITH ASKED with exaggerated patience. "What have you learned?"

Sophia pushed her half-eaten slice of pie away from her and mourned the loss of the rest of the delightful dessert. After that huge breakfast a couple of mornings ago, she couldn't justify eating the whole thing.

At just after two, they were sitting in Dilly's Bakery—supporting a beaming Cora who worked enthusiastically behind the counter—and going over the latest developments. Sophia would have preferred a three-way phone call—she'd needed to be pruning an out-of-control butterfly bush—but Bitsy didn't trust "the airwaves." Who knew who might be listening in? she'd argued, so they'd agreed to meet for tea at the bakery.

"I called Jolie last night," Sophia told them. "She went in yesterday and closed the business. She's repaid the investors—and Fran, of course—and is planning on meeting someone from Moon Valley Realty about selling her old house and buying that little bungalow on Lelia Street that she mentioned at last week's meeting."

Bitsy whistled low and beamed. "Why she's not wasting any time at all, is she?"

"It would seem not," Meredith said. But she didn't

seem to share Bitsy's enthusiasm for Jolie's swift actions. A line of worry emerged between her brows. "Don't you think that she ought to be a little more careful, Sophia? You know…in light of her involvement with us?"

Sophia had thought that as well, but couldn't fault Jolie for moving as quickly as she had. She told Meredith and Bitsy about Jolie's concern over the possibility of frozen accounts. "If she'd waited on that, who knows when she'd have been able to give everyone their money back, most importantly her mother's."

Bitsy shoveled another bite of lemon-blueberry pound cake into her mouth and swallowed thickly. Her chins jiggled as she bobbed her head in a sanctimonious little nod. "Sounds to me like she's using her head."

Sophia resisted the urge to reclaim her plate and finish her pie. "She's just ready for it all to be over with."

"I know," Meredith sighed, propping her chin up with her hand. "I just wish she didn't have to be so…hasty. Makes her look guilty."

"Jake knows about the pre-burial plan and the life insurance," Sophia told them gravely.

Meredith gasped and her eyes widened. "Already?" she breathed, straightening in her seat. "But how?"

She gave them both a droll look. "Apparently Andy called wanting the body and mentioned the plans to Jake."

Bitsy's doughy face folded into a disgusted scowl. "I swear, if it weren't for having to go to another county to be laid to rest, I'd be damned before I'd let those morbid vultures have my business."

She could always pay them in coupons, Sophia thought.

"How did he find out about the life insurance?" Meredith asked.

Sophia shrugged. "Put two and two together, I suppose." She released a heavy sigh. "But he still doesn't know about the Club, and Jolie has assured me that she isn't going to tell him. He tried to pump Sadie for information yesterday afternoon, but thankfully she didn't tell him anything, either."

Bitsy snorted. "She better not. I save my best coupons for her. Those dollar-off's will dry up in a heartbeat if she opens her mouth, I can tell you that."

Sophia resisted the urge to roll her eyes, certain that Sadie fervently wished those coupons *would* dry up. Everybody who worked in any sort of service capacity within a fifty mile radius of Moon Valley certainly did.

"What will we do if he finds out?" Meredith asked, blithely ignoring Bitsy's dire coupon warning.

"We'll cross that bridge when we come to it," Sophia said. And pray they didn't come to it.

"I don't think we have anything to worry about," Bitsy interjected, seemingly unconcerned as usual. "She's not going to tell. If she doesn't tell, then he can't find out about us, right? I mean, we've been careful. We've had to be to keep it together for so long, right?" Her gaze bounced to Meredith. "Stop worrying, Meri. Everything's gonna be fine. Are you going to eat the rest of that cake?"

A faint grin tugged at Meredith's mouth as she slid Bitsy her leftover dessert. "You're right, I suppose," she relented. "Still, I can't help but be nervous."

Her thin face red with pleasant exertion and

wreathed in a smile, Cora appeared at Sophia's elbow. "Can I get you anything else, ladies? Mary just pulled some hot apple fritters out a few minutes ago. They're divine."

Sophia's mouth watered, but she imagined having to buy all new support hose and woefully shook her head. "No, thanks, Cora. I'm good. How are things going here? You look happy."

Cora's smile glowed with delight and just the smallest hint of much-needed pride. "Oh, Sophia, I am. Mary's just a joy to work with, and I've always loved to bake." Her grin turned downright triumphant. "Then there's having my own money, of course. I bought a new cake pan last week. It's shaped like a rose and it's just lovely. I can't wait to—" She drew up short and ducked her head. "I know it's just a cake pan, but it was so nice to get something just because I wanted it."

Meredith offered Cora a warm smile. "We're proud of you, Cora. You always had it in you, you know."

"You don't know how much I appreciate being a part of our *bridge group*," she said earnestly, her fingers twisting into her apron hem. "Don't know what I'd do without it."

Sophia, Bitsy and Meredith all shared a significant look. "We're glad to have you, Cora," Bitsy told her.

Cora looked over her shoulder. "Well, I'd better get back to work. The mayor's coming in shortly to pick up his order and I haven't gotten it together yet." She wrinkled her nose. "He smells terrible," she whispered, leaning down where only they could hear her. "But what can you do? Poor man still hasn't gotten rid of those skunks." With a shake of her head, she turned and walked back behind the counter.

Meredith sniggered. "And he won't until one of us wins the Beautification Award," she muttered under her breath. "It's my turn, right?"

Bitsy nodded. "I've got it—" *it* being their secret skunk attractor "—in the trunk of my car. Don't let me forget to give it to you before we leave."

"Oh, don't worry," Meredith assured her. "I won't. I swear if he doesn't give you that Award next week, I'll figure out a way to get those stinky suckers *inside* his house. Or maybe I'll just plant the stuff all around his house—at the rate we're going through it, it would probably be cheaper."

"He could give the award to one of you two," Bitsy demurred, preening. "You both have lovely lawns as well."

Sophia snorted. "Not as nice as yours, but I appreciate the compliment."

Admittedly her yard was looking a lot better this spring—she'd certainly spent a great deal more time outside working it…but it hadn't been because she'd been angling for the Beautification Award.

More like she'd been angling for Edward.

Sophia still flushed like a school girl every time she thought about their delightful breakfast the other morning. Edward had been excellent company, complimenting her—even though she'd looked like a total hag, she thought, mentally writhing with remembered mortification—and had praised her cooking, then had even insisted on staying until they'd finished all of the dishes.

That had been refreshing, Sophia thought, grudgingly impressed. God knows her own lazy, shiftless husband had never so much as put a coffee cup in the sink, much less taken the trouble to wash it. Once everything had been done, every excuse to linger used, Edward had thanked her and promised to reciprocate the gesture. He could make a decent biscuit, he'd told her, if she'd be willing to try one.

Sophia had been stunned—if she wasn't completely off her rocker, he'd essentially asked her for a date—and had merely toyed nervously with her hair and nodded. So far the invitation hadn't come through, but she'd purposely stayed indoors the past couple of mornings because she loathed the idea of looking eager, or God forbid, needy.

Furthermore, though she hadn't determined precisely how just yet, Sophia wanted to make sure that all of Edward's…parts were in working order. She didn't want to get too attached to him—or the idea of having sex with him—if he wasn't going to be able to seal the deal. She hated to be callous or unfeeling, but she wasn't buying a pig in a poke here. Time was running out. If she was ever going to have an honest-to-goodness bonafide orgasm again, she had to act quickly. And if you asked her poor neglected—intensely rejuvenated—hormones, the sooner the better.

Bitsy fished a couple of coupons from her purse and laid them on the table. One was for fifty-cents off a roll of paper towels, the other for a Lean Cuisine.

Sophia heaved an exasperated sigh. "Honestly, Bitsy, can't you just put down some change? Cora's thin as a rail! What does she want with a low-calorie meal?"

Bitsy's eyes rounded. "Oh, you're right. Here," she said. She replaced it with a quarter off a half-gallon of ice cream. "She could use that a whole lot more, eh?"

Sophia looked to Meredith. "Can't you do something about her?"

"I was instrumental in talking her out of the motorcycle. You'll have to tackle the coupon issue."

Bitsy's gasped as though just remembering something important. Eyes gleaming behind her purple glasses, she rummaged around in her purse until she'd found a mangled newspaper clipping. "You only *think* you've talked me out of the motorcycle," she said, sliding the paper to Meredith. "The idea of getting a motorcycle license was the deciding factor against making that purchase. But this," she said, her voice ringing with satisfied excitement, "this is what I'm getting. It's on order. Acid green with purple racing stripes." She practically wriggled in her seat. "Isn't it wonderful? We should all have one. Then we could ride together. Get matching helmets and jackets. We could be the Moon Valley Marauders or something."

Meredith frowned, adjusted her reading glasses, then her mouth dropped open. "You can't be serious," she said faintly. With a disgusted huff, she handed the paper to Sophia.

"A pocket rocket?" Sophia asked her, inspecting the ad. "Isn't this a kid's toy?"

"Technically, yes," Bitsy admitted, not the least bit embarrassed or chagrined. "But it doesn't require a license, it's gas and electric, will go up to thirty-five miles an hour, and it'll hold up to two-hundred-and-fifty pounds."

Sophia quirked a brow.

Bitsy scowled at the quiet recrimination. "I'm dieting," she said, irritated.

"Bitsy, be that as it may, I don't think this is a good idea. You could get hurt."

She shrugged, unconcerned. "If it's safe for kids, then it's safe for me." She bobbed her head determinedly. "I want it. I'm gonna have it."

"Do as you please," Meredith said stiffly, "but don't say we didn't warn you." She removed her napkin from her lap, wadded it up and tossed it on the table. "You're blind as a bat. You don't have any business trying to ride something like that. You'll end up getting yourself killed."

Bitsy grinned and raised her palm. "Talk to the hand 'cause the head's not listening."

Meredith harrumphed. "You'll be listening when your kids try to have you committed."

"Nah," Bitsy said, blithely unconcerned. "They're too afraid I'll leave my money to my cat and my coupons to them."

Sophia suppressed a grin. Knowing Bitsy, her kids better realize that very scenario wasn't completely out of the realm of possibility.

"But I do appreciate your concern, Meri," Bitsy told her, leaning over to give her an air kiss. "It's nice to be loved. Now what say we do a little shopping, eh?" Her smile turned a wee bit sly. "We'll need a new outfit for the funeral, won't we?"

Oh, she hadn't even thought of that, Sophia realized with a pleased start. Per tradition, every member of the

FWC attended the funeral in support and appreciation of the newly widowed. To the casual observer, they merely looked like concerned friends, paying their last respects, but in truth the event officially kicked off their celebration. Sophia smiled.

And if there was one thing the FWC knew how to do it was party.

CHAPTER TWENTY-ONE

JOLIE FINGERED the single long-stemmed rose loosely held between her gloved fingers and waited for Reverend Hollis to finish the final prayer said over Chris's casket. The warm afternoon sun beat down on her back and a slight breeze ruffled her veiled hat.

Flanked by her mom and Sadie—both of them wearing somber but relieved expressions—and the entire FWC at her back, Jolie finally felt the beginnings of true closure wrap around her, felt it clawing away at two years of misery and regret, and by the time Hollis muttered the final amen, she had to suppress a triumphant whoop of joy.

It was over.

Or as over as it was going to be until Chris's murderer was found, but at least this was an official beginning to the rest of her life.

"And that's it," Sadie whispered quietly as she turned and wrapped Jolie in a warm hug. "You made it."

Sadie had no more than let her go when her mother gathered her up. "It's over, hon," her mom breathed. She could feel her soothing relief washing over both of them, could feel her mom trembling with it.

Jolie smiled, but didn't speak. She couldn't. She was

too overcome. The past several days had been a flurry of activity for her. She'd closed the business, satisfied the investors—most especially her mom—and the profound sense of comfort that doing that brought her had made it worth every miserable moment of the past two years. Just knowing that she'd made things right, that she'd have made her father proud, and that her mother wouldn't have to worry, wouldn't have to scrimp or scrape to get by anymore, had lifted a tremendous weight off her shoulders.

In addition to all of that, she'd cleaned out her things from the house she'd shared with Chris and, despite Jake's dire warnings about being hasty, she'd listed it with a Realtor, the same one who'd negotiated the deal for her for the house on Lelia Street.

Her mom had told her that she was welcome to stay at home with her, of course, and, while Jolie appreciated the offer, she wanted *her* own space, something that was hers and hers alone. She couldn't wait to move in, set up her office and flex her neglected decorating muscle. Other than her bedroom, she'd never been able to arrange things to suit her own tastes. She liked rich colors and the combination of old and new, and she couldn't wait to pick out paint samples and furniture.

Sophia, Bitsy and Meredith, all of them looking polished and gorgeous in varying spring shades, moved toward her. "You look smashing, dear," Sophia told her with an approving nod. "Like a true widow."

Meredith leaned in. "Plan on staying a little longer this week. It's customary in our little group to celebrate a new official's status."

"That's right," Bitsy chimed in. She did a little hip-roll shimmy dance move. "We're gonna *party.*"

Meredith frowned and looked to Sophia who whacked Bitsy on the upper arm. "Cut it out, fool," she admonished. "We're at a bloody funeral, for Pete's sake," she hissed, looking around to make sure no one was paying attention.

Bitsy blinked and straightened, properly chastised. "Oh, right. Sorry."

Jolie barely smothered a chuckle. The trio moved aside and slowly the rest of the FWC members came by and, their faces arranged in purposely somber expressions that in no way matched the delight in their eyes, wished her a softly spoken congratulations. Several mentioned the upcoming party and like Bitsy, seemed to want to dance. Thankfully, they refrained because from the corner of her eye—prompted by a not-so-gentle nudge from Sadie—Jolie caught sight of Jake. A tremble shook her belly, forcing a shuddering breath to escape her lungs.

He wore his trademark khaki pants and a cuffed white oxford cloth shirt. His dark brown hair was tousled and a pair of trendy shades covered his eyes. The prerequisite cell phone was clipped at his waist and she could tell by the flat shape of that usually carnal mouth that he was supremely displeased.

In fact, *pissed* was probably more accurate.

Jolie drew in a careful breath as a combination of fluttery air and dread wrestled in her belly. He'd obviously made a new discovery, possibly more, she thought warily, hoping that it didn't crush the bud of newfound neutral ground they seemed to have found.

Every time she thought about him offering to call her when Marzipan went to foal, a light hopeful feeling swelled in her chest and a tingle of tentative happiness sizzled through her blood.

Jolie knew better than to start entertaining the idea of a belated happily-ever-after with Jake. Even if he were willing, quite frankly she didn't know if she'd be able to pony up the emotional investment to pull it off. She'd given everything she'd had to him and the one time she'd really needed him he'd wavered. Which was what had ultimately sent her down the path she'd just gotten off of.

Did she love Jake? Jolie swallowed tightly as the truth readily rose in her heart. Yes, she did. Always had, always would. She ached for him, yearned for him, longed for that sense of closeness and familiarity—being his friend, and oh, God, being his lover. She wanted that back more than anything. But could they go back? Could *she* go back? Jolie frowned. She didn't know.

Granted she knew that Jake was sorry, that he regretted letting her go, then not having the nerve to try and reclaim her after she'd come back with Chris. He could have, too, Jolie thought. She'd been hurt and angry and miserable, but if he'd asked—just asked—she would have culled Chris in a heartbeat to have Jake back. He had to know it, Jolie thought. And he surely must have known it then…yet he hadn't so much as lifted a finger when he could have merely crooked it and she'd have come running.

Pride was a funny thing, she knew, because it had propelled her to bring Chris home in the first place.

God, she'd been so stupid. It was amazing what two years of sheer hell could do to make one see things clearly.

Jake strolled toward her, stopped, then lazily looked her up and down. She felt that keen caressing gaze move up her legs, over her hips, linger over her breasts, then finally find her face.

"Nice dress," he said. "Bought that last week, didn't you?"

It had been in her closet, with the receipt stapled to the bag. He knew exactly when she'd bought it, and now he knew what she'd bought it for. Her breakfast rolled. "I did," she returned, albeit shakily.

Jake swore and looked away. "I need to talk to you when you have a moment."

Jolie shrugged, twirled her rose and refused to be intimidated. Dammit, she'd told him she was moving on. What exactly had he expected? "Now's good," she said, pretending to be unconcerned. "Mom will want to go on. Can you give me a ride home?"

"To which one?" Jake asked tightly. "The one I encouraged you not to sell—which you've put on the market anyway—or the one you just bought?"

Ah, so that was it. "Neither at the moment, unless you're interested in seeing my new house," she said. "It's on Lelia Street. Right off the—"

"I know where it's at," Jake interrupted, his voice throbbing with pent-up anger. He told her mother that he'd see her home—in a considerably warmer tone than what he was using with her—then slid his hand around her upper arm and propelled her toward his car.

It was the first time in more than two years that he'd touched her and despite the fact that it wasn't the gentle caress she'd longed for, her body responded all the same. Her breath hitched in her throat, her mouth lost its moisture and a pulsing ache commenced in her nipples and between her thighs.

He opened the truck door for her, rounded the hood, then joined her inside. He waited for her to finish buckling her seat belt, then started the engine and bolted out of the cemetery.

"I came into work this morning and was immediately called into Dean's office. His sister works at the bank and she mentioned to him over the weekend that you'd cleaned out Marshall's accounts."

Jolie swallowed. "That's right."

His nostrils flared. *"The night he died."*

"It was after midnight, so technically it was the next day," Jolie clarified despite his thunderous expression.

"She also mentioned that you've closed all the business accounts." His tone was edged with disgust. "I saw you putting a sign up in the window last week. I just assumed that you'd put up a notice about Chris's death." He chuckled darkly. "I assumed wrong. You didn't put up a death notice—you put up a damned out-of-business sign!" He wheeled around the square, then waited for a stream of pedestrians to make it across to the corner. "What the hell were you thinking? Do you have any idea how guilty you're making yourself look? Do you even care?" He glanced over at her, moodily inspected her outfit once more and seemed to get even angrier. "So help me God, if you've got on that black corset underneath that, I'm gonna have a friggin' stroke."

Jolie felt a flash of feminine pleasure hit the tops of her thighs and her lips rolled into a droll smile. "You went through my underwear drawer? Take your detective work seriously, don't you, Jake?"

Jake edged the car up to the curb in front of her new house, shifted into park, then cast her another glance and let go a seemingly tortured sigh. "Are you wearing it?"

She smiled. "It matches."

His gaze dropped to her breasts again and he swallowed. From the looks of things it was taking every ounce of patience he possessed to get through this encounter.

Strangely enough, she was finding it funny, a fact she knew she'd better keep to herself.

"Let me paint a picture for you," Jake said. "We've got a dead husband with a wife who A.) has a credible yet curious alibi for the time of the murder, B.) researched pre-burial plans a week before his death, C.) took out one-hundred grand in additional life insurance the week before he died."

His expression blackened accordingly with his tone of voice as he continued to tick off her offenses.

"D.) bought the outfit she planned to wear to his funeral the week before he died, E.) cleaned out his accounts before the body had even been moved from the scene, F.) closed his business before the M.E. even finished the autopsy, G.) put the house up for sale, and H.) bought another one." Jake plucked his glasses off and slung them up on the dash. "If you were the detective on this case—or just any regular old citizen, for that matter," he added sarcastically, "what would you infer from this woman's actions?"

Yes, well, when you put it like that, she would admit that she looked a little guilty, Jolie decided. Nevertheless, she wasn't guilty and regardless of how bizarre her alibi looked, the fact remained that she had one. Furthermore, she was innocent.

"I'd infer that this wife had been married to a miserable SOB who'd delighted in making her wretched, and who'd stolen money from her mother and other hard-working citizens. I'd infer that the bastard had absolutely no redeeming qualities and that the wife—who'd had her life on hold for the past twenty-four months—was ready to move on as swiftly as possible, to wash the stench of her nasty, sorry-assed husband's life out of her own and endeavor to create a new one as soon as possible." Her veil quivered as she bobbed her head. "If I *knew* her," she said pointedly, "*that's* what I'd infer." She paused, punctuating the thought, then let herself out of the truck and, head held high and stilettos clicking, made her way up the sidewalk.

Gratifyingly, she felt his gaze on her backside as she made her way to the door…and she liked what she could *infer* from that.

JAKE SLAMMED his palm against the steering wheel, then snagged the keys and met Jolie on the porch. He did know her and, dammit, he did understand. He just wished that she could use a little bit of discretion. He'd walked into that meeting with Dean this morning and, for all intents and purposes, might as well have had his pants down.

Not only had Dean informed him—*the damned Detective,* by the way—that Jolie had cleaned out the accounts, but he'd also known that she'd closed the business, put the house up for sale and bought a new one. Things weren't looking good, Dean had said. Did Jake want to let this one go?

Not no, but hell no.

In light of everything that had been uncovered—and, dammit, he knew there was more—he couldn't afford to let it go. Guilty or not, she'd go to jail. There was too much circumstantial evidence floating around to prevent otherwise. It wouldn't matter that she had an alibi and the thick-headed, stubborn…Jake's gaze drifted over the backs of her legs—her fishnet hose, specifically—up over her gorgeous rump and slim back, and he felt another blast of heat detonate in his loins. He blinked. Aw, hell…what had he been thinking?

Oh, yeah.

"Jolie, I didn't say that I didn't understand it," he said with an exasperated sigh. "I'm just asking you to at least consider how it looks."

She inserted a key into the lock and, smiling, let herself inside. "That's just it. I don't care how it looks."

And therein lay the rub, he thought, exhaling a weary sigh. She'd made up her mind and that was that. Jake followed her into the living room, noting the worn heart-of-pine floors and custom built-ins. The spacious room had lots of nice molding, plenty of architectural detail. He caught her gaze and nodded. "It's nice."

She pulled that femme fatale hat off, ruffled her hair

and let it fall loose around her shoulders. "I thought so," she said with a satisfied sigh.

It was certainly homier than that sterile colonial she'd called home on Poplar Street, that was for damned sure. She gave him the guided tour, getting more and more excited as they moved from room to room. Other than her bedroom suite and office equipment, she had no furniture to speak of. She ticked off decorating ideas, and mentioned several improvements and upgrades she'd like to install.

"It needs a little TLC, but I can see myself here," she said, rubbing a hand over the mantle. "I can see myself calling it home."

A curiously unpleasant sensation twisted like barbed-wire in his chest and an awkward moment passed between them. There'd been a time when they'd both assumed that they'd make their home together, namely the one he'd built after she'd married Marshall.

Though Mike had called him a fool and his mother had asked him to stop torturing himself, when it had come time to build his farmhouse, he'd carried on with the plans that he and Jolie had put together. Granted, building it without her—not to mention living in it without her—had never been part of the plan, but Jake had genuinely liked what they'd put together and he couldn't see changing it simply to avoid thinking about her.

That, he knew, was never going to happen.

Furthermore, there was no point in being unsatisfied with a house just because every time he pulled into the driveway he'd think about her.

Hell, that had always been a foregone conclusion. They'd grown up together, had been through every first together. There wasn't a spot in this county that they hadn't explored, a place on the planet where he could escape from her. No matter where he lived, what he did, he couldn't outrun his memories. She'd had his heart since third grade and he didn't anticipate ever getting it back.

Jake finally swallowed. "I'm, uh… I'm sure you'll be happy here."

Jolie toyed with the netting on her hat, and glanced up at him. "I'm sorry I put you in a bad position with Dean," she said. "That was not my intention. I just knew I had to get the money out before the accounts were frozen. That's what I'd been working on, you know. Why I'd stuck it out. It was to return Mom's money, and the other investors, of course. If Dean's sister mentioned that I'd cleaned out the accounts, then she had to have mentioned what I'd done with it."

Jake nodded. He couldn't fault why she did it—noble intentions, he knew—but that didn't change the fact that he wished she'd just confide in him now. Dammit, he hated being out of the loop. She needed to let him know what the hell was going on. How did she expect him to protect her otherwise?

"She did," he admitted. "But that doesn't change the fact that I looked like a fool. I can't afford those kinds of mistakes—and neither can you. Do you understand what I'm saying?"

He watched her chest flutter with an awkward breath. "Yes."

Jake pinned her with the full force of his gaze. "Then tell me what I need to know."

Jake waited, watched a host of emotion race across her face, her mouth work up and down. "I—"

His cell chirped at his waist. He swore and checked the read-out. It was Mike, so he had to take it. "What's up?" he asked, cursing the timing of this damned call.

"We've got a twenty on the penis," Mike said grimly.

Jake blinked. "Come again?"

"We've found Marshall's dick." Something that sounded suspiciously like a chuckle sounded into his ear. "You'll, uh… You'll have to see it to believe it."

CHAPTER TWENTY-TWO

TEN MINUTES LATER Jake, Jolie, Mike, Dean and Todd, as well as a crowd of morbidly curious onlookers, stood at the base of the statue of Jebediah Moon and, dour faced, stared in abject fascination at the sight in front of them.

"Somehow I don't think this is w-what the City Council would c-consider an improvement," Mike commented, once again sounding perilously close to laughter.

Dean shot him a firm look and Mike flushed. "Sorry," he muttered.

Marshall's apparently semi-frozen penis had been glued—with what, Todd would have to determine, thank God—to Jebediah in a position that, if not anatomically correct, was at least in the general vicinity of where a penis should belong.

This case had just left Interstate Weird and exited onto Highway Bizarre.

"Who noticed it?" Jake asked, passing a hand over his face.

"Martin Mashburn," Mike told him. "He said he was just strolling by and noticed a part of Jeb that wasn't tarnished. Said he almost fell down when he realized what it was."

He supposed so, Jake thought, still shocked. He'd had advance knowledge and it was still pretty damned hard to believe. Who in the hell could have done such a thing? he wondered. And more importantly, why?

Though he dreaded it, he knew he had to ask. He shot Jolie an uncomfortable look. "Is this—" He cleared his throat. "Is this Marshall's—"

Thankfully, she didn't let him finish. "Limp and little," she said coolly. "That's definitely his."

The comment drew a shocked chuckle from them all, most especially Dean, who smothered his laugh with an unconvincing cough. "Well, Todd," said the Sheriff, "I don't envy your job on this one."

Looking distinctly unenthusiastic, Todd grimaced. "Yeah, me neither."

"What are you going to do with it?" Mike wanted to know. "They've already buried him."

Todd shifted uncomfortably, darting a hesitant look at Jolie. "I guess it needs to be given to Mrs. Marshall."

"It's Caplan," Jolie corrected, much to Jake's surprise. "I've taken back my maiden name. And I don't want it," she said. Her face had folded into a frown of disgusted distaste. "I don't care what you do with it."

Jake slid a veiled glance at Dean. He had a grim suspicion what fate awaited Marshall's severed penis. "Er…don't you need to process it first? Maybe see if you can figure out what was used to—"

"Yeah, I'll do that. Though frankly, I don't think I'm gonna find much."

"Yeah, that happens when you don't have much to work with, eh?" Mike jibed.

Dean's brows lowered again, prompting Mike to make another red-faced apology.

"Mike, you want to help me start questioning?" Jake asked, looking around the square. "I'll take one side, you take the other."

Surely to God, this time they'd find some sort of witness. No one could have possibly walked into the square and glued Marshall's dick to Jebediah completely unnoticed. Someone had to have seen something. The square was the hub of Moon Valley commerce. It was usually packed, Monday being especially busy.

Though looking at the slowly thawing grayish penis made his stomach roil, this could actually end up being the break in the case that he needed.

Mike nodded. "Sure. So long as I don't have to look at it anymore—or touch it—I'll do whatever you ask me to."

Jake turned to Jolie. "Do you need a ride to your Mom's?"

"I'll call her," Jolie told him.

"No need," Dean interrupted smoothly. "I'll give you a lift."

Though Jake didn't particularly like the idea, he couldn't very well object, and if Jolie was the least bit intimidated by riding with the Sheriff, she didn't betray so much as a blink of disquiet.

"I'll be in touch later," he told Jolie, a subtle warning that their interrupted conversation was by no means over.

She nodded and walked away with Dean. Jake looked back at Marshall's drooping dick and shuddered. Whoever did this was either really sick…or had one supremely twisted sense of humor.

For whatever reason, he suspected the latter.

JOLIE DIDN'T KNOW exactly what she'd expected Dean to say to her when they were alone in the car, but the apology she got on behalf of his estranged wife was definitely not it.

"I know there was no love lost between you and your husband, but as far as my wife's—soon to be ex-wife's," he corrected "—part in it, I'm really sorry."

Jolie blinked, somewhat stunned. "Well, I'm sorry for Chris's part in it as well." She stared at the radio, pretending to be interested in the other gadgets and gizmos she wasn't accustomed to seeing in her own car. For reasons that escaped her, something about his sincerity made her feel worse instead of better. Then she knew why. "I should have come to you as soon as I found out, but…" Somehow telling him that shoring up her grounds for divorce was more important to her than his right to know didn't seem very palatable.

"Jake explained," Dean told her, letting her off the hook. "Don't worry about it. It's done."

"Still… I'm really sorry."

"No hard feelings." He negotiated a turn and his dark brown gaze shifted to her. "I guess Jake told you she moved out."

"He did."

"Ah, well. It's for the best."

He was probably right, but agreeing felt like bad form, so she kept her mouth shut.

"He's still in love with you, you know," Dean said conversationally.

Jolie felt her heart trip, then race.

"It was against my better judgment to leave him on this case, but he's convinced that you're innocent and any other detective may might not be so inclined to keep your best interests at heart."

"I *am* innocent," Jolie felt compelled to point out. "And I'm very thankful that he believes me."

Dean flicked her a glance. "A thankful person wouldn't let him get called on the carpet for things that he's too close to the investigation to see." He pulled into her mother's drive, shoved the gearshift into park, then turned to face her. "I don't think you killed Marshall, Jolie. Aside from your alibi, you were working too hard to get away from him legally without having to resort to murder." A weak smile caught the corner of his mouth. "Besides, you protested dissecting a dead frog in biology—I can't see you having the wherewithal to shoot Chris." He shifted. "That said, there are other issues that make you look damned guilty and if there's anything else that's likely to crop up, you ought to have enough respect for Jake to let him know. He's not the enemy. He's trying to help you." He lifted one shoulder in a negligent shrug and smiled. "Just think about it. End of sermon."

Slightly surprised by the unexpected lecture, Jolie nodded and moved to get out of the car. "I will. Thanks for the ride home."

"Anytime," Dean told her.

Her stomach knotted with tension, she straightened

and watched him drive away. Good grief, what a damned mess, Jolie thought, wishing she had some idea as to how to fix it. She could either betray the FWC, or betray Jake.

Either way someone got hurt.

Aside from listening to him tell her not to do the things she'd wanted to do—like closing the accounts and business, putting the Poplar Street house up for sale and buying another—there was really no reason why she shouldn't have told him. Furthermore, after she'd shifted the money, there was really no reason—apart from catering to her own comfort—not to tell him that it had been done.

By keeping those things from him, she'd indirectly escalated the importance of the one thing she *had* to hide—the Future Widows' Club.

She could not—*would not*—out them, no matter how much Jake felt betrayed.

There was too much at risk for them, for past, present and future members. For women like Cora, Gladys and Margaret. The Officials—like her, Jolie realized with an odd start—didn't have as much to lose. Their lives were their own now, their miserable husbands dead and buried.

But what about the Futures? It's what made their lives bearable, what made them keep going from week to week. And the minute the group became public that would all be over with. Oh, there were some people who'd laugh it off, think that it was funny, even some she suspected who'd want to join.

But then there'd be a select few who had good decent husbands who wouldn't understand and it would be those few who would turn the FWC and all of its members into social outcasts or morally bankrupt second-class citizens. The anonymity was its only protection, what made it especially unique.

Jolie shook her head, firmed her resolve as she walked up the steps. She wouldn't be responsible for taking that away from them. Not to save her own skin and certainly not to spare Jake's feelings. She was sorry, but that was simply the way it had to be.

Her mother stood at the stove stirring a pot of marinara as Jolie walked into the kitchen. She'd been to see Sadie and a fresh new color had replaced the faded shade she'd had just the day before. A container of gourmet coffee sat proudly next to the pot, causing Jolie's lips to slip into a pleased smile.

"Looked like there was a big brouhaha down at the square when I came through," her mother said. "I tried to call Sadie and see what was going on, but no one answered the phone at The Spa."

Jolie sank down into a chair at the kitchen table. "I didn't see her, but she was probably there. Someone, presumably the killer, glued Chris's missing penis to the statue of Jebediah Moon." Though she knew it was inappropriate, Jolie felt her lips twitch and she forcibly quelled a laugh.

Her mother stilled, then slowly turned around. Marinara dripped from the wooden spoon in her hand unheeded onto the floor. For a moment she appeared as if she'd been cryogenically frozen.

Then she burst out laughing.

Jolie let the laughter she'd been holding back explode

into a hysterical peal of guffaws that made her lose her breath.

"Oh, my God," her mother wheezed brokenly. "I know it's horrible, but I just think it's too funny. He was always so proud of that p-penis and…there's just some-thing…poetic about him being buried w-without it." She wiped her streaming eyes, struggling to get herself under control, but like Jolie, didn't seem to be making much progress.

"Oh, Mom, it was horrible," she told her. She pulled in a deep breath in a vain attempt to stem the humor still lingering in the back of her throat. She swallowed, re-calling the sight of his pitiful little dick stuck awkwardly to that statue. "It had been frozen."

"Shrinkage, then," her mom deadpanned. "What a tragedy."

Jolie shook with silent laughter until her sides hurt. "Yes, well. That poor Nathan Todd was left to 'process' it, and Mike and Jake were charged with the duty of in-terrogating passersby to try and determine who'd glued the penis to the statue." She snickered again. "Should be interesting to hear how they tactfully broach that subject, huh?"

Her mother's smile turned thoughtful. "It was glued, you say?"

"Yep."

She hummed under her breath. "Wonder how they pulled that off. Must be *some* glue if it held a frozen penis in place."

Jolie rested her head against her palm. She hadn't thought of it that way. "I guess so."

"Probably used that Mega-glue, you know that kind they show on the commercials that can hold a three-ton truck by a broken chain."

Her mother turned back to the stove and tended to her sauce. "Has Jake gotten any more leads on who might have killed Chris? Is that what he wanted to talk to you about?"

"No. He'd gotten wind of some of my recent activities," Jolie said drolly, "and wanted to express his displeasure."

"Can't blame him, can you?" she asked. "He is trying to help you."

For the love of God, how many more times was she going to hear that today? "I know," Jolie told her, trying to sound grateful rather than exasperated.

"I understand why you can't tell him about the FWC," she said lightly, "but there wouldn't have been any harm in sharing the other stuff with him."

Jolie felt her jaw drop.

Her mother turned around and smiled benignly. "Who do you think encouraged your invitation?" she asked. "You know Sophia and I are friends."

She did, Jolie thought, still shocked and dumbfounded, but she'd never put it together. Actually, come to think of it, she'd never really put any thought into why Sophia, Bitsy and Meredith had approached her. Nor had she thought anything about the entire FWC attending the funeral. Her mother hadn't batted an eye…and no wonder, Jolie thought, her gaze swinging to her mom.

She'd known.

Undoubtedly she'd known everything, all along, she suddenly realized. And Jolie had gone to so much trouble to avoid her, to hide the gruesome details that weren't common knowledge at The Spa, at the Garden Center. In the nanosecond it took to make that deduction, the truth dawned and she gasped.

Sadie.

"Don't be mad at her, dear," her intuitive mother said gently. "She was just being a good friend."

She knew, still… She and Sadie—who was ordinarily very trustworthy when it came to keeping a secret—were going to have to have a little talk about exercising discretion.

"Don't you say anything to her," her mother admonished, evidently reading her line of thought. "She knew I was worried about you, and you couldn't look me in the eye." Her mother tsked. "It was heartbreakingly dreadful."

Jolie swallowed. "It was too hard, Mom," she confessed. "I was so ashamed."

"And I understood that, which is why I never pushed it." Her expression softened. "But I can't tell you what a relief it is to put all of this behind us, and though I know it's awful of me to say this—which is why you'd better not ever repeat it—I hope they never find who killed Chris." She shrugged and turned back around. "Far as I'm concerned, that person did the world a favor, and most assuredly did you one. Whether you'd divorced him or not, he'd never have been completely out of your life. People like him—soul suckers—they just hang around forever, feeding off other people's misery."

She'd never spoken it aloud either, but her mother had just neatly described how she felt about Chris's killer as well. She hadn't wanted Chris to die, had certainly never wanted him to be murdered. But she was not sorry that he was out of her life, and she was definitely better off as a widow than she would have been as a divorcee. Her mother was right. Divorce wouldn't have been the end of it. He would have dropped back into her life, sprinkling the acid of his presence and infecting everything she ever touched. She knew it.

This way it was over. She'd buried him today and she could finally move on, an action she intended to embrace beginning right now. Jolie felt a slow grin move across her lips.

After all, if Jake kept her out of jail, she'd have a house to decorate.

CHAPTER TWENTY-THREE

HER INSIDES QUIVERING with pent-up anxiety, Sophia patted her hair and smoothed away a non-existent wrinkle from her trendy linen pantsuit as she made her way up Edward's carefully manicured walk. Bulbs, vines and delicate flowers and shrubs bloomed in perfect harmony around his garden and every blade of grass had been tended with razor-perfection.

A closer look at his flower beds showed not a single weed and from the looks of things, he'd made his own mulch because, unlike some of the cheaper bagged varieties, every piece was uniform in shape and size, giving each cultivated inch a more polished quality.

Sophia pursed her lips and reluctantly acknowledged the bit of grudging admiration trying to worm its way into her jealous heart. And he didn't just plant the no-brainers—pinks, petunias and impatiens—he'd chosen finicky plants which required a great deal of time and maintenance, ones that had to be nursed and coaxed.

Edward opened the front door and a welcoming smile spread across his lips and infected those Paul Newman blues. "Ah," he sighed. "I thought I saw a new flower out here. You look lovely, Sophia."

Again she found herself resisting the ridiculous urge

to preen. She was in her early sixties. She had stretch marks, varicose veins, wrinkles and cellulite. At best she'd held up well, but she knew she was far from lovely. Nevertheless, she smiled and said thank you, and did her best to hold her ground and not bolt like the frightened coward she suddenly felt like. "I was just admiring your garden, Edward, and I must confess I have to take back every uncharitable thing I've ever said about your being undeserving of the Presidency of the Garden Club." She cast an approving eye around his lawn. "You've done a wonderful job here and from now on when you offer advice, I daresay I'll be listening a little more closely."

Those blue eyes twinkled with mischief and he gave his jaw a thoughtful stroke. "No longer 'insufferable with an exalted opinion of my own wit' then?"

Sophia flushed, but lifted her chin. "That's right. It would appear that you do know it all and I stand corrected."

"Well, I'd like it better if you'd stand inside. Come on in," he told her, opening the door. "My biscuits are going to burn."

"That would be a tragedy," she replied drolly.

He looked back at her over his shoulder and a smile that affected only one side of his mouth shaped his lips. "Tragedy is a bit dramatic, but it would definitely be unfortunate seeing as that's what I promised you for breakfast." His gaze caught and held hers. "Disappointing you would be the tragedy."

His low voice resonated with a combination of innuendo and sincerity and once again her body experienced another slow simmering burn. Sophia knew she had absolutely no business checking into Edward's private affairs, but that hadn't kept her from contacting a good friend who worked at the local doctor's office. She'd asked her to check Edward's charts and, while Sophia had waited with bated breath, the woman had come back on the line with a good report. Everything seemed to be in good working order and he'd never been prescribed any sexual enhancement aids.

She'd hung up the phone, let go a small shuddering breath, then raided her refrigerator until she'd soothed the nerves she'd wrecked by making the call in the first place.

Edward's kitchen was large and spacious with high ceilings, glass-fronted cabinets and antique reproduction appliances. A long trestle table served double duty as a work island and dozens of worn, gleaming pots and pans hung from an old door that had been fashioned with big hooks for easy storage.

The scent of buttery biscuits filled the room and the table had been loaded down with all of her favorite foods, the very ones she'd made for herself the morning he'd shown up and joined her for breakfast.

He saw her looking at the table and a flash of red color hit his cheeks. "I, uh… I just wanted to make sure that I had everything here that you liked."

Touched, Sophia struggled to find her voice. "Thanks, Edward. My mouth thanks you, but my hips are pissed."

He chuckled, the sound warm and intimate in the fragrant kitchen. "There's nothing wrong with your hips. They're perfect." He turned around and tended to a pan of scrambled eggs on the stove. "I should know. I've been admiring them for months."

Sophia blinked. "For months?"

He shot her another look over his shoulder. "I've been coming by your house for months, which is blocks out of the way from my own. What did you think I was doing?"

"Walking for your health."

He grunted. "If I wanted to walk for my health, then I damned sure wouldn't be strolling past your house. Seeing your rump sticking out of a flower bed does things to my old heart that could be downright dangerous at my age."

"Do you have a heart condition?" she asked, grateful for the sentiment but suddenly wary of possible…problems.

"Not in the literal sense, no," he told her cryptically. "I'm healthy as a horse."

Sophia released a relieved sigh. "That's good."

"Thank you. I wasn't aware that you were concerned." He turned around once more and emptied the pan onto an awaiting plate. "At least, I hadn't been until Janice Lowery told me that you'd asked about my general health. She's a friend of mine as well."

Sophia's tongue stuck to the roof of her mouth and every ounce of blood she possessed raced to her face. Her heart tripped and emptying her stomach became a genuine fear. She'd kill her, Sophia decided. The minute she left here, she fully intended to run Janice to ground and rip every salt-and-pepper hair out of her head.

He grinned. "Did I pass muster?"

"You did," Sophia told him tightly. "Right up until this moment." She snatched her purse from the counter and hurried from the room. God, she was so embarrassed. She wanted to crawl into the nearest hole and die.

"Sophia, wait!" Edward called, hurrying after her. "Please wait. I'm sorry. I shouldn't have said anything. I just— Aw, hell, I was flattered and I—"

Sophia felt mortified tears burn the backs of her eyes and, muttering a string of dire curses, darted through the dining room. She'd almost reached the door when Edward caught up with her. He snagged her arm and turned her around.

"Sophia, please," he said softly. "I'm sorry. I shouldn't have said anything. It's just you've given me *hell* all spring and I—" His voice turned into a tortured growl. "You make me crazy. Half the time I can't make up my mind if I want to kiss you or throttle you. You're prickly, but sweet, and you're unlike any woman I've ever known…and I've wanted you for…forever."

Startled by the confession, Sophia glanced up. Edward tenderly cupped her cheek and before she could form a protest—or even prepare herself for that matter—his gaze dropped to her lips, and his mouth followed suit and she suddenly found herself being kissed. Her knees all but buckled and the tears that had been borne of mortification suddenly turned to tears of joy. She tore her mouth away from his. "Your biscuits will burn," she warned breathlessly.

He kissed her lids, then her nose, then the corner of her mouth. "To hell with the biscuits."

Sophia sagged against him, smiled against his lips

and with a slow, desperate groan of surrender, she wrapped her arms around his neck and simply gave herself up to the exquisite perfection of the moment.

After all these years of being alone—and being with the wrong man—she'd earned it.

CHAPTER TWENTY-FOUR

JAKE SHIFTED tiredly in his seat, continuing to watch Jolie roll dark gold paint onto her living room walls. The smooth tunes of Norah Jones wafted out her open windows, weaving around his senses.

Wearing a pair of frayed denim cut-offs and a white tank top, her hair pulled up into a messy ponytail, she looked like a poster girl for home-improvement. Watching her stretch and reach, seeing her belly-button play peek-a-boo every time she moved, had turned into a sadistic form of torture for him.

Hell, he should just go home, Jake thought, wearily rubbing a hand over his face. He'd left work this afternoon, had dropped by the barn long enough to feed and determine that tonight probably wasn't going to be the night for Marzipan, then remembering Dean's latest edict to "watch her every move," he'd driven back and parked across the street from her house.

She knew he was there, of course. She'd looked out the window, seen him sitting there, then when she'd figured out that he'd put her under surveillance, she'd smiled and waggled her fingers at him.

Smart-ass, Jake thought, feeling a faint grin tug at his lips. The best he could tell, other than working on her house and doing away with all the extra office furniture and equipment she didn't need from Marshall Inc., she'd done exactly what she'd told him she planned to do— move on. If it wasn't for the lingering fear that haunted those pale green eyes, he'd buy into her whole unconcerned facade, but he knew better. She might be moving on…but that hadn't kept her from having a healthy fear of going to jail.

He'd checked back with the insurance companies that had covered Chris and so far she didn't seem to be in any hurry to meet with them and satisfy her claim. He'd followed her around town the past couple of days, watching her load her car down with various domestic goods. He'd tailed her to Moore's Furniture on the square, had pulled his truck up in front of the huge glass-paned windows and watched her select her furniture. At one point she'd held up a couple of pillows, pointed at each in turn and quirked a brow, soliciting his opinion.

Typical Jolie, Jake thought. She wasn't going to let him know that she was the least bit worried about who'd killed Chris or about being pinned with his murder. Pretending to be confident in her innocence, she was moving blithely along seemingly without a care in the world, completely oblivious to the fact that her sweet little ass was on the line and that becoming someone's bitch in prison could too easily become a reality if this case didn't break soon.

As he'd predicted, the D.A. had sought him out, wanting to know all of the particulars on the case. Jake had filled him in, making certain that he realized Jolie's alibi was tight, even if everything else had been shaky. But true to form, the D.A. had been skeptical. "If it walks like a duck, talks like a duck, it's a damned duck," he'd argued. Jake had held his ground and presented a host of other suspects—each of which Jake had culled as well, though he'd neglected to share that—and hoped that something significant happened soon. If it didn't, he didn't know what would happen.

The case was getting cold, and frankly, no one seemed particularly interested in seeing Marshall's killer brought to justice, himself included. Nevertheless, a crime had been committed and he was bound by the law to do everything in his power to see that the person responsible was punished to the fullest extent of that law.

Rather than risk Jolie's wrath, he'd covertly scoped out Fran and ruled her out as a suspect. She'd been at the Methodist Church Bazaar the night of the murder and dozens of people had confirmed her whereabouts. Dean had vouched for Emily, and the mayor's daughter had been off with Tad Ralston, the county agent who'd been trying to solve the mayor's skunk problems. To no avail, Jake thought, grimacing as he remembered the stench. His eyes had watered while he'd waited at the door. Jesus, he didn't know how they stood it. It was awful.

As for working the money angle, Jolie had done such a good job of covering up for most of Chris's antics that the majority of the investors hadn't realized until she'd paid them back in full that Chris had been screwing them. That had derailed that potential train of thought.

Aside from a single green thread and a few fibers that

were consistent with the other hand towel left in the bathroom, Marshall's dick had been a dead end as well. He and Mike had canvassed the square, talked to practically every resident in Moon Valley and none of them had seen a thing.

Either the person he was looking for was damned good, or Moon Valley residents were the most unobservant people on the planet. In fact, most people had been more interested in knowing what sort of adhesive had been used to glue the dick to the friggin' statue. Had to have been good glue, Otis Harper had remarked thoughtfully. He'd like to have some of—

Jake started as a knock sounded at his driver's side window. He looked up to see Jolie's smiling, paint-smeared face and swore. Feeling his cheeks flame with embarrassment, he lowered the window.

"You might want to take another course on stealth tactics, Detective," she remarked, her voice laden with droll humor.

"I was thinking."

"I noticed. It looked painful."

"It is painful," Jake told her, shifting uncomfortably. "My ass is numb."

Jolie held up a wet paint brush and cocked her head. "I have a cure. If you're going to have to watch me, the least you could do is help."

Jake smiled at her, shook his head. "Not dressed for it. I could ruin my shirt." As if that would be such a loss. Like he didn't have a dozen more white shirts. What the hell. It kept laundry simple.

To his slack-jawed astonishment, Jolie reached

through the window and painted his sleeve. "Oh, darn," she deadpanned, eyes wide in mock innocence. "There goes that excuse."

A stunned chuckle bubbled up his throat. "You're evil, you know that?"

"I prefer resourceful." Eyes twinkling with devilish humor, she jerked her head toward the house. "Come in and help me, you big jerk," she admonished. "You've been sitting out here watching me for hours. What sort of man are you, anyway?"

Jake followed her, letting his gaze drop to her back-side and felt an arrow of heat land in his groin. "The kind who hates to paint."

"Oh, you won't feel that way once you're high from the fumes."

Jake sighed. "So long as there's something to look forward to."

"You mean the pleasure of my company isn't enough?" she teased.

Just watching her had been enough, Jake thought, accepting a roller from her. "I'm still mad at you."

He heard a protracted sigh. "I'm sorry."

"Sorry that I'm mad or sorry that you're hiding something from me?"

"Both."

Jake methodically rolled paint onto the wall, admiring the color. "You could remedy that easily enough by telling me what I need to know."

"That's just it," she said, a hint of frustration entering that cool, lyrical voice. "You *don't* need to know. It won't help you, won't do anything for the investigation…but it could hurt a lot of innocent people and I—" She stopped short, dashed a stray strand of hair off her cheek. "I can't be responsible for that."

"Just because you don't think that it's relevant to the investigation doesn't mean that I wouldn't."

"Believe me, Jake. It's not."

He paused and let his gaze trace the familiar slope of her cheek, the delicate arch of her brow. A landslide of emotion and heat swept through him. "If you hadn't hidden everything else, Jo, I might."

She looked away, silently acknowledging the truth of that statement, then growled low in her throat. "I know that I should have told you about the accounts and whatnot, but I just didn't want to deal with the unpleasantness of it all."

His lips curled. "Translate: you didn't want to hear a lecture."

She turned around, darted a look at him and the corner of her mouth tucked into a grin. "That's probably an accurate assessment. But I was just tired of it, dammit. I told you from the get-go that I planned to move on, that I wasn't wasting another minute of my life. Is that so hard to understand?"

"I do understand," Jake told her. "I just wish you'd confided in me."

"We all make mistakes," she said, subtlety reminding him of his. She gestured toward a ladder. "Would you mind helping me move this?"

Jake nodded, grabbed one end and helped her position it where she wanted. For a while they worked without the noise of conversation, merely listened to Norah's smooth voice sing "Come Away With Me" and other poignant ballads, which undoubtedly made them both think about what they'd lost, what they'd missed. Jolie worked on cutting in the trim, occasionally asking for his assistance with the ladder.

When she'd finally finished the last corner, she paused and inspected her handiwork. "You think it's going to need a second coat?"

Without a doubt, Jake thought. He shook his head. "No."

She grinned and he felt that smile land in his heart, then settle behind his zipper. God, she was gorgeous. Simply breathtaking.

"Yes, it does," she said with wry exasperation. "But I'm willing to feed you first. How about I order a pizza?"

He wasn't hungry, but any reason to avoid painting appealed to him, so he nodded. "Pizza sounds good."

Her shrewd gaze narrowed and her smile widened. "You're not even hungry are you?"

"Oh, yes I am. I'm starving." He eagerly set his paint roller aside, affecting a frown. "In fact, I'm gonna faint from hunger. I don't think I can work anymore until I've had something to eat."

Jolie rolled her eyes, then set her brush length-wise over the bowl she'd been working from and started down the ladder. "You're so full of sh—"

She squealed as her foot slipped three rungs from the bottom. Lucky for her, he'd been admiring her ass, otherwise he might not have lunged in time to catch her.

She'd instinctively turned around to brace her fall and

landed smack dab against his chest. The impact knocked the breath from his lungs in a startled whoosh, he lost his footing and toppled backward, landing painfully on his previously numb ass, Jolie right on top of him.

Her small body aligned perfectly against his and he barely had time to note the fit of her hips over his groin, the lush mounds of her breasts against his chest before she braced her hands on either side of his head and her eyes widened in shock-delayed humor. Laughter fizzed up her throat in a long infectious stream that made him chuckle, too, and soon they were both howling like a couple of psychotic hyenas. He settled his hands at her waist and absorbed the delectable feel of her shaking frame above his.

After a moment, her laughter petered out and she seemed to realize their position. Her light green gaze darkened to a mossy hue, then dropped to his mouth and she moistened her lips. He caught the faint fluttering of her pulse in her neck, carefully drawing in a vanilla scented breath and resisting the urge to kiss her, to align his mouth to hers and eat every breath she exhaled, to roll her over onto her back and make long, slow beautiful love to her.

The desire was there, of course, the pressing need to firmly root himself between her thighs, but with Jolie it was more than that. Always had been. There was something painfully sweet about being with her, where love met lust and turned the generic act of sex into a commingling of souls, a meeting of the minds, ritual instead of rote.

He wanted to taste her—needed to—more than his

next breath, and yet he didn't. That move had to be hers. Given what she'd been through and how he'd indirectly contributed to it, Jake couldn't allow himself to take that decision out of her hands. He was hers for the taking, when and if she was ever ready.

And it wouldn't be tonight, he realized, squashing an immediate sense of disappointment as she ultimately rolled away. She covered the move with another laugh, tried to pretend the awkward moment away. "That was graceless, eh?"

"Not really," Jake told her, forcing a chuckle for her benefit. "You *swan-dived* into me."

"Are you hurt?"

"Yes," he said. He closed his eyes and massaged the bridge of his nose, barely resisted the urge to massage another part of his anatomy. "My painting arm is broken."

She snorted, leaned up on her elbow and glared at him accusingly. "Fraud. You just don't like painting."

He turned his head toward her and offered an unrepentant grin. "There is that."

"Fine," she said with a dramatic sigh. "You can watch me paint. Without my pizza. From your truck."

Jake laughed, lifted his right hand and wiggled it around. "Look at that," he told her, feigning delighted surprise. "I'm healed."

Her lips slid into a wry grin. "A miraculous recovery. I expected as much."

Jake gingerly got to his feet and offered her a hand up. "Must be nice," he told her. "With you, I never know what to expect."

She batted her lashes shamelessly at him. "It's part of my charm."

Indeed it was, Jake thought, hopelessly in love with her. He picked up his roller and set back to work while she called in the pizza.

Indeed it was…

CHAPTER TWENTY-FIVE

JOLIE WALKED outside, waved at Jake who'd been parked at her curb the majority of the day and, smiling, got into her car. Predictably, he dropped his shades in place and fell in behind her. He'd lessened his so-called surveillance over the past couple of days, had taken to driving by a couple of times a day, checking on Marzipan, then coming over after his shift.

Jolie felt a smile tug at her lips. For someone who didn't enjoy painting, he'd shown up each night this week in an old T-shirt and shorts, ready to get started. As a result of his help, they'd managed to get every room in the house painted except for the spare bedroom. He'd mentioned knocking that room out tonight and she'd very casually reminded him of her *bridge* meeting. Those carnal lips had slid into a knowing smile and he'd merely inclined his head. Maybe you could teach me, he'd said, a careless taunt that had made her heart skip an unsteady beat.

Jolie caught sight of him in her rearview mirror and felt a flutter of heat wing around her belly, then nestle between her legs. She let go a stuttering breath. Being with him every night, being able to covertly study the familiar cut of his jaw, those silvery gray eyes, and the way his muscles rippled beneath his shirt as he pushed his hands through those dark chocolate locks had been a feast for her senses. Every move he made was unhurried and sensual and reeked of familiarity. His presence warmed her in neglected places, making her shake like an addict in withdrawal.

The night she'd literally fallen into him had been the sweetest form of torture imaginable. Feeling that hard body beneath hers, that husky intimate laugh breezing across her neck and vibrating her nipples had all but made her come unglued. She'd been mentally praying—wishing—that he'd kiss her, and though she knew he'd wanted to, he'd held back.

As much as Jolie wished he'd have taken the decision out of her hands at the time, in retrospect she appreciated that he hadn't and the respect for her behind the decision. If things moved forward for them, it would be completely up to her. She knew him well enough to realize that he'd held back because he understood her desire to make her own decisions.

It hardly seemed real that Chris was gone and she was actually thinking about a tentative future with Jake. Madness, she knew, but she couldn't seem to help herself. She'd wanted control of her life and in just under a week she'd managed to put the majority of what Chris had ruined over the course of two years back to rights. She'd sold his car yesterday and, while the house hadn't garnered an offer yet, she knew it was just a matter of time. Hell, whoever bought it was getting the damned thing practically furnished.

Since Jake had been so against her moving things

along as swiftly as she had, Jolie had held off meeting with the life insurance agent. She'd been in a hurry to give everybody else's money back and therefore hadn't been too concerned with her own. Once that was done, there wouldn't be anything left to do.

When not working on her house, she'd managed to get her office up and running and fully anticipated officially opening for business in a couple of weeks. She'd already had a couple of potential clients drop by, the majority of them wondering why she hadn't simply converted Marshall Inc. into her headquarters, but as much as she liked the square atmosphere, she thought she'd enjoy the privacy of being one block removed from the hub of activity. She could reap the benefits without being in the middle of things.

Jolie pulled up in front of Meredith's house, snagged her purse and apple dumplings from the car and made her way up the walk. She turned to wave at Jake, who'd pulled in a couple of car lengths behind her, but paused as the thump of music reached her ears.

It didn't take long to recognize the tune and once she did, a bark of laughter erupted from her throat. Gloria Gaynor's "I Will Survive" vibrated through the walls, then practically knocked her down when Meredith opened the door. Decked out in black sweats, her black hat—which had been topped with a party hat—and a kazoo in her hand, Meredith smiled, darted a look over Jolie's shoulder, then spotting Jake, jerked Jolie inside.

"What's he doing?" she shouted above the din. "Why's he out there?"

"He's following me," Jolie explained. "I'm under

surveillance." Which admittedly was nice, but a complete waste of his time if he planned on finding the real killer.

Meredith's perfectly lined brows folded into a faint scowl. "Oh, well. Let him sit there. We're going to party."

Jolie followed Meredith into the living room and when she walked in, every member of the FWC whooped with joy. Then they killed Gloria and started singing their own custom version of "Ding Dong the Witch Is Dead!"

"Ding dong the bastard's dead,
the mean old bastard's dead!
Who's old bastard? Jolie's old bastard!
Ding dong—and he was missing his dong—
Ha! Ha! Ha!
The mean old bastard's dead!"

They finished the end with a flourish, dragging "dead" out until Jolie was certain every pair of ears in a ten mile radius had heard them.

Which was particularly unsettling when she knew Jake was outside.

Before she could think about it anymore, however, someone turned the music back up, pressed a drink in her hand, and they formed a train, dancing around the living room.

Like Meredith everyone had donned black—except for her, Jolie thought wryly, who'd apparently missed the memo—and had placed a party hat on top of their regular widow hats. Looking even more lovely than usual—there was a certain glow about her—Sophia cha-cha-cha-ed up next to her, then pulled her out of the line.

"How's everything going, dear?"

"Great," Jolie called above the noise. She thought she'd better tell her about Jake, but Meredith had already beaten her to the punch.

"I've already been outside and taken him a drink and a couple of petite fours—had to practically wrestle the damned things away from Bitsy," she said, exasperated. "I told him that we were having an anniversary party for the Club."

Jolie grinned at her ingenuity. "He bought it?"

She snorted indelicately. "Of course, not," she scoffed. "He's a smart man…but he's got too much class to argue with an old woman."

Ah, yes, Jolie thought, inclining her head. That sounded about right.

"Anyway," Sophia told her, "tonight is your night, dear. This is your 'official' party."

She took Jolie's hand and tugged her toward the living room, leading her to a chair that had been moved to the middle of the room where Sophia typically stood, then urged her to sit down. Somewhat baffled, Jolie sat patiently while the rest of the members crowded into the room.

Sophia waited for someone to turn down the music, then snapped at Bitsy—who was doing a disjointed Egyptian Walk around the room while trying to eat a piece of coconut cake—to do it. *For the love of God, Bitsy, would you turn that down?"*

Startled, Bitsy stopped and quickly moved to do as she asked. When the music was finally turned off, Sophia smoothed her hair, gathered her thoughts, and smiled. "Now then. As we all know, making the transition to Official status is an important milestone in a Future Widows' Club member's life. It's a rebirth of sorts, a new beginning. From here on out, Jolie will enjoy the privileges of her new status. She'll be revered, admired, even pitied by the unenlightened who don't realize that she's better off." Sophia shook her head at this presumed tragedy, then continued. "Tonight, we'll celebrate her newfound freedom by presenting her with this pin—" Sophia reached down and attached a small rhinestone hat and gloves pin—the same logo she'd noted on her handbook, Jolie realized—onto her collar "—and party!"

Bitsy cranked the music back up—the Dixie Chicks' "Goodbye Earl"—and, like her first meeting, everyone came by and paid their respects once again.

"May he rot in hell."

"May he never rest in peace."

"I envy your loss."

Bitsy started the train again, someone pressed another drink in Jolie's hand, and the entire congregation proceeded to get smashed, herself included. Meredith proved very adept at making Daiquiris, and Cora, of all people, ended up doing a table dance before the night was over. Most of the ladies had either planned to spend the night or had arranged for someone to pick them up, but Jolie, unaware that she'd need to do one or the other, ended up walking outside and asking Jake to take her home.

His eyes widened comically. *"You're drunk?"*

Jolie's lips were numb and the warm, languid slide of the alcohol in her blood loosened her tongue. "Yes," she said, climbing clumsily into the cab of his truck. "I think I am."

Jake pulled away from the curb. "Some bridge club," he muttered. "Tell me, Jo. Do you usually get hammered at these meetings?"

Jolie let her head loll back against the seat. "Nope. First time."

"Well, that's a relief."

"Poor Jake. You've been bored out here, haven't you?" She glanced at him, then stared transfixed at the way the dashlights illuminated the strangely beautiful lines of his face. "You should be looking for the real killer, not wasting your time with me."

He shot her an inscrutable, almost wistful look. "Being with you—or even near you—isn't a waste of time," he returned softly.

Her silly heart melted. That was too sweet not to offer a small reward, so she leaned over and pressed a kiss against his woefully familiar cheek. "I've missed you," Jolie told him, then unable to make her neck support her head any longer, she let it drop against his shoulder and dozed off, the comforting scent of Jake and fresh hay in her nostrils.

The next morning when she awoke, she found herself in her bed, stripped down to her bra and undies and a note attached to her pillow.

I've missed you, too. Yours, Jake.

CHAPTER TWENTY-SIX

"HOW DO YOU THINK it's going?"

Jake dropped into one of the chairs flanking Dean's desk and tried to think of some way to tell his boss that he'd researched every angle and wasn't any closer to finding who'd killed Marshall than he'd been the night the man had been murdered.

He finally shrugged helplessly. "It's going...nowhere," he admitted, letting go a resigned whoosh of air. "I've followed every lead, checked every alibi, followed procedure and...nothing. Nobody saw anything, nobody knows anything. It's as if a ghost waltzed into that house and shot him."

Dean tapped his pen against his desk. "What about the penis?"

Yeah, what about it? Jake wanted to ask. All he knew was that Todd hadn't found anything significant. He'd refrained from asking what the evidence tech had ultimately done with it for fear he might not want to know.

Jake told him about the thread and the fibers Todd had found on Marshall's dick. "That's all I've got, Dean, and it's not from lack of trying." Jake ticked off everybody that he'd investigated, then shook his head. "I don't know what else to do."

"Sounds to me like you've done everything you can," Dean told him, his voice measured.

Jake knew he was supposed to infer something from that careful tone, but exactly what he didn't know. He arched a brow, silently asking his boss to spell it out for him.

"I'd say you don't have any other choice but to let this case go inactive, at least until new information surfaces."

"She didn't do it, Dean," Jake felt compelled to point out.

"I don't think she did."

So long as they were on the same page, Jake thought. Still, he couldn't help but feel like he hadn't done enough, that he should have looked harder. Quite frankly, he'd gotten so caught up in keeping Jolie under surveillance—translate: watching her for the sheer sport of it—that he hadn't devoted as much time to the case as he probably could have. Then again, he did think that he'd followed every possible lead. There simply wasn't enough evidence to continue.

Which meant that she was finally in the clear.

Jake took a deep breath, but when another thought surfaced the air stuck in his throat. If she was in the clear, then he didn't have to stick to her like glue anymore. He didn't have any legitimate reason to keep hanging around her, absorbing her presence, sharing her space.

Except for the reason that he was still head over heels in love with her.

Last night when she'd leaned over and kissed his cheek, Jake had felt the world shift back into brighter focus. The innocent unaffected gesture might have landed on the side of his face, but he'd felt it all the way down to the bottoms of his feet. His belly had filled with air, then flipped, and a shiver had worked its way up his spine.

And she'd barely touched him.

Christ.

He ran a shaky hand through his hair. "What about the D.A.?" Jake asked.

Dean leaned back in his chair. "I'll talk to him."

He didn't know what Dean could tell him that Jake hadn't already, but he supposed his boss's opinion carried more weight than his. At any rate, he didn't care because it was over. She was safe and that's all that mattered. He thanked Dean, then grabbed his portfolio and made the trek home. He'd planned on following the routine he'd started this week—change clothes, check on the horse, then head back to town, to her house specifically—but after watching Marzipan for a few minutes, Jake decided that going anywhere tonight was out of the question. He unclipped his cell from his belt and keyed in Jolie's number. "It's happening," he told her. "Do you still want to come out?"

JOLIE WHEELED her car down the narrow dirt drive that would deliver her to Jake's house and felt the strangest sense of anxiety and homecoming push into her throat. She knew this land and its owner as well as she knew herself and yet something about driving here now made her feel like her insides were too big for her body. She topped a little hill and, backlit by a beautiful setting sun, the house and barn rose in the distance.

The old farmhouse replica was white with green shutters, with full sweeping porches and tall multi-paned windows. Instead of going with modern asphalt shingles, Jake had opted for a green metal roof, one that would make beautiful music when it rained. A bittersweet pang squeezed her chest. From the looks of things, he'd built precisely what they'd planned. He could have modified things on the inside, Jolie knew, but if he'd kept the facade the same, then she thought it was relatively safe to assume that he'd left everything else as it was as well.

She pulled around back, close to the barn, then snagged the picnic basket she'd packed from the back seat. Evidently hearing her drive up, Jake stepped into the wide doorway of the barn.

"Hey," he called.

Jolie smiled, gestured toward the basket as she made her way toward him. "I thought we might get hungry."

Wearing a pair of faded jeans, beat-up boots and a navy blue T-shirt with a hole in the sleeve, he walked out and took the basket from her. "Thanks. Since it's her first, we could be in for a long night."

That's what she'd figured. As Jolie fell into step beside him, she felt the brush of his sleeve against her arm. A tingle hit her breasts, causing the air to thin in her lungs. "Er…how's she doing?"

Jake set the basket on a tack table, walked over to Marzipan's stall and put a boot up on the bottom rail of her door. "She can't get comfortable. Keeps circling, twitching her tail."

Jolie moved in beside him, put a hand over the top of the door and, throat tight with emotion, called the horse. Her ears pricked at the sound of Jolie's voice, then she walked over and nudged her muzzle beneath Jolie's palm.

Smiling, she rubbed the horse's velvety nose. "Look at you, Mama," Jolie told her softly. "Big, beautiful girl," she soothed. The horse sidled closer for more attention, nipped at Jolie's hair.

A deep masculine chuckle sounded beside her. "Looks like she's missed you."

Stroking her neck, Jolie darted a glance at Jake. "It's a feeling that's reciprocated." She paused, scoping out some of the other stalls. "So who's the proud papa?"

"Smoke."

Jolie turned her attention back to the horse. "Ah," she sighed. "Then we can expect a beautiful baby then, eh?"

Seemingly unable to stand still any longer, Marzipan resumed her pacing, absently nibbled at the feed in her bin.

Jake picked up the picnic basket and pilfered through what she'd brought.

"If you're expecting prime rib, then you're out of luck," she said. "I brought what I had on hand—peanut butter and banana sandwiches, chips and beer."

Jake looked up and a slow grin slid across those incredibly sexy lips. "Ah," he sighed. "A feast fit for a king."

Jolie rolled her eyes and helped him spread a horse blanket on the ground in front of Marzipan's stall. "Does that make you the king, then?"

He laughed. "That goes without saying."

"I suppose so," she agreed. "You've always been a royal pain the ass."

He opened a beer and handed it to her, then tutted under his breath. "Ah, now. That's a fine way to talk to the man who's saved yours."

Jolie bit into her sandwich and shot him a look. "What are you talking about?"

"I talked with Dean today."

"Oh?" she asked, intrigued by an indiscernible note in his voice.

"Yeah. He told me he thought that Marshall's case should go inactive until new leads or evidence surfaces."

Jolie frowned. "Inactive? What does that mean?"

"It means the case isn't closed, but we're no longer *actively* pursuing it." He smiled at her, but something about that half-hearted grin seemed…off. "In laymen's terms, it means you're in the clear." He took another bite of his sandwich.

"Oh," Jolie said, her eyes widening as the import sunk in. *Now* it was over. She felt her spine sag with relief. Her gaze slid to Jake's impassive profile and the reason he'd seemed off about the new status of the case surfaced belatedly in her sluggish mind.

If she was in the clear…then there was no reason for him to "stick to her like glue" anymore.

A sickening sensation swelled in her gut, pushing the bite of sandwich she'd just taken back up her throat.

No reason for him to come to her house every night.

No reason for him to be with her.

Jolie knew that she should say something, should pretend she was happy that she was no longer the prime suspect in a murder investigation, but she couldn't seem to muster the enthusiasm for the required response. The silence swelled between them, a grim reminder of the wedge that had been in place just a little over a week ago. She swallowed a whimper and tried to steady her suddenly shaking hands.

God, she didn't want to go back to that. She wanted to go back to him, for them to find their way back to each other.

Jake took a long draw from his beer, and then that silvery gaze drifted to her, causing her breath to hitch. "There's something that I want to say to you that's long overdue."

Jolie knew what he wanted to say, knew that it had to be said for them to move forward and, God, how she'd waited for it. She felt tears burn the backs of her lids and nodded at him.

"I'm sorry," he said simply. He didn't elaborate because he didn't have to. They both knew what had happened, both knew that he'd been primarily at fault. "I don't know what the hell I was thinking," he told her, his voice riddled with self-disgust, "and if it makes you feel any better, I've regretted asking for that time more than you can ever know." A bitter laugh spilled from his mouth, punctuating the truth of that statement. "So much more than you can ever know."

Every cell in her body warmed with delight and once again she was hit with the urge to simply rest her head on his shoulder, to feel those beautiful hands against her face. Jolie took a pull from her own beer. "Oh, I think I've got a pretty good idea. I've certainly regretted some choices I made, one in particular." She shot him a tentative look, then asked him the one thing that she'd always wondered. "Why'd you ask for it, Jake?" She moistened her lips. "Were you that unsure of me?"

She felt his soft gaze trace her face. "Oh, babe, I was never unsure of you. I was unsure of myself." He picked up a piece of hay and twirled it around his fingers. "After your dad died, I guess it all just sort of hit me, you know, how important I was in your life…and I wasn't sure I could live up to the expectation. I was afraid I'd fail you." He shrugged helplessly. "I got scared, and thought I'd better get my head on straight." He looked away and swore softly. "Stupid."

"You were stupid for thinking that you'd ever fail me."

"But I did," Jake said.

"Only because you walked away. If you'd stuck it out, I would have been happy no matter what." Jolie swallowed, then made a face. "Besides, you weren't the only one to blame. I should have had enough faith in you to wait it out. Instead, I got pissed off, then decided to get even." She grimaced. "And look what happened."

Seeming to mull it over, Jake took another drink. "And I regret that, too."

"We were both stupid," she said magnanimously.

He inclined his head.

She slid him a smile, relieved that they'd had this talk. "But you were more stupid."

He laughed. "Gotta have the last word, don't you?"

She shrugged unrepentantly. "Just tell it like it is."

A noise from the stall drew their attention and Jake's gaze sharpened, and then he bolted into action. He leapt up, then offered her a hand. "She's down," he said quietly. "Here we go."

An excited thrill whipped through her as she moved into place next to Jake. Marzipan had indeed lain down, fortunately in the center of the stall.

Jake lowered his head toward hers and she caught a whiff of his woodsy cologne. "That's a contraction," he whispered, inadvertently sending a chill down her spine.

Jolie watched, not realizing she was holding her breath until she was forced to let it go. Then something amazing happened. She grabbed Jake's arm. "I see hooves!"

He chuckled softly at her. "That's a good sign. Hooves first, then head, then the rest of the body."

She moved in closer, inadvertently—but oh so pleasantly—putting herself in front of him. Jake dropped his chin on top of her head, wrapped his arms around her waist and absorbed her weight against him. Jolie felt his breath leak slowly out of him, then her eyes fluttered shut, and she drank in the sensation of coming home. *This* was where she belonged, she thought.

Right here. With him.

Just as he'd predicted, the foal's head emerged next and though the baby was covered in placenta, it was easily recognizable as Marzipan's. "Oh, it's white," she said softly.

"I wouldn't be so sure," Jake hedged. "We'll have to wait until it's dry to really tell."

"Come on, Mama," Jolie softly crooned to the horse. "Almost there."

And then it was. The rest of the body emerged. Marzipan made quick work of the placenta and the baby horse started to move around.

Absolutely awed and delighted, Jolie impulsively turned and hugged Jake. "Oh, my God," she breathed, bouncing on the balls of her feet. "That was…amazing."

Jake laughed, wrapping his arms even more firmly around her. His lips curling into an inherently sexy grin, he looked down and those twinkling silvery-gray eyes captured hers. And in that instant the mood changed. Her belly trembled, gooseflesh raced down her back, and the air leaked out of her lungs.

The hug might have been impulsive, but her kiss wouldn't be. She wanted him—wanted *them*—and wanted him to know it. Jolie reached up and tenderly framed his face with her hands, watching as his lids dropped at her touch, then ever so gently—reverently— pressed her lips to his.

The feeling was so exquisite, so perfect that for a moment she forgot to breathe.

The sky could have fallen, the earth could have opened up beneath her feet and she wouldn't have noticed.

Jake sighed into her mouth and she savored that breath, then slipped her tongue against his and silently asked for more.

With a low growl of almost desperate approval, he pulled her closer, tunneled his fingers into her hair, then tilted her head to better align their mouths. He fed at her, sucked at her tongue, her bottom lip, then came back for more.

"God, I've missed you," he growled softly. "Missed you so damned much."

Jolie's heart melted…along with other parts of her. Her nipples tingled, her sex pulsed and every nerve seemed to vibrate. She couldn't feel enough of him, couldn't taste enough of him. It had been so long, so very, very long.

To her immense regret and frustration, Jake very tenderly ended the kiss, and breathing heavily, rested his forehead against hers. "Will you spend the night with me?" he asked softly. "Stay here and let me love you?"

Feeling a slow smile drift across her lips, Jolie nodded.

Jake kissed her again, seemingly unable to keep from tasting her. Then after checking on Marzipan and the foal, he threaded his fingers through hers and took his time leading her through the house.

As impatient as she was, she couldn't help but appreciate that he wanted to take things slowly, savor their reunion and honor it with the respect that it deserved. Her hand in his, he led her through the house, and just as she'd suspected, he'd stayed true to their plan, almost as if he'd prepared it for her return. Pressed copper tiles lined the ceiling in the kitchen and a small wood-burning fireplace sat in the corner of the room. The living room had been equipped with built-in bookshelves and big open windows that caught the late afternoon breeze.

It was beautiful, Jolie thought. Every bit as wonderful as she'd always imagined it would be. Despite the fact that she'd spent the past couple of weeks making her little house on Lelia Street a home, she suddenly didn't care if she ever went back there. This was where she belonged.

Right here, with him.

Jake tugged her toward the bedroom. "Do you have any idea how many times I've imagined you here?" he said, his gaze, hot with desire and warm with affection, slipping over her, feasting on her. Loving her. "How many times I've been driven from this room—this house—because being in it without you felt so wrong?"

Jolie felt tears mist her eyes. "Oh, Jake," she said unable to elaborate as her heart pushed into her aching throat. She knew what he meant because she'd felt it, too. She'd been like a ship without an anchor for years, drifting miserably through life without him, and the idea that she didn't have to anymore—that he was hers again—burrowed into her tripping heart and sent a warm tingle to her very fingertips.

He slipped the pad of his thumb over her cheek, guided her into the bathroom where he turned on the tap and adjusted the shower, then slowly set about undressing her. His fingers skimmed over her rib cage as he pulled off her shirt, sent gooseflesh racing up her back as he unbuttoned her shorts and pushed them down her hips. Soon she was naked, mesmerized by the sweet sensual brush of his hot hands slipping reverently over her body.

It had been so long and yet being with him was like stepping back into a long, slow beautiful dance. Easy, effortless...perfect.

Her breasts heavy, her sex wet and her heart racing, Jolie tugged his shirt from his waistband, drew it over the top of his head and cast it aside, then drank in the sight of him. Soft skin, hard perfectly sculpted muscle and bone. Crisp masculine hair, flat male nipples. Familiar. Loved. Hers.

She offered her mouth up for a kiss and savored the

intoxicating taste of his tongue against hers, blinking back another hot rush of redeeming tears as he gently nudged her into the glassed-in shower. She let her hands drift over his back, feeling the muscle bunch beneath her fingertips. Then he bent and latched his greedy mouth onto her breast, pulling a startled gasp from deep in her throat.

Jolie closed her eyes and arched her back, purposely pushing her aching nipple farther into his mouth. His masculine growl vibrated against her, sending a cascade of hot fizzies through her blood, all of which raced to her heavy womb. She could feel his hot length prod her belly and purposely opened her legs and rocked her hips forward, pushing him through her drenched folds, then gasped when he bumped the most sensitive part of her.

Jake drew back, and his fevered gaze tangled with hers. "I've dreamed about this," he confessed, his voice a sweet rough whisper. "I wanted to go slowly, but I—"

"Don't," Jolie said, rocking against him once more. She didn't want to go slowly. She wanted to feel him deep inside her, desired that connection more than her next breath. She'd missed him so much and needed him even more. "We've got time, right?"

He knew what she was asking. What she wanted. Jake's gaze softened, drifted lovingly over her face, then he very carefully, very slowly lifted her up and pushed into her. Her lungs deflated as he slid into her and wrapping her arms around him, she clenched her feminine muscles, claiming him as her own. "All the time in the world, Jo," he said, wincing with pleasure as he filled her. "And you own every second."

Her eyes misted with emotion and he leaned forward and sipped up her tears. "I love you," he murmured. He bent and kissed her again. "Here," he said, his voice a soft husky whisper fraught with emotion. "Let me show you."

And as the water beat down upon them, washing away their mistakes, he did.

CHAPTER TWENTY-SEVEN

"THANK GOD," Sophia muttered irritably as the mayor's car finally pulled out of the drive. She, Bitsy and Meredith had made a point of learning his schedule and this was the only night of the week that both he and his wife were gone. They had a standing reservation at Zeus', which gave Sophia plenty of time to make sure that the coast was clear before she left her hiding place next to the garage and moved behind the heavy shrubbery around the foundation of the house. Yew, Sophia thought, battling her way inside. If she ever planted another hedge, she'd definitely plant yew.

Once in position, she lifted the scarf from around her neck and slipped it up over her nose. She didn't know why she bothered anymore. The stench of skunk was so horrible that she'd had to start throwing away her clothes after she came here. Honestly, she didn't know how they stood it. If it had been her house, she'd have moved out a long time ago.

Frankly, she'd hoped that Greene would come to his senses before it had come back around to her turn, but true to his ignorant, asinine form, the mayor had attended the Garden Club meeting this morning and bestowed another Beautification Award to yet another city council member, one whose idea of gardening extended to bought potted plants—*blasphemy!*—and plastic pink flamingoes.

It was outside of enough.

She, Bitsy—who'd ridden her new Pocket Rocket to the meeting—and Meredith, had gotten together after the meeting, and fuming, Meredith had given her their skunk attractant. If it wouldn't make too much noise, Sophia would fill her Shop-Vac and blow the stuff under the house so thick that every skunk in the state would congregate there, but alas it would make too much racket, so she stuck to the usual method. After duck walking around the house, she opened the foundation vents and starting tossing handfuls underneath. At least it was good exercise, she thought, deciding that she'd have another slice of cake when she got home.

Besides, over the past couple of days, she'd been getting a *different* kind of workout. Sophia's lips slid into a smile and she barely suppressed a giggle. She'd never been a giggler.

Or at least she hadn't until she'd started having sex again.

And not just any kind of sex. Wonderful, sweaty, down and dirty, sometimes tender sex. That first kiss from Edward had done something to her. Flipped an on switch that she hadn't known she possessed.

One minute he'd been pressing his lips to hers, and the next minute they were in his bed going at it like a couple of teenagers who were trying to get laid before anyone got home. It had been wild and wicked and later, when she'd begun to get embarrassed over her rash behavior, Edward had smiled at her, then kissed her again. "We're old," he'd said. "We don't have to play by the usual rules."

And he'd been right. She could be dead by the time they finished what would be considered a proper courtship. Furthermore, she'd waited long enough. She didn't want to wait anymore.

A flashlight blinked on right in front of her, blinding her, and with a startled yelp, she fell backward on her ass. What the hell?

"Good evening, Sophia."

Edward?

Horrified, Sophia scrambled up and goggled at him. "What— How—"

"I followed you." His gaze dropped to the bag in her hand and he chuckled softly. "Catnip. Very crafty. I suspected as much."

Sophia had never been good with feminine wiles, so when she found herself in this horrible position, she didn't even bother. Instead, she threatened him. "Look, Edward. I don't know what you hope to gain by following me here, but if you've enjoyed our recent exercise—"

"Exercise?"

"You know what I mean," she snapped, blushing to the roots of her hair.

"It's sex, Sophia. We're having sex."

Though they were hidden behind eight feet of dense shrubbery, Sophia glanced around to make sure no one could see them. "Would you hush, please?" she begged, scandalized. "Sweet Jesus. What the hell are you doing here?"

He blinked at her. "I came to help."

Once again she found herself dumbfounded. "What?"

"Jimmy Pickens, the Beautification Award?" he scoffed, his usually amiable face dressed in a frown. "The man doesn't know his mulch from molasses. It's outrageous." He reached for the bag. "Give me some of that, would ya? I'll take the other side of the house."

True to his word, Edward moved around to the other side and left a shocked but delighted Sophia squatted behind the mayor's shrubs.

That settles it, she thought as the smell of skunk all but choked her. She'd found her man.

After all, it wasn't just any guy who'd be willing to vandalize with her.

CHAPTER TWENTY-EIGHT

"AMAZING, ISN'T IT?" Jake asked. "Just a couple of weeks old and already the little guy is showing attitude."

Marzipan's colt, whom they'd named Ash because he'd ended up being a paler version of his father, galloped clumsily around the enclosure on tall, spindly legs.

Jolie chuckled, pressing her head against his upper arm, and the tender, unexpected warmth moved into his chest.

Contentment, Jake realized.

For the first time since they'd broken up, he was happy. Despite the two-year gap in their relationship, amazingly they'd picked up almost precisely where they'd left off, only at a better place because they both knew how precious their time together—their relationship, specifically—was.

Since the evening the colt was born, they hadn't spent a night apart. For all the work that Jolie had done on her little house, she'd easily started calling his place home—which was only fitting because it should have been hers all along—and had quickly relegated the Lelia Street house as a full-fledged office.

Aside from the bed—which they'd left to accommodate nooners—everything else had been moved to the farm. Coming home to her was the highlight of his day.

Be it in sweats or a negligee—and admittedly he had a thing for the black merry widow—when he walked through that door, she made him feel like she'd been waiting for him all day, whether she had been or not. Those slim arms would come around his waist, she'd lean up and kiss his chin, and regardless of what had happened during the course of the day, at that moment, everything became right in his world.

Because he was with her.

Jake curled his arm around her neck, propelling her reluctantly away from the paddock. "Come on. I've got a surprise for you."

Her hip bumped his as they walked along. "You do? What is it?"

"If I told you it wouldn't be a surprise."

He opened the truck door for her and waited for her to slide in. "Can't fault a girl for tryin', can you?"

Jake joined her in the truck, aimed it toward one of their favorite hang-outs and waited for her to realize where they were going. When it turned off on Rabbit Trail Lane, she figured it out and sent him a sidelong glance. "The fire tower?" she asked, surprised. "Wow," she breathed. "I haven't been out here in years."

Him either. He hadn't been able to go once they'd broken up. It had been too hard. He and Jolie had spent hours up in the loft, had plotted, planned, necked and loved up there and somehow making the trek up the stairs alone had never been something he could do.

He wheeled the truck off the main road and followed the rutted dirt lane until they were parked right next to it. Jolie didn't wait for him to open the door, but got out, shaded her eyes and looked up. "Yep. It's still tall."

Jake felt a chuckle bubble up his throat. "What? You think it's gonna shrink?"

She shot him a droll look. "Smart ass."

He put a hand over his heart, pretending to be wounded. "You go first," he said as they walked to the steps.

She turned, green eyes twinkling with warm affection. "So you can catch me if I fall?"

That was the plan, Jake thought, falling in behind her. They'd always done it that way. She went up first, so that he could catch her, and he came down first for the very same reason. He wanted his body between her and possible danger.

Jolie hurried up ahead of him and mere minutes later they were at the top looking out over Moon Valley. It was gorgeous. The late afternoon sun gilded the trees and sparkled over the river, painting it bright orange.

Jolie braced her elbows against the rail and let go a soft sigh that hissed through his blood. Jake moved in behind and wrapped his arms around her.

"I'm not going to fall," she admonished softly.

"I know that," he told her. "I just want to hold you."

In fact, he wanted to hold her forever. He'd proposed to her in this very spot when they were sixteen, and somehow it seemed only fitting that they revisit it for the encore. Jake gripped her shoulders and slowly turned her around, then pulled in a shuddering breath and groped in his front pocket for the ring he'd placed there.

She gasped when she saw it and her hands flew to

her mouth. "Oh, Jake," she said, her voice clogged with emotion.

He chuckled nervously, took her hand and slipped it on her finger. "You're gonna marry me."

She blinked, smiled. "Is that a proposal?"

He cocked his head. "More like an edict."

She pulled back and glared at him. *"Oh, really."*

"Someone told me to start as I meant to go on." He winced. "It's not gonna work, is it? The whole lord-of-the-manor, do-as-I-say-woman approach?"

She ducked her head and bit her lip to hide a smile. "No."

Jake heaved a dramatic sigh. "Fine. In that case, Jolie Michelle Caplan...will you marry me?"

Her misty eyes searched his. "Yes," she breathed, then tilted her chin up and offered him her lips. He didn't know how long they kissed, how long they stood there. Time, at least in this dimension of happiness, didn't exist.

When the sun finally slipped beneath the tree tops, Jake decided they'd better go down. He placed another lingering kiss on her mouth, then reluctantly made the trip back to the ground.

He was debating the merit of going out for dinner versus staying in and feasting on her, when he opened the car door and her purse fell to the ground, spilling all the contents.

Jake swore. "Sorry," he muttered and instantly dropped down and starting gathering up her things. He picked up a compact, a tube of lipstick, her wallet and...his gaze zeroed in on a little pink book with a hat and gloves on the cover, similar to the pin she'd taken to wearing since the night she'd gotten hammered at her so-called bridge meeting.

"Don't worry about..." Her voice trailed off as she looked up and saw what he held. She swallowed. "Jake, could I have that back, please?"

Jake looked away, summoning patience. This was the key to what she'd been hiding, he knew it. And yet despite the fact that she'd just agreed to marry him, she still wanted to keep secrets? "Jolie, you can trust me. Let me prove it," he implored.

Looking like she couldn't decide whether to puke or bolt, she chewed her bottom lip and whimpered.

"Jolie."

She finally met his gaze. "Jake, if you look inside that little book, you have to swear to me that you'll never— and I repeat *never*—repeat a word of it to another living soul."

Geez, from the way she was carrying on you'd think she had the map to the Holy Grail in there. Jake nodded. "Okay."

She let go a breath. "Then you can look at it. But brace yourself," she added direly.

Jake flipped the little book open, read the title page and felt his eyes widen in shock. *"The Future Widows' Club?* What the hell is the Future Widows' Club?"

"Read on," she said miserably. "You'll figure it out."

Five minutes later, he closed the little book and though he knew what it was—and better still why she'd added the life insurance, checked out the burial plans and bought the outfit—he wasn't any closer to understanding it. "Let me get this straight," Jake said, trying to wrap his mind around the concept. "You're in a secret society of women who are *anxiously waiting* for their husband's to die?"

She nodded.

He frowned. "And this is where you were the night Chris was murdered? At one of these meetings?"

She nodded again.

"Christ." Jake looked away. "Jolie, for the love of God, why didn't you think this was relevant?"

"Because I didn't do it."

"I know that. Still…"

"I needed them," she said simply. "I was only a member for a couple of weeks before Chris died, but they were the best weeks of my life in the past two years." Seemingly exasperated, she looked away. "You're a guy. You're just not going to get it. I didn't want Chris to be dead, not really…but until I could file for divorce it was the best thing I had." She swallowed. "And it's all they've got. You can't take it away from them."

Knowing how miserable she'd been, Jake did understand. Did he agree with it? No. But, in all honesty, he didn't see the harm. He let go a breath. "I just have one question."

She looked up and quirked a cautious brow. "What?"

"Are you going to remain a member when *I'm* your husband?"

Her lips curled and she pulled a lazy shrug. "Lifetime membership," she said. "But I'll be mentoring to future widows rather than preparing to be one."

Jake cocked his head. "Fair enough, I suppose."

She gazed at him questioningly. "That's it? That's all you've got to say about it?"

"Was I supposed to say more? They're not hurting anybody, are they?"

"No."

"Then I don't see the problem."

A slow grin spread across her lips and those pale green eyes danced with affection. "I love you."

"I know," he said, placing a quick but tender kiss on her lips. "Which is the only reason you get to keep *playing bridge*."

EPILOGUE

Six months later...

"I'LL BE HOME before nine."

Jolie's heart warmed as Jake kissed her cheek and then rubbed her belly. "You'd better be," he told her. "Mothers-to-be need their rest." He frowned. "And try not to get too upset, would you? Are you sure you don't want me to come with you? I could—"

Jolie blinked back tears and shook her head. "No. You can't. You know that." No one in the FWC was aware that Jake knew about them. They'd worry, and in light of recent events, they had all of that they could handle at the moment. Jolie swallowed tightly.

They'd buried Bitsy today.

"At least let me take you. You can call when you're ready and I'll come pick you up."

"I can drive, Jake," she said. "I'm only pregnant, not on medication."

"I know. I'd just feel better if—"

She gave him another peck and grabbed her purse. "I'll be fine. Don't worry."

Jolie slid behind the wheel and made her way to Meredith's on autopilot. She still couldn't believe it, couldn't believe that Bitsy was really gone. Granted Jolie had known her for a little over six months, but she'd grown very fond of the eccentric older woman. But the worst part was looking at Sophia and Meredith. They were shattered, particularly Meredith who'd warned Bitsy about getting the little motorcycle which had ultimately caused her death. Too vain to wear her glasses beneath the helmet, she'd crashed it through Dilly's Bakery. The impact hadn't killed her, but the heart attack which had immediately followed had.

Sophia had come up to Jolie at the funeral and told her that Bitsy's attorney had been to see her and that apparently Bitsy had left a box to be opened in the event of her death. Per Bitsy's written instructions, only Sophia, Meredith, Jolie and curiously, Sadie, were allowed to be present when the box was opened. Meredith had asked her to come early tonight. They were going to go through it before the rest of the FWC arrived. Jolie couldn't imagine what on earth could be in the box that could pertain to her, but wasn't about to ignore one of Bitsy's last wishes.

Eyes puffy and her face generally wracked with grief, Meredith answered Jolie's knock. "Come in, dear," she said. "We're gonna open it in the back parlor."

Jolie nodded and somberly followed her to a room she'd never been in before. Windows lined the back wall, which overlooked a small enclosed garden with a big brick barbeque pit. "How are you feeling?" she asked, no doubt referring to the pregnancy.

Jolie managed a genuine smile. "Huge." Finding out that she was pregnant with Jake's baby had been a dream come true. She'd taken a broken road, but had finally ended up on the right one.

With him.

It seemed like a lifetime ago that she'd been involved with Chris, embroiled in a horrible nightmare of a marriage. As a result of that disaster, there wasn't a day that went by that she wasn't thankful for Jake, for his love and the relationship they shared.

He completed her.

There were times when she just looked at him and her heart would expand and she could barely catch her breath. Times when he dozed off, and she lay awake in their bed just so she could watch him sleep. Times when she woke him up because sleeping was the furthest thing from her mind. Be it merely holding hands or making love, he moved her in a way that defied reason and trumped logic. She could feel him in her bones, in her blood, and knowing that they'd created this little life inside her belly was a divine joy that often brought tears to her eyes.

Managing to look both strong and shattered, Sophia stood when they walked in. "Hello, dear."

Jolie's eyes misted and she crossed the room and hugged her. "I'm so sorry," she said, knowing it was inadequate. She couldn't even imagine a life without her best friend, couldn't think of going on in a world where Sadie didn't exist. As if on cue, Sadie made her way into the room.

"Thanks for coming, Sadie," Meredith told her.

Looking slightly bewildered, Sadie nodded, then sent Jolie a curiously nervous look.

Sophia pulled in a bolstering breath. "Well, the suspense has been killing me all day, so let's just go ahead and get it over with. Knowing Bitsy, it's her damned coupons," she said, her voice a poignant cross between a laugh and a sob.

Openly crying, Meredith giggled. "You open it, Sophia."

Sophia nodded, picked up a pair of scissors and cut into the box, then lifted the lid and pulled out a letter.

"Dear girls,
If you're reading this letter, then I'm dead. (Well, that goes without saying, doesn't it?) Anyway, now that I'm gone there's no reason to keep hiding these things from you. In this box you will find some things that, at first, will appear odd—a couple of syringes, a crochet mallet, a gun, a pair of scissors and a bath towel."

Sophia looked up and frowned, then resumed reading.

"For the past decade or so I've kept a secret, one that I knew that I'd have to take to my grave. (Somebody see to it every once in a while, would you? I like daisies.) Sophia, Meredith, I know you think your husbands—and even mine—died of natural causes. Well, you thought wrong. I killed them. A healthy shot of vitamin K induced those random heart attacks mine and yours had, Sophia, and the crocket mallet sent your husband down that mountain, Meri. (He was drunk. The

damned fool would have eventually done it to him-
self anyway, goin' on all those infernal nature
hikes.)"

Meredith inhaled sharply, Sophia's face had gone
chalk white and Jolie had had to find a place to sit. She
knew what was coming, but she simply couldn't believe it.

Sweet little scattered Bitsy? A cold-blooded killer?

Her gaze shot to Sadie, who seemed curiously reluctant to look at her.

"As for you, Jolie, I just felt so sorry for you that
I had to do something. That SOB you were mar-
ried to didn't deserve to live. Shooting him was
planned. Cutting his penis off with my sewing
shears and gluing it to the statue wasn't, but it was
pure genius if you ask me. Sadie, you're here be-
cause I know you saw me altering dear old Jebe-
diah and yet you never told."

Jolie inhaled sharply and her gaze swung to Sadie.
"You knew?" she breathed.

Sadie shrugged helplessly. "I couldn't tell on her for
having the courage to do what I couldn't," she explained. "It wasn't right."

Sophia and Meredith shared a look, then Sophia let
go a small breath and continued reading.

"Sadie, you are truly the best secret keeper in the
county and therefore deserve to be an honorary

member of the Club. (Sophia, see to it, would you?
This is my last nomination, after all.)

"Finally, don't be mad at me, girls, and I hope
this doesn't change your opinion of me. We were
all married to bastards who needed killin'—I was
just the one to do it. I'll see you in the hereafter.
Until then...
Much love from your Bitsy
"P.S. I glued the dick to the bloody statue with
denture adhesive. Brilliant, eh? I've left a sizable
fund that should take care of old Jeb, by the way.
In coupons, of course. Ha! Just kidding."

Hands shaking, lips twitching, Sophia lowered the
letter and looked at both of them in turn. "Well."

"My God," Meredith breathed. "I never dreamed—
Never imagined."

Sophia shook her head, seemingly lost in her
thoughts. "Me neither." She looked heavenward and
blinked back tears, and Jolie listened as she said the one
thing that neither she nor Meredith had the courage to
say. "Thank you, Bitsy," she whispered softly.

"What are we going to do with all this stuff?" Meredith asked, typically moving on to practical matters.
"Everybody thinks our husbands died of natural causes,
but Jolie's is a different story."

Jolie knew that going to the police would probably
be the right thing to do, but she couldn't bring herself
to suggest it. Bitsy was dead and buried—they couldn't
do anything to her. Furthermore, going to the police
would involve outing the FWC, and Bitsy had worked

too hard to protect it and to protect them, specifically. She gazed out the window, not really looking at anything, trying to think.

Then the barbeque pit seemed to swell before her eyes and she smiled and looked back at Sophia and Meredith. "How about a bonfire?" Jolie suggested. "It's a chilly night, after all."

Instantly taking the hint, Sophia and Meredith and Sadie shared a smile and five minutes later a big fire burned in the pit. Smiling, they each held a petite four in honor of Bitsy's favorite dessert, then lifted them up for a toast of sorts.

"Our un-dearly departed..." Sophia said softly.

"...may he never rest in peace."

Everything you love about romance...
and more!

Please turn the page for Signature Select™
Bonus Features.

Bonus Features:

BONUS FEATURES

the
Future
Widows'
Club

A conversation with
Rhonda Nelson

Rhonda Nelson says she can't imagine herself doing anything else. And if *The Future Widows' Club* is any indication, then we can't imagine her doing anything else, either!

4

Tell us a bit about how you began your writing career.

Eek. I'm going to commit a cardinal sin among authors and admit that I read a bad book...and thought I could do a better job. Guess what? I was wrong. At least to begin with, anyway—and I still have the rejection letters to prove it. But I'd always been a reader, had taken a couple of creative writing courses in college, and things just sort of clicked from there. Writing is like breathing for me. I have to do it.

Do you have a writing routine?
I do. It's called get-out-of-bed-and-hit-the-ground-running. In all seriousness, I work better in the morning, when it's quiet and the house is empty. The problem is, I'm also a neat freak, so everything has to be done in the house before I can start. Beds are made, laundry's started, dishes are done, etc...so that after I drop the kids off at school, I can come in, sit down and work without any distractions until it's time to pick them up from school. Ideally, I like to get my pages done for the day before they get home, but it doesn't always work out that way. When that happens, I barricade myself in my bedroom with Diet Mountain Dew and sugar-free cookies, and I don't come out until I've done as much as I can possibly do for that day.

When you're not writing, what do you love to do?
Oh, that's an easy one—read! While I'm working on a book, I always make these grandiose plans for what I'm going to do when I get finished. Top of the list is always to read. For instance, with this book, I'm telling myself that when I get done I can read all five Harry Potter books again, that I can read Janet Evanovich's Stephanie Plum series again, that I can watch all 110 episodes of *Northern Exposure*, and then the *Anne of Green Gables* movies again. Like I said, grandiose plans, but it's nice to dream.

What or who inspires you?

Ah, a hard one. I'm inspired by many things. When it comes to my writing or book ideas, anything can inspire me. Usually it's an article I read, or a throwaway comment, or an interesting story that begs the question *What if?* I'm inspired by the innocence of children, the clean smell of a spring rain, roasting marshmallows over a campfire, good friends, good family, my husband's laugh and my faith in God.

Is there one book that you've read that changed your life somehow?

Well, er...the bad book mentioned in question one, and the Bible, of course.

What are your top five favorite books?

Oh, wow. Only five? Well, let's see. My absolute favorite book is *Lord of Scoundrels* by Loretta Chase. Loved, loved, loved that book. It's falling apart I've read it so many times. Others, in no particular order, would be *Solitary Soldier* by Debra Webb, *Son of the Morning* by Linda Howard, the Stephanie Plum series by Janet Evanovich and J. K. Rowling's Harry Potter series.

What matters most in life?

My faith and my family. Everything else is secondary.

If you weren't a writer, what would you be doing?
More reading? Honestly, I don't know. I can't imagine doing anything else. Even when I'm on deadline and I'm tired and my arms are aching, it's still not work. It's writing, and there's nothing quite so perfect as finding the exact phrase to say what I want to say, to breathe a character to life on a page. Do I get tired? Of course. It can be exhausting, but it's a pleasant sort of exhaustion. It's a solitary thing, and a host of insecurities come along with it—I invariably go through a this-is-complete-junk phase, one that thankfully a few words of praise from my wonderful, inspired editor can magically undo—but I wouldn't want to do anything else. Can't even wrap my mind around it.

Marsha Zinberg Executive Editor, Signature Select, spoke with Rhonda last winter.

TOP TEN

Reasons Widowhood Is Preferable

to Divorce

1 Instead of losing half—half your assets and half your friends—a widow keeps it all.

2 People offer sympathy.

3 Those same people usually bring food.

4 Black is slimming.

5 Less risk of humiliation—a dead husband can't remarry a twentysomething yoga coach barely out of braces with better breasts and a belly-button ring.

6 A widow is a martyr, whereas a divorcee is often unfairly deemed damaged goods or viewed with suspicion.

7 Life insurance.

8 More life insurance.

9 Death is permanent—no Jerry Springer-like meetings, courtroom brawls or bitter debates over who was right or wrong. (You were right, of course.)

10 The ultimate last word...and you have it.

TIPS & TRICKS

A page torn from the Future Widows' Club handbook.

Preparing for your future role as a widow requires a few prerequisites.

10

FINDING THE OUTFIT—The perfect ensemble for the funeral is simply a must. It puts you in the "widow" mindset and gives you something to look forward to. The perfect veiled hat—to hide your tears of joy and small satisfied smirk—is particularly difficult to find. Start early!

SHOW ME THE MONEY—Regardless of present insurance and assets, another half mil is prudent. Contact your agent at once.

X MARKS THE SPOT—Think of a treasure map, and The Will as your treasure. In this case, you don't want it to be a buried treasure that requires a long and possibly fruitless search. Make sure you're properly provided for—being sole beneficiary is best—and that the document is signed and stowed in a safe place.

PREPAY IS THE BEST WAY—Planning a funeral nowadays before one kicks the bucket is completely acceptable, even deemed considerate, thoughtful and prudent. Take advantage of this perk, ladies! Have fun with it! Pick a plot, pick a casket, pick a service. Graveside or chapel? Efficiency now will make your special day run more smoothly. Your *un*-dearly departed...may he never rest in peace.

Here's a sneak peek...

MAKING WAVES
by
Julie Elizabeth Leto

She's got a reputation for being bad...

Tessa Dalton used to be a celebrated author of erotic fairy tales...until her ex-husband used them against her in a highly publicized divorce case. He said she had an insatiable appetite for men—any men. But in truth, Tessa's erotica was inspired by her personal fantasies, fantasies her ex-husband never came close to fulfilling...and fantasies that are suddenly fueled when she meets journalist Colt Granger...

CHAPTER 1

"IS THE COAST CLEAR?"

Parked a half block away, Tessa Dalton watched her attorney's house, her chest tight. The front window sheers fluttered. Karen stepped into view and scanned the street outside, lending a second pair of eyes to confirm that Tessa was safe to leave the confines of her rental car. Damn, she resented taking such paranoid precautions, but she hated ambushes even more. Most of the guests had already arrived at Karen's party, and if Tessa could just slip inside the house relatively unnoticed, she might actually have a good time.

Switching her cell phone to her other ear, Tessa listened to the tropical Jimmy Buffett beat playing in the background, the perfect sound track for small talk and laughter on a hot Miami night. A mortgage-payoff party should have been the last place Tessa wanted to be, but with every measure of music, she longed to dash inside. Escape. Enjoy. Relax. Besides, Karen deserved Tessa's support for the long hours her attorney had logged while working on her high-profile divorce, not to mention the even longer hours she'd spent bolstering Tessa's confidence in the human race. Karen had promised an evening of good music, food and laughter with people who had enough class to ignore Tessa's current situation. A night like that could go a long way toward restoring her faith in her fellow man.

Well, maybe not her fellow *man,* but her fellow women at least had a decent shot. And after nearly six months of self-imposed exile—protection from her world as it unraveled around her—Tessa wasn't about to let an opportunity for some long-earned fun slip away.

Still, caution couldn't hurt.

Karen's sheers skimmed back into place. "Looks clear to me," her attorney concluded. "I'll send a friend out to meet you. I'm so sorry about today at the courthouse. I don't know what happened to your bodyguards."

Tessa smirked. "Yes, you do. You're just too devoted to that *innocent until proven guilty* credo to speak your suspicion out loud."

Tessa had no doubt her wily, soon-to-be ex-husband and his powerful father had been behind the defection of her bodyguards. Daniel had likely doubled their salary so they'd leave her vulnerable to the reporters hovering around the Palm Beach County Courthouse. The ravenous swarm couldn't have anticipated that she'd have no more meat to give them. Since she'd announced her separation from the prince of West Palm Beach and then had had the audacity to deny his claim to her wealth, the press had picked her clean.

Which didn't mean the insects didn't return to the carcass every so often, to make sure they hadn't missed a morsel of muscle, a prime cut of cartilage—anything they could grind into another outrageous lie.

Tessa scanned the street one last time, hating the fact that she felt like a prisoner in such a wide-open space. A van caught her attention, causing a prickle along the back of her neck. "Who's catering your party?" she asked, apprehensive.

"Lido's from South Beach. Why?"

The Lido's logo, complete with palm trees and a setting sun, spanned the side of the van. So much for trusting her instincts.

"I have a serious craving for strong Cuban coffee," she said, covered her anxiety.

Karen chuckled. "I've got a whole carafe here, just for you. I'll mingle by the front door," Karen said, her inflexible attorney voice replaced by her more natural, feminine inflection. "I can't believe you came all the way to Miami to celebrate with me. Means a lot, Tess."

"Hey, I owe you," Tessa said. "And more than just your retainer and fees, you know?"

"You've paid in full. If you hadn't, I wouldn't have been able to pay off this mortgage," she joked. "Now get in here so we can party."

"I'm on my way."

Tessa disconnected the call, pocketed the phone and pulled the keys out of the ignition. She took a deep breath, exhaled. God, this could be such a mistake. Going out in public, opening herself up to the snide remarks and speculative glances of strangers. She knew that sooner or later she wouldn't give a damn about what other people thought. That, at least, was her goal. Might as well be sooner rather than later—as in tonight.

Besides, she owed Karen, and couldn't blame her attorney for the mess she now faced. It wasn't Karen's fault that Tessa had preferred to bank on love instead of legalities, ignoring her attorney's advice about a prenuptial agreement just after her engagement. It also wasn't Karen's fault that Tessa had thought she'd found that love with a rotten, double-dealing son of a bitch who'd sucked the magic out of Tessa's romantic heart just like the pool vacuum hose he'd accused her in court of using as a sex toy. The least she owed Karen was to show up at her party.

Tessa was tired of hiding. She had only one more day left until the judge issued a final ruling in her divorce. For over three weeks she'd sat in the courtroom listening to Daniel, his family, his attorneys and his lying private investigators paint her as a sexual deviant, an insatiable seductress who'd fucked everyone from the pool boy—emphasis on the word *boy*—to the elderly cook, a woman, no less. They'd used her secret love, the erotic stories she wrote under a pseudonym, as the main evidence against her.

Only Tessa's editor and agent had come to her defense, but they lived in New York. Daniel's attorney had made a strong case that they couldn't have known about Tessa's sordid West Palm Beach life of excess. Of course they didn't know. No such life existed. Except for the fact that she wrote erotic stories, Daniel's claims had been fabricated, bought and paid for to ensure that Daniel not only got his hands on the money she'd inherited from her father, but that he kept every dime of his. He wanted everything. Homes, cars, cash—spoils he'd purchased from business deals Tessa had helped arrange through her contacts or had at least supported with her impeccable social aptitude.

She'd been the perfect corporate wife, and now she'd be the perfect social pariah. Her so-called West Palm Beach friends had either deserted her long before the trial or they'd bolstered Daniel's salacious tales with misinterpretations of their own.

Vilified and crucified in the courtroom, on television newsmagazines and in the tabloids, Tessa could either run or hide. Or she could say, "screw 'em," and go have a good time. If reporters came after her again, the worst they could do now was slow her progress to the java.

She checked her makeup in the rearview mirror under the dome light, unlocked the car and opened the door. No sooner had her foot met the pavement than someone yanked the handle out of her hand and shoved a microphone in her face.

"Mrs. Reese, is it true you're writing a memoir of your sexual exploits? Who is the publisher? Do you have a release date?"

Tessa grabbed for the door, but the reporter placed her body between Tessa and the handle.

"Get out of my way," Tessa demanded. Enough was enough. Pushing out of the car, she swung her purse, only half trying to hide her grin when the heavy leather bag punched the reporter in the gut.

Luckily the piranha had quick reflexes or Tessa might have flattened her when she slammed her door.

Tessa ducked under the symbiotic cameraman and hurried toward Karen's house, not giving a damn if the woman followed. Or pressed assault charges. Chances were, after tomorrow she'd have nothing left to be sued for.

A quick glance to her left verified Tessa's earlier suspicions. Another cache of reporters rolled out of the Lido's van, armed with lights, cameras and microphones. She judged the distance to Karen's front gate, but didn't sprint fast enough. In seconds she was surrounded. Bulbs blinded her. Microphones poked her in the face, ribs. Questions, accusations and lurid, disgusting suggestions assailed her from all angles, all volumes. She wanted to stand her ground, scream, fight—but she settled for a startled cry when a strong hand grabbed hers and yanked her out of the melee.

18

Within moments she was through Karen's gate and darting to the backyard with her rescuer. Behind her, Karen barked above the din, threatening lawsuits if one member of the uninvited press set foot on her private property. Only after they rounded the corner into the quiet backyard did she take a minute to identify her knight in shining armor.

"You!" she said, disbelieving.

She'd seen her Galahad in the courtroom, taking notes and weaving his stories with the rest of the media. He was a hard guy to miss. Six foot two, rakish dark hair, pewter eyes that missed nothing. Karen had told her his name. Granger. Colton Granger. With the *Chicago Sun-Times*.

"Are you okay?" he asked.

Tessa quickly traded one bout of shock for another, but glanced down to find her clothes in place and her body unhurt. Unhurt, but not unaffected. Colton Granger was one fine specimen of male flesh—and her female flesh couldn't help but tingle whenever they shared less than ten feet of space, even in the courtroom. Another woman might have wondered how the heck she could feel anything remotely associated with sexual interest after what Daniel had put her through, but Tessa rather liked knowing her slimy ex-husband hadn't entirely squelched her natural-born passions.

"I'm fine, thanks," she answered. "Why are you here?"

"Karen sent me out to meet you."

She slung her purse over her shoulder. Close by. Ready to strike in case her instincts to trust this man—even briefly—were off by a country mile.

"Where's your press pass?" she cracked.

He ignored her question and slipped his hands into the front pockets of his loose-fitting khakis. "Karen said you craved coffee."

She couldn't resist. The press had played her up to be the poster girl for fallen women. Why not live up to the reputation a little?

"I crave a lot of things—haven't you heard?"

His eyes narrowed, darkened. When he tightened his jaw, the clench emphasized the rugged, square shape of his chin, the full curve of his generous mouth. Tessa swallowed and remained silent, no moisture in her throat, her tongue thick.

He wanted her.

Instinctively she took a half step backward. She'd thought she knew what a man looked like when his concealed desire broke through to the surface. She'd thought her current situation with her divorce and trashed reputation had given her ample armor to protect her from succumbing to even a little hint of want or need.

She'd thought wrong. In a flash Colton revealed a depth of hunger she'd only dreamed up in her books. Then just as quickly, the look was gone. Clearing her throat, she grabbed control of the situation before he grabbed her—with her intrigued permission.

She stepped forward, reclaiming the ground she'd nearly lost. "Why are you here again? No, wait. Don't bother answering unless you know why I'm here, too. I'm betting only my therapist can answer that one."

He chuckled; she rolled her eyes. She hated men who found her funny. No, that wasn't true. She simply hated men in general. But she wasn't so possessed with loathing that she'd blindly lump Colton Granger into the whole rotten barrel. He had just pulled her from the throng. So far as she knew, he'd been the one reporter to give her a fair shake in the press, questioning the veracity of Daniel's claims in the respected print of the *Chicago Sun-Times*.

This incredibly handsome man had taken her side. Twice now. She could at least produce a civil response. And if he rewarded her with another glimpse of his intense appetite… For what? Her? Her story?

"Thanks for the escort," she said.

"You're welcome."

She waited, but though his jaw clenched again, nothing flashed in his eyes except compassion. "How about you grab a step on the porch and catch your breath? I'll track down your drink of choice."

"I should go in. I promised Karen."

"She'll understand if you take a minute to get yourself together first."

She tugged at the sleeves of her blouse, a sheer purple confection she hadn't been able to resist pairing with tight jeans and ankle boots. Panels of silk hid her bra from view, but revealed her bare tummy through a potent plum haze. Never in her life had she had the audacity to buy such sexy clothes, much less wear them, but she'd already been publicly pegged as a slut. Why not enjoy some of the benefits?

"Don't I look together?" she asked, wide-eyed with feigned innocence. She smoothed her hands down her sides, emphasizing the curves beneath the blouse, the slim cut of her jeans.

The return of his hunger, so clear in his dark gray gaze, surged through her like electricity. And her reaction—a tiny prickle of heat between her thighs, so unexpected and overwhelming—nearly sent her running. Luckily Colton seemed to wield great control over his needs.

Yet when he licked his lips just seconds before he spoke, he jolted her with another wave of hot awareness.

"You look like you could take on the world," he answered.

She allowed a half smile to quirk through. "Maybe I'll just take you on."

He tilted his head to the left, his expression doubtful. And right on target. "Promises, promises."

She couldn't help but laugh, and the light, tinkling echo sounded so strange coming from her. She had no intention of taking him on, or any other man for that matter, but for the first time in forever she at least felt comfortable in her skin.

When was the last time she'd allowed herself the freedom to indulge in a round of harmless flirting? When was the last time she'd allowed a man into her personal space at all? Maybe having her life torn to the point where she had nothing to lose and everything to gain wasn't so much a tragedy as an opportunity. For change. For liberation.

She followed Colton up to the gleaming white wraparound porch of Karen's Cape Cod–style minimanse and sank to the bottom step, overwhelmed by the prospects. Behind her the screen door creaked, and she closed her eyes. The sound of the party surged, waned, then surged again less than a minute later, finally dulled by his firm slam.

"This ought to smooth out the rough spots," he offered.

She turned to accept her coffee, but instead, her hand met the cold glass of a long-necked beer. Mexican, with lime. She thought she might cry with gratitude.

"You read my mind," she confessed, swiping lime around the lip of the bottle before taking a long, cold sip. The beer eased down her throat, icing her frazzled nerves into cool submission.

"I have a knack for anticipating what a woman wants."

She laughed, shaking her head. "My turn to say, 'promises, promises.'"

His grin had no hint of contrition or capitulation. "You do that to men, don't you? Incite the natural male instinct to show a woman a good time?"

She smiled. "I'm just sitting here, innocently drinking my beer."

Gray eyes—gray, intense eyes, she amended—cast a glance toward the long-necked bottle she dangled suggestively between her knees. Oh, that. Maybe his instincts weren't the only ones rising unbidden to the surface, simply from their shared company. To counteract the effect of her inadvertent sensuality, she lifted the beer to her lips and took a most unladylike, nonseductive swill.

With a chuckle he twisted the top off his own brew and matched her swig for swig. The atmosphere alternately crackled between charged and comfortable, and surprisingly, Tessa didn't know which she liked better.

"You've been quite the rescuer tonight."

He tilted his head again, and this time an errant sweep of thick black hair swung down over one eye much like a pirate's signature patch. He raked the lock back with a strong, long-fingered hand decorated with a gold college ring. Now who was trying to be seductive?

"Right place, right time." His voice hinted at an accent buried deep within his sultry baritone.

"And I don't suppose you want an exclusive interview for your trouble?" she suggested, unable to tone down the not-so-subtle bite in her question.

"That would be crass."

"Isn't Crass 101 a required course at journalism school?"

He chuckled again, the warm sound inspiring Tessa to take another long, cooling drink from her beer.

"Where I was born, crass is a horrible offense."

She placed the accent. Southern, but carefully hidden beneath a Midwesterner's cadence.

"I'll have to visit your Oz someday," she joked. "Be a nice change of scenery."

24   They remained silent on the porch, her sitting on the step, him standing along the rail. After she'd downed half the bottle, she turned and gave him a good once-over one last time. As intrigued as she was by Colton Granger, Tessa couldn't allow a foolish dalliance right now—not even with a sexy reporter who seemed to be on her side. She had hard decisions to make about her life—decisions she had to make with a clear head. And she'd learned the hard way that even the smallest hint of passion tended to muddle her brain worse than San Francisco fog.

The light from the porch sconces rimmed Colton's broad shoulders with a glimmering sheen, casting his face in shadow, causing Tessa to instantly compare him to the mysterious warriors and princes she wrote about in her novels. Or used to write about. Before Daniel blew her cover. Before he sucked the joy out of her one talent in life.

Tessa took another sip. She knew she'd had too much beer too fast, but she needed the fortification. Under any other circumstances, she would have cut off this inter-action with Colton immediately after she'd thanked him for his help. She didn't need strange men in her life. She was having enough trouble with the guys she knew. Better to nip this in the bud. Nothing like a little reality to drown the last of the heat sizzling between them.

"You don't want an interview. Good for me," she said.

"You could ask me a question."

She eyed him skeptically, but his expression re-mained open, honest.

"Okay," she said, willing to give him a shot at the truth. "Why is a Chicago reporter following a divorce case in West Palm Beach? Other than as means to annoy my soon-to-be former father-in-law?"

Martin Reese's company had recently relocated to the Windy City and he spent a good deal of time and money buying whatever political favors he could there. But he was a newcomer in a town that prided itself on two mayors from the same political dynasty. Colton's columns had to have fueled public speculation that old Marty didn't want to deal with. In Florida he could con-trol the damage. In Illinois he was out of his element.

Colton didn't answer her question, but cleared his throat guiltily.

Bingo.

"Well, whatever your reason for sticking up for me,

thanks. You got the old man's goat, too." She remembered the scene so clearly—someone shoving the newspaper in Martin's face just after a lunch recess a few days into the divorce hearing. Controlled, cool Martin Reese had turned a particularly bright shade of red and barked several interesting expletives at no one in particular. At the time she hadn't understood her father-in-law's ire, but after she'd found out that Granger had raked him over the coals for his attacks on his daughter-in-law, she'd considered Colton Granger to be a brave, if not brilliant man.

Now she could add sexy to the list. Lucky, lucky her.

"I'm surprised he didn't have you fired," she added.

"Oh, he tried."

She raised her bottle. "Kudos to your editor, then."

"Have you read my articles?"

She sighed. "Funny, but I've been avoiding newspapers and television lately."

"My stuff is good. I'll send you copies. Though they would have been better with that exclusive interview."

She swiped her tongue over the lime, closing her eyes and enjoying the tangy bite. "So that is what this is about, then."

"Nope. Tonight is off the record."

One glance told her he was serious. "Damn, but those fifteen minutes go by quick. From the crowd out front, I figured I had at least another five left."

"You have a smart mouth, you know that?"

Too bad she didn't have a smart heart to match. "Betrayal tends to make a woman a little bitchy. I shouldn't take it out on you."

"I can handle justified resentment."

Good, because she had that in spades. "So tell me. What *do* you want, Colton Granger, defender and rescuer of women in desperate need of privacy and beer?"

He grinned, but didn't hesitate. "Just one answer to one question. Off the record."

She smiled. Of course. A journalistic veteran like him could probably pack one heck of a punch into one question. Oh, well. What did she have to lose? Tessa had had enough of trying to project the right image to the court, of defending herself against Daniel's ludicrous accusations and, mostly, of running from the tabloid press that seemed to follow her everywhere. She'd had more fun in these very few minutes with Colton when she'd slipped into the role Daniel had created to destroy her—the flirt, the seductress, the insatiable woman with a thousand secret needs—than she had in months. And she'd definitely had Colton's interest, which also felt very, very good.

Colton seemed to handle her transformations with aplomb, as if he expected no less than her cold quips one minute, hot innuendos the next. And as a reporter, he was legit. Why not answer his question? Could be a real kick.

"Fire away," she challenged.

He eased down next to her and placed one boot—comfortably worn tanned leather—beside her foot on the lowest step. He watched her squeeze lime juice into the bottle, then stuff in the rind until it floated in the last of the amber lager.

His smile would have been devastating on someone

completely sober. Luckily Tessa had achieved a light buzz. She blamed her heightened awareness on the stress, the beer. Colton's irrepressible magnetism.

Yet she wasn't so loopy that she'd forgotten the uncertain life she now faced thanks to her inexperience and naiveté with men—especially the handsome and charming ones. Though what Colton might or might not ask— and what he might or might not print in the paper tomorrow, despite his off-the-record promise—couldn't possibly affect the outcome of her case.

She curled her hair behind her ears, wishing for something to tie the thick tresses away from her neck. The Miami night had cooled to a humid eighty-five degrees. The acrid scent of citronella burned her nostrils, but kept the buzzing swarms of mosquitoes at an impotent distance. Salsa music danced into the cigar-scented air through a newly opened window and she watched Colton's fingers tap a rival beat on the bottle.

"Are you game to discuss Charlene Perrault?"

She shifted in her seat. Her "secret identity" wasn't a favorite topic. For the past month she'd tried to convince the court she was a writer of fiction, not a crazed nymphomaniac. Her task hadn't been easy, particularly after Daniel revealed with lascivious glee that Tessa Dalton Reese, socialite, was the force behind Charlene Perrault, the writer of the edgiest erotica published in the mainstream market since Anne Rice donned the penname A. N. Roquelaure and sent Sleeping Beauty into sexual servitude.

As Charlene Perrault, Tessa had taken up the gauntlet where Rice had left off. With a lighter touch and a strong spirit of romance, her carnal fairy tales fired the imaginations of men and women alike. And thanks to her Pulitzer-prize-like divorce, the books, produced by a small press publisher, were selling like proverbial hot-cakes on a cold day.

"Is that your *one* question?" she asked.

"Not exactly. What I want to know is, *are* you Charlene Perrault?"

She glanced at him sideways, but when her vantage point proved ineffective, she twisted her entire body. She searched his face, his blank, cool expression. Handsome, yet set in serious stone. She'd expected another glimpse of his lascivious nature, and for an instant she suspected he'd used this opportunity alone with her to see if the nympho-author wanted a quickie on the back porch.

With a sting of disappointment she realized that wasn't why he'd asked.

"Everyone in the free world knows I'm Perrault, Mr. Granger. Wouldn't you rather ask me why I married Daniel in the first place? Why I didn't sign a prenuptial agreement to protect myself? Why I didn't just pay off the putz when I had a chance with the millions my daddy left me?"

He shook his head. "I'm not interested in your past. Just your future."

He scooted back on the wooden porch step, his jeans rasping against the painted pine, so smug and comfortable with who he was. Tessa couldn't control the sudden quiver rattling her insides, until she harnessed a flash of anger. How dare he, a perfect stranger, care

about her tomorrows when she wasn't yet sure there'd
be anything to care about? How dare he ignite fires she
had no business burning?

"How about if I ask you another question first?"

"Why not?" He drank a draft from his beer. "I have
nothing to hide."

"Everyone has something to hide." She punctuated
her insight with a snort, a cynical grunt that she might
have contained in the past, simply because such an expression wasn't refined. Too fucking bad. The sound expressed a hard-won wisdom she planned to hold on to
for the rest of her life.

"I won't make it too hard," she promised. "You're a
reporter…"

"A columnist," he corrected.

"Even better! You spout opinions, probably hang
tight to some single-minded agenda."

He nodded, tipped back his beer. "You could say
that."

"Okay, then. Do you believe every word you write?
Every idea? Every judgment?"

"I try."

Honest, but noncommittal. How lucky for him. She
took one last drink from her beer, then set it down in the
inch or so of space that separated them. Standing, she
rubbed her hands down the front of her jeans, then
hooked her thumbs in the empty belt loops.

He wanted to know if Charlene Perrault was the
manifestation of her private fantasies or a real part of
her personality. Thanks to Daniel and journalists like
Colton—not to mention her own naiveté—she might

never know how much of her nom de plume came from her secret desires or from a latent part of her soul she'd only lightly tapped into. Since the separation, she'd forced her needs into a deep hiding place. For protection. For one last attempt at privacy.

The anger simmering inside her now shot to the surface in hot arcs. "You have no secrets and you believe every word you write? Then you're one lucky guy. Either that or you're too good to be true."

She'd meant her words to sting with sarcasm, but he had the cool audacity to drain the rest of his beer without looking the least bit offended. Either he didn't give a damn what other people thought of him or he was a true master of controlling his reactions.

After tamping down her admiration, she rolled her eyes and headed toward the door. Like everyone else, he'd believe whatever he wanted to believe about her, accurate or not. In court and in the news, Tessa Dalton now personified the ultimate seductress, a voracious sexual deviant with no scruples and no honor. She might one day take advantage of that persona, but she'd never be easy. Not even with a dreamboat like Granger.

She peeked through the half-moon window on the door and spied the kitchen, relatively empty. She'd go in, exchange the required small talk, then find one of the five bedrooms in Karen's house and crash until court tomorrow, when some self-righteous judge would decide if she'd at least hold on to the legacy her father had left her. She had her hand on the screen door handle when a business card flicked in front of her.

"For the record," Colton said. "I'm too good to be

true just the same as you're too bad to be believed. If you ever want to really answer my question or just set the record straight, get in touch."

Tessa snatched the card, stuffed it into her pocket and forced her gaze forward at the glossy white panels in the door. She ignored the powerful draw of his body heat, the lingering lure of his musky scent. After she heard those sexy boots of his depart down the steps and across the walkway, she risked a glance over her shoulder. He was just as hot on the flip side, and she was just as determined to stay away.

Hmm. In less than ten minutes he'd jump-started her libido and had given her food for thought. Either she was drunker than she realized after just one beer, or this Colton Granger knew how to fascinate and entice a woman recently convinced she'd be jaded and lonely for the rest of her life.

With a groan Tessa opened the door. She couldn't help leaning toward the second theory, even though every fiber of her being hoped like hell for the first.

...NOT THE END...

Look for Making Waves *by Julie Elizabeth Leto, in bookstores July 2005 from Signature Select™.*

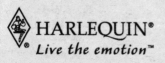

MINISERIES

Love—not-exactly-American-style!

That's Amore!

USA TODAY bestselling author

Janelle Denison

and

Tori Carrington
Leslie Kelly

For three couples planning a wedding with a little family "help," it's way too late to elope, in this humorous new collection from three favorite Harlequin authors.

HARLEQUIN®
Live the emotion™

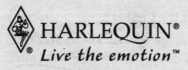

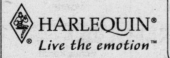

MINISERIES

These are men you'll want to come home to.
National bestselling author

MURIEL JENSEN

Two full-length novels in
her bestselling miniseries...

THE MEN OF MAPLE HILL

Maple Hill, Massachusetts, is the kind of small
town that makes men like Cameron Trent and
Hank Whitcomb want to settle down...even
when neither has any intention of doing so!

Look for these men...coming in May.

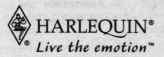

HARLEQUIN®
Live the emotion™

Bonus Features
include:
Author Interview,
Sneak Peek and
Bonus Read!